# STANLEY SAVES THE UNIVERSE

by Bill Muir

# Stanley Saves the Universe

## Bill Muir

### Methinx Publishing

MeThinx Publishing

Methinx Publishing
methinxentertainment.com

Printed in the United States of America
First paper edition by Methinx Publishing
ISBN: 978-1-7347696-3-0

Art & Design:
Contributing Editor: Kathryn Tedrick
Cover Art: Digital Coast Media, LLC

# Chapter One

## Attack from Outer Space

From the western scarlet sky, five silver flying saucers flew in a V-shape formation. They came to a standstill, hovering in silence over Washington, D.C. Government employees left their metal desks and darted over to the windows, others poured outside onto the sidewalks to get a better look at the giant saucers filling the sky above the city.

Suddenly without warning, the alien ships began firing green laser beams at government buildings, exploding whole sections into nothing but hot dust. People trampled each other, trying to escape the falling granite, marble, and concrete. Sirens blared throughout the city. A brilliant flash of light struck the Capital Building, blowing open the top and leaving a gaping crater in the center of the building. The Pentagon took the next devastating blow. Several saucers hit it at once with their beams, setting the entire structure on fire with flames that leaped as high as the Washington Monument.

Military personnel in camouflage tanks, jeeps, and trucks quickly rolled into position. It began firing large shelled bombs at the silver saucers. They did no damage. Air Force jets streaked across the sky, firing missiles at the saucers. The missiles exploded when they hit the invisible force fields of the alien saucers, preventing damage to the ships. The alien lasers turned their attention to the jets, and they were picked off one-by-one until none remained. The sky rained burning metal.

Police and military personnel herded the civilians away from the burning buildings and firestorm in the streets, into whatever hovel of protection they could find. Emergency vehicles rushed to the scene, sirens blaring a non-stop chorus of terror. Chaos ensued as people screamed, shouted, cried, and prayed that God would somehow save them.

At the White House, Secret Service agents rushed the President and his family into a secure bunker beneath the building. It was built to withstand a nuclear attack, but no one knew if it would hold up against the aliens' advanced weaponry.

"Notify as many of our allies as you can reach," the President ordered the men escorting him. He kissed his wife and two daughters, who were then taken to private quarters. Then he continued down the hallway to the Situation Room.

"I want to know if other countries are undattack or just ours."

"What if they aren't?" His chief of staff asked.

"If they aren't, we'll need all the military support they can send."

"And if they are?"

"Then may God have mercy on us all."

Once the primary defense system was destroyed, the saucer located at the point of the V, drifted down from the formation and landed on the White House front lawn. Secret Service agents fired everything they had at it, but their bullets could not penetrate their invisible shield.

Then after what seemed forever, the battlefield became as silent as a tomb. The Army and Air Force were out of ammo, the Marines as well. The soldiers remained standing where they were, their expressions hard and unreadable. They had been trained to show no emotion. They didn't. Internally, they watched in despair, anger, and hopelessness as the spaceship landed. Lights around the rim of the saucer searched for weapons. Then the door of the alien ship slowly slid open. The helpless U.S. military simply stared at the opening. Nothing happened, and no one emerged. The earth seemed to stand still in those moments.

Two eight-foot-tall aliens eventually walked out in shiny spacesuits. Silver helmets with opaque face plates wholly covered their heads, preventing anyone from seeing what the enemy looked like. They headed for the front doors of the White House. The two figures confidently walked through the White House, searching for the president. As they swaggered through the halls, their compact blasters eliminated anything and everyone in their way.

***

In 1964, Invasion from Mars was showing in Habsburg, Kansas. The Palace Movie Theater was filled to max capacity with teenagers staring at the massive silver screen in the town's only theater. Seated in the middle row of the crowded theater, sixteen-year-old Stanley Adams and his friends, Rick and Roger, sat on the edge of their worn burgundy seats. Their eyes glued to the giant theater screen, their mouths open in awe. Their hands, filled with buttery popcorn, seemed frozen in mid-air. They were so enthralled by the movie that they no longer noticed the smell of mildew that was always present in the old theater.

"How are they going to stop the aliens?" A girl in the row behind them asked.

"Shh!" Was the response from someone farther back in the theater.

Ten minutes later, the audience discovered that the world was saved through a new military weapon that destroyed the aliens and saved the president. The crowd cheered the heroes, clapping enthusiastically as the credits rolled.

Outside the theater, the sidewalk filled with teenagers leaving the theater. Stanley and his friends shielded their eyes from the bright afternoon sun. Going to the Saturday Matinee was a weekly ritual for most kids in the small farming town.

Stanley and his buddies loved science fiction movies. Ever since the late President John F. Kennedy announced that the U.S. would be sending a man to the moon. The boys had shown an avid interest in everything that had to do with outer space.

"Wow, that was worth the $0.93 ticket price," Stanley said to his friends.

"Indeed," Rick added.

"It would be worth more than that if you had a girlfriend, Stanley," the handsome Mark Whitfield said, as he walked past him, heading toward his red 1962 Corvette. Mark was the prize quarterback of the local high school, and next to him was Mary Guthrie, head cheerleader and the prettiest, sweetest, and the smartest girl at the school.

Stanley's buddy, Roger, was still trying hard to get the last remains from his soda cup.

"Hey, Roger, why don't you just get a refill before you suck your tonsils up the straw?" Mark laughed.

Mary looked disgusted. "Was that really necessary, Mark?" Boy, I hate this, she thought. Mark is such a creep. I wish I had never accepted a ride home with him.

"Hey, if the truth fits…."

"I'm sorry, Roger," Mary said, giving the heavy-set boy a sympathetic look. "Just ignore him."

As Mark and Mary walked to his car, Stanley couldn't take his eyes off her. He had been in love with Mary since the first grade, but she didn't know it. Neither did anyone else. Stanley knew he had no chance of having a girlfriend as pretty and popular as Mary. Not when you're just another average looking guy, Stanley thought.

***

Monday morning was a cold fall day. Stanley walked to his locker in the first-floor hallway of two-story high school, Habsburg High. He wore a blue sweater shirt with grey and white stripes and grey plaid dress pants; however, this was due to the school's dress code. The young man walked through the hallway and passed a large banner that was painted by the student council. He read the words as he walked by: Go Habsburg High! Goooo Havocs! There were numbers painted representing the athletes and a large, almost comical drawing of a tornado, the school's mascot.

As he approached his locker, he couldn't help noticing Mary at her locker near his. She turned and smiled. She wore a soft ivory sweater and brown pleated skirt. A heart-shaped pearl necklace was her only jewelry. He started to smile back until he saw Mark and his buddies walk up to her. Mark had seen him staring at Mary and immediately crossed the scuffed linoleum floor to confront him.

Stanley quickly turned back to his locker and grabbed his science book for the next class. Mark moved his face up close to Stanley, so Mary could not hear their conversation.

"You're not staring at my girl, are you?" Mark threatened in a whispering tone. In reality, he knew Mary wasn't his girlfriend, but he hoped to change that.

"No, not at all," Stanley said, staring at his locker. Mark had given Stanley a black eye in the third grade, and he didn't want the humiliation repeated.

The jock looked back at Mary with a smile and then moved his face even closer to Stanley's. "Good. Keep it that way."

Mark returned to Mary and his buddies.

"What did you say to Stanley?" Mary asked.

"I asked him if he enjoyed the movie."

"What did he say?"

"What would a science nerd with a crazy, grandfather say? He loved it."

"He's not a nerd, and his grandfather isn't crazy," Mary defended.

Mark and his friends only laughed, and Stanley knew why.

Stanley's friends, unaware of what had just happened, wandered up to his locker. While Mark's friends had athletic bodies, Stanley's buddies were different shapes and sizes.

Rick Turner was the first to arrive because he was always in a hurry. He was a lanky kid with ears too big for the size of his head and black-rimmed glasses that helped cover some of his pimples. He was the last kid picked for anything unless you needed someone smart to help you with your homework or a school project. He weighed less than 130 pounds soaking wet.

Roger, on the other hand, was short, barely over 5'4", even though he told everyone he was almost 5'10". He was also fat, around 250 pounds. His body was almost a perfect circle. He had red hair, and freckles splashed across his small nose. Kids who didn't like him called him St. Nick due to his appearance.

Stanley loved his buddies, but that didn't stop him from being embarrassed by their obvious and talkative love for space and aliens. Stanley was just as interested in space and aliens as they were, but he kept it as much of a secret as possible.

The three of them headed to Mr. Stuart's first-period science class. Stanley often walked a few steps behind Rick and Roger, trying to save as much of his image as possible.

The students in Mr. Stuart's physics class sat at their wooden desks, making small talk until the teacher called the class to order. The room was painted an uninteresting shade of green, and tall windows ran the length of the outside wall. One boy threw a spitball across the room where it landed on a girl whose brown unruly locks seemed to absorb it, bringing a guffaw from the kid who had thrown it.

Three girls talked about the newest hit record, Oh Pretty Woman by Roy Orbison. Another girl in the back of the classroom chewed gum while checking her makeup in a compact mirror. On the blackboard, the teacher drew a series of orbits around the sun with a \ dot that represented each of the planets in the solar system.

When he turned around, he called the class to order. "All right, class, let's quiet down." He glanced around the room. "Linda, deposit your chewing gum into the wastebasket now or wear it on the tip of your nose."

Linda made a face, took the gum from her mouth, and put it back into the original wrapper. Then she got up and dropped it into the wastebasket next to the teacher's desk, sashaying back to her desk to whistles and catcalls from the boys.

"That's enough, boys," Mr. Stuart said. "Linda, that mini skirt is too short. Dress code states that your hemline cannot be any higher than an inch above the knees. Go to the principal's office and get a slip to return home and change."

Linda shrugged her shoulders. She knew she would get sent home, which was why she wore it. Swinging her hips, which drew more wolf whistles, she headed for the principal's office. She had no intention of returning to school that day. She was going shopping.

Once Mr. Stuart had everyone's attention, he began to teach about the planets of the solar system. "Today, we are going to study Pluto."

"Are you going to show us the cartoon first?" Mark asked.

The kids laughed.

"Not the animated dog, the planet Pluto."

Seated in front of Stanley, Mary raised her hand. She loved science and everything about it.

"Yes, Mary?" The teacher asked.

"Most of us saw Invasion From Mars this weekend. Do you think there is life on Mars?"

Stanley was amazed by Mary's confidence. If she liked something, she was not afraid of what anyone would think. Stanley was just the opposite.

"Unfortunately, we don't know yet. Russia has sent four probes to Mars, two in 1960, and another two in 1962. All four failed their mission. The United States will be sending Mariner 3 and Mariner 4 in November, which is right around the corner.

Hopefully, at least one will arrive successfully and be able to transmit the first-ever pictures of the planet back to Earth."

"That will be so exciting," Mary replied, dreaming of what the probe would find there and what the people would look like. "I hope we're able to make contact with the aliens."

"That might not be such a good idea," the overweight Roger spoke up. "You wouldn't want what happened in that movie Saturday to actually come true."

Mark and several classmates laughed.

"Yeah, Roger, who knows what they would do. Maybe they'd come here looking for food...human food."

This brought another laugh from the class.

"After all, Roger, you'd be a feast!" Mark added.

Roger was the fattest kid in the school. That didn't matter to Stanley and the rest of their group. However, that did not help in this embarrassing moment.

Mr. Stuart's expression darkened. "That's enough, Mark! Quiet down the rest of you. You are here to learn, not make fun of people."

\*\*\*

The day continued until the bell rang, ending the eighth period. It was time to go home. As the students streamed for the front door of the school, Stanley, Rick, and Roger gathered together on the steps.

"That creep, Mark," Roger seethed. "Someday, I'm going to...."

"Forget it, Roger," Stanley said. "He's not worth it."

"No, I'm not going to forget it. He puts me down every chance he gets. If he doesn't watch it, we'll just have to beat him up."

"We?" Stanley asked.

"Yeah. We could if we all fought him at the same time."

"You're dreaming," Rick said, pushing his large black-framed glasses higher on his nose. He alone, with his arms tied behind his back, could drop the four of us. He wouldn't even need his friends."

"He's right," Stanley smiled, "just let it go."

"Hey, the planet Jupiter is supposed to be visible tonight," Rick said, trying to change the subject.

"If anyone spots it, make sure to call the others," Stanley urged. And with that, they all headed for the school buses hoping that tonight they would see something special.

# Chapter Two

## Unidentified Flying Object

The evening started as just another regular night for Stanley in his modest one-story house inside the city limits of Habsburg. He lay on his bed, reading a comic book, The Red Planet. The cover showed a silver spaceship flying toward Mars. As Stanley read, he had two significant concerns: Would the astronauts on their way to Mars have enough fuel to get there? Would his mother call him down to finish washing the dinner dishes before he finished reading? He turned the pages of his comic at the speed of light.

It was the sixth comic book he had read this week, along with a 300-page technical book titled Living in Outer Space and Cultivating Food There. Neither the size of the book nor its title had stopped Stanley from reading it. He loved anything to do with outer space. While he received his share of C's on his report card, he always received straight A's in science, astronomy, creative writing, and chemistry.

Stenciled on the wall next to his bed were the words: The best things in life are out of this world. Giant movie posters of old science fiction movies covered his walls. His bookcase was filled with twenty-three models of different U.F.O.'s. On his nightstand, a blue light pointed upward, highlighting the solar system he had painted on the ceiling. His bedroom reflected his love of the stars, which was something he shared with his three closest friends.

Stanley didn't want people comparing him to his grandfather, whom everyone thought was a crazy old coot because of what had happened five years earlier. He even kept his fascination with outer space a secret from his mother. She, too, was embarrassed by what her father claimed. Even at a young age, Stanley remembered kids calling him "Space Boy" because of his crazy grandfather. Even though he loved space, he had to conceal it, especially from his mom. He didn't want to bring her any more embarrassment. It was better to hide his truth than face the pain of being laughed at and ridiculed.

After he finished reading and before washing the dishes, he retrieved his telescope from the closet and peered through it at the dark, cloudless sky. He wondered if he would see Jupiter. While scanning the sky, he noticed something bright racing toward the Earth's atmosphere. His mind briefly drifted back to the comic book and its bug-eyed creatures, making his heart race. He shivered, just at the thought.

The idea of an alien spaceship visiting Earth made him think about the 1947 incident at Roswell, New Mexico. When ordinary citizens spotted an alien spaceship crashing outside the city on a nearby ranch. Before anyone could get to the crash, soldiers from a nearby Army base quickly removed every piece of evidence. Later, they said it was a weather balloon that fell back to earth. Rumor, in any space-related group or publication, was that they had even captured an alien and kept it alive.

Focusing on the sky once more, Stanley watched in fascination as the object sped toward Earth. His instinct told him it was merely a meteor. His imagination told him it was a spaceship.

***

Five miles away at a popular spot where high school kids often went to make-out, a red 1962 Corvette Convertible was parked on a narrow dirt road. Mary stared at the stars. Mark stared at Mary. She studied the constellations in her book before peering through the windshield at the stars. Her eyes danced between the sky and the page open in the book on her lap. Her long brown ponytail swung back and forth, nearly hitting Mark in the face as he inched closer to her.

"That's Orion," she said. Her sky-blue eyes sparkled with interest. "Did you know that it's often called 'The Hunter' and is one of the most recognizable constellations in the night sky?"

Mark Whitfield wasn't interested in stars or the sky for that matter. He only pretended to be interested in space to get Mary to this lookout. While everyone saw her as the kindest, most caring girl at school, Mark saw her as another status symbol of how great he was.

After tuning in to his favor rock station on the radio, he yawned and stretched, using it as an excuse to slide one arm around her shoulders. He figured Mary was too interested in the night sky to notice, and as he leaned toward her with his eyes closed, he puckered his lips. Mary bent down to get another book on constellations from the floor of the car. With his lips in midair and not making contact with anything, he quickly opened his eyes and realized how stupid he looked. He quickly leaned back in his seat before she saw his failed attempt and to save his reputation as irresistible to the girls.

Actually, Mary knew exactly what he was trying to do, and she wanted no part of it. He was not her type. The only reason she was in the car with him now was that he had offered to take her somewhere nice to look at the stars. She hadn't really believed him, but her mother thought she spent too much time with her nose in a book and suggested that she give him a chance. Mary continued to study the stars as Mark continued to study her.

Looking out the front windshield, Mary spotted a series of colorful lights that seemed to be coming straight down toward the car. At a distance, they looked like those of a plane. She leaned closer toward the windshield to get a better look. Just as Mark leaned toward her for another attempt at a kiss.

"What are you looking at?" he asked, trying to keep the frustration he felt out his voice.

"Those lights, in the sky, they're coming right toward us," she said.

Mark finally took his eyes off her and looked at the sky but in the wrong direction. He didn't see anything and looked back at her.

"I don't see anything. Are you teasing me?"

"No, look!"

Instead of looking at the stars, Mark focused on the radio and tried to find another station. When he looked up, the lights were no longer visible.

"I don't see anything."

"No, really, something was racing this way."

Mary then looked out all the windows of the car for what she had seen. There was a soft light around them, but she couldn't figure out where it was coming from.

On the car radio, The Beatles song I Want to Hold Your Hand suddenly turned to static before the radio went dead.

"What's going on?" Mark asked, annoyed as he tried to turn the radio back on by pounding on the front of it.

"I think a meteor just entered our atmosphere."

"I mean, what's going on with my radio?"

"The same answer," Mary responded.

Mary jumped out of the car and looked just above the trees. She saw it again but was barely able to follow the object. Mark was still trying to figure out what was wrong on his radio.

The lights disappeared from Mary's sight at the very moment Mark's radio came back on.

"I fixed it," Mark yelled

"It must have crashed!" She exclaimed.

The sky returned to its usual darkness.

Mary sighed. "Boy, that was close."

"Yeah, I thought I would never get that radio working again."

***

Stanley lowered his telescope and stared out his bedroom window. The meteor, plane, or spaceship had crashed nearby. Before leaving his room to use the only phone in the house, he stashed his telescope back in the closet and tucked the comic book under his pillow as though he had been doing something wrong. Then he pushed down on a lever by his desk, causing a series of objects connected to fishing lines to drop. Football posters unrolled and covered his alien space movie posters, and a large black cloth with a logo of a pro football team dropped over his 3D space globe. He spun his bookshelf on wheels around, hiding his models of spaceships and U.F.O. Comic books. The backside of the bookshelf was filled with models of cars and school books. Suddenly, his room decorated to reflect his interest in space became a room filled with football décor.

He ran down the hallway to the kitchen. Attached to the wall was the house phone. Stanley dialed the rotary dial phone as fast as it would turn. When the dial finished its last slow turn, he waited for his friend Rick to answer his phone.

Their little group depended on Rick's vehicle for transportation. He was also a devoted friend to Stanley. Rick worked weekends as a dishwasher at a local restaurant. The money he earned paid for gas and the upkeep on his car.

"Your dime."

Rick never said hello. He thought it was funnier to say, 'your dime,' which is what a local call cost in a phone booth.

"Rick! Did you see it?" Stanley asked.

"The approaching light? Yeah, it happened when we were looking for Jupiter."

"What do you think it is?" Stanley asked.

"I think it's a meteor," Rick replied, "but Roger thinks it's a spaceship."

Roger's voice came through in the background. "Is that Stanley?"

Stanley could tell he was eating something from the mumbled sound of his words.

"Tell him there's no question in my mind that it was a spaceship," Roger said, speaking loudly enough so that Stanley could hear his excited words through the phone. When Roger got excited, he stuttered and began sweating. He was also a bit girl crazy, and whenever he was around them, the same thing would happen. The sweating made it difficult to get a date.

"Whatever it is, it went down not far from here," Stanley said.

"We'd better check it out," Roger insisted. "If it isn't a meteor, we need to notify the authorities. It's our civic duty."

Rick was no risk-taker. He was practically the only kid in school who had never been called to the principal's office. The boys thought Rick's parents were really strict. They were right. Rick seemed to be on restriction more than he was off, and that gave him a lot of time to read novels. He was smart and had a vivid imagination. He knew by heart every line of dialog from every sci-fi movie. He even said them with the same accent as they were delivered in the film. Everyone at school figured he would be a screenwriter in Hollywood one day.

"There is only one way to find out," Rick said, "we'll pick you up and check it out, Stanley. If nothing else, we can have fun looking."

"Okay, just don't tell my Mom when you get here what we're doing. If she knew, she would never let me go."

The phone had already gone dead before Stanley finished his sentence. He slowly slid down into the wooden chair at the kitchen table, his mind racing. Never in all the group years of studying the sky did anything hit the ground near Habsburg. The fact of the matter was nothing exciting ever happened in this tiny farming town.

***

Twelve hundred miles away in the Pentagon building just outside Washington D.C., forty officers sat in a large room with state-of-the-art tracking equipment. Their mission was to protect the United States from anything entering the country's airspace. The men sat in front of their green screens; each screen showed five yellow circles, each one bigger than the next. A straight line rotated around the screen like a minute hand on a clock.

One of the men staring at a screen noticed an object entering Earth's atmosphere over Kansas. The hair on the back of his neck stood straight up as he rose out of his chair. He had been trained for this day. He just never believed that the day would come.

"Code Green! Code Green!" He yelled.

Code Green was an indication that something from outer space had entered the Earth's atmosphere. It was the only thing that scared the Pentagon more than something coming in from the Russians.

Lieutenant Stone, sitting at a metal desk nearby, slowly but deliberately left his chair and walked over to the man.

"What do you have, Sergeant?"

The sergeant's trembling index finger pointed to the upper left side of his green screen.

"There's an unidentified flying object, right here, sir."

The lieutenant studied the screen.

Everyone in the room left their seats and scurried toward the sergeant's screen to get a look at something they hadn't seen for five years. Each straining to spot the U.F.O. And hoping to tell their grandkids about it someday.

"Back to your desks, men," Lieutenant Stone ordered. "There may be more."

The lieutenant gently pushed the sergeant back into his chair. "Put the image on the large screen and create a printout of all the activity on your screen in the last ten minutes. I need to deliver it to the general immediately."

Lieutenant Stone, a caring individual, stood in front of the room's large screen. He was as still as a statue as he watched the radar track the blip across the sky.

"So, you've finally back, my friends," he said. "It's been a while."

"Excuse me, sir?" A second lieutenant standing nearby asked.

He turned to the officer. "Just thinking about the last time this happened."

Then another officer shouted, "We have a second ship, lieutenant."

This time the room was quiet, not as excited as before. There was a sense in the room that this might be the beginning of a war, something they had been trained for but hoped never to experience.

"Put it on the large screen," Lieutenant Stone commanded.

The men studied the image and wondered if this was the beginning of the end.

# Chapter Three

## It Begins

Stanley stood alone, looking out his window. As he thought about what they might find, a sense of doom threatened to douse his enthusiasm. What if it really was a flying saucer? Would he end up like his grandfather? Stanley lived in two worlds. In a word, he was a secret space and alien nerd, in the other, a typical teenager. He was athletic, a place-kicker for his high school football team. He was interested in girls, although Stanley felt awkward and clumsy around them. He thought of himself kind of invisible and had no idea how good looking he was. But the girls? They all thought he was a hottie. More than one note had been passed around study hall about cute, smart Stanley Adams.

Stanley saw Rick coming down dirt driveway in a red, two-door 1954 Chevrolet Bel Air with hooded headlights, tail fins, wraparound windshield, and rear fender skirts. At least, that is what it looked like ten years ago, now it was rusted and barely holding itself together.

Seeing Rick's car coming down the dirt driveway, Stanley opened the door of his closet and began looking for his binoculars.

Rick stopped his car in front of the detached garage on the two-acre lot. The boys piled out of the vehicle, their excited chatter disturbing the quiet evening. Walking toward the front door, they heard a strange noise coming from the garage. Roger and Rick froze in their tracks and clammed up.

They stared in the direction of the sound. They studied the strange colored lights seeping out between the cracks of the dilapidated detached garage. Roger slowly took a step backward, knowing that with his slow speed, he would need a head start running if whatever was in the garage attacked them. Something was clearly alive inside the garage.

Then a figure stepped out from the garage door, the creature was dressed in a gray cloth jumpsuit, and a metal helmet encased its head. In its gloved right hand, it held a bizarre weapon that looked like a ray gun attached to a twelve-inch canister.

The boys threw up their hands and froze, unable to move and too afraid to run for fear of being disintegrated by a death ray. They wanted to scream, but it died in their throats. The terrifying being continued marching toward them, weapon in hand. Unlike Roger's step back, Rick stepped toward the figure.

"Take us to your leader," Rick said, using a line that was in every science fiction movie ever made.

The alien reached up. The boys jumped back. Roger made a funny squeak when the creature started to remove its helmet to reveal Mrs. Adams, Stanley's mom.

"Rick, that's really funny," she said. "That may be the first time I have ever heard a joke from you.

Rick's face turned red as he pretended to laugh and act like he knew all along it was her. It was apparent that she held a welding torch in her hand, not a ray gun. She had been welding her latest metal sculpture in the barn. A gifted artist, people all across the state of Kansas, bought her art.

"Oh hi, Mrs. Adams." Roger found his voice as he stepped up next to Rick.

"What are you boys doing here?" She asked.

Roger was about to tell her all about the invasion. Though Rick knew what he was going to say and kicked him in the foot.

"We wanted to talk to Stanley," Rick said.

"Why didn't you just call?" Mrs. Adams inquired.

The boys exchanged looks. They knew better than to tell her that her son had called them after his sighting had crashed to Earth.

"We are going teepeeing. We'll be back in no time," Rick said.

"Go on in, Stanley's probably in his room reading."

"Yes, ma'am," Rick replied.

The boys headed for the door, but Roger stopped and turned around. "We saw something from space."

Rick could have strangled him. Roger was so impulsive that at times, he felt like bursting inside if he didn't say what was on his mind.

Mrs. Adams gave him an odd look, and a quiver of dread shot through her. The last thing she needed was for these boys to get Stanley riled up about space and aliens. She'd had enough of that nonsense with her father.

Seeing her expression, Rick said, "Roger was spoofing ya, Mrs. Adams. It was just a meteor." The tension left her face, and Mrs. Adams smiled.

Stanley was stepping out of the house when Rick reached the front door.

"Where's the toilet paper Stanley," Rick said, winking at him.

"What?"

"Remember, we're teepeeing Julie's house, and that tree in the front yard is huge."

Stanley darted back inside and returned with four rolls.

"Hurry! We have to check out the flying …"

"Toilet paper," Rick shouted, cutting off Roger from finishing his sentence.

All three boys sat in the front seat of the Bel Air and started talking at the same time.

"This is out of sight! I'll bet the aliens have gray skin and large eyes," Roger interjected. "I'll bet they don't like the light. That's why you only see them at night."

"Those are vampires, not aliens," Stanley corrected.

"They're probably from Mars," Rick added.

"Maybe they're friendly," Roger said. He was so excited, he began sweating.

"I'll bet they want to enslave us, or maybe they want to eat us," Rick added. "Historically speaking, invading cultures arrive unannounced right before initiating a hostile takeover." He hated to be wrong and would often pull wild ideas out of thin air to cover his mistakes.

Their imaginations continued to run wild.

"What are we going to do if we see aliens?" Roger asked. "Should we call the sheriff?"

"Not the sheriff," Rick said. "We need to contact the Army or maybe the Air Force!"

"Nuthin' doing!" Stanley shook his head. "They'll never believe us."

"Then what are we going to do?" Roger asked.

"Let's just wait till we know what it was that we saw. Then we will make a decision on what to do," said Stanley in a calm voice.

Stanley's excitement was mixed with dread. What if what they saw really was a flying saucer? Would he end up being labeled the town crazy like his grandfather?

While the car sped down the first one street and then the next, the boys yelled directions to Rick. Everyone was contradicting each other. The truth was that no one in the car really knew where the 'thing' had hit.

"Go straight," Roger yelled, unable to contain his excitement.

"No, turn left," Stanley shouted as Rick drove past the indicated road.

Rick slammed on the brakes, threw the car in reverse, and backed up. Shifting again, he turned down the road and sped on. There was so much excitement in the car that Stanley soon left his personal thoughts behind. Like his friends, his emotions went from confident and quiet to afraid and nervous. What if they were right? Did they really see a flying saucer?

As the car sped down the dirt road, they spotted something odd in the distance.

***

Mary jumped back in the car.

"We have to see what that was," she said. She could barely contain her excitement.

"Let's go to Bill's Drive-In Burgers instead," Mark responded, thinking that it would be a complete waste of time driving after something that didn't exist.

"You're kidding, right? This may just be the biggest thing to happen to our town. No, to Kansas! Come to think of it, the United States! No wait, I mean the world," Mary said with her voice getting higher with each new phrase.

"Have you been hanging out with Stanley's crazy grandfather?"

"His grandfather isn't crazy. I believe him when he said aliens visited him."

"Well, you're the only one. Everyone else in this town thinks he's off his rocker. Even Space Boy thinks his grandfather is crazy."

"Why do you do that, Mark? You know Stanley hates to be called that."

"Oh, I'm sorry I didn't know he was around." Mark looked around with an exaggerated gesture.

"Mark, how can you be so blind?"Mary asked. "Do you really want to go get a burger when something from space just landed over there? Something that may just impact the universe?"

"Earth to Mary, time to come back."

"Mark, if you don't want to, just take me home. I'll use my father's car."

"Okay," he agreed with a sigh, "but afterward, can we go get burgers?"

"Deal."

"Which way?"

"In the direction of Stanley's grandfather's farm."

Mark rolled his eyes and peeled out, filling the area behind him with dust.

***

Standing outside his barn, Professor Charles Anderson, Stanley's grandfather, was ecstatic at what he had just seen through his telescope. From the age of six, he had

27

studied the stars. He was seventy-five now. He had become a world-famous astrologer with the government. In 1944, he taught at an Ivy League University on the East Coast. When he retired in 1954, he was awarded the President's Award for Science. When his wife became sick, they moved to Habsburg, the town where she had grown up. Their daughter's family also lived there. Anderson's wife died two years later. Then a year after that, Stanley's dad was killed in a car accident. Stanley and his mom moved in with him.

In 1959, while his daughter and grandson were on vacation, Anderson told the town that he had been visited by aliens on a scouting mission. His story was amazing. He said the aliens spent a week on the farm, and they had become friends. What he didn't tell anyone was that they had honored him with a gift; a beautiful crystal they had told him could power an entire country. He was never able to make it work.

Everyone started calling him a crazy old coot. At first, Stanley's mom tried to get him to admit that the aliens had never visited his farm. Despite her pleas, being ridiculed by the press, and detained and questioned by the military, he wouldn't change his story.

Then things grew worse when he started building communication dishes on the farm. Every month, he added another dish until he had over two dozen of them. He wanted to get in touch with them and invite them back to salvage his reputation. It was too much for Stanley's mother, so she moved Stanley and herself to the other side of town.

All that was in the past. Today, now, something else was happening! After observing the objects through his telescope, Anderson ran into his garage. He grabbed one of his inventions, a detector of foreign metal. If he was about to meet more aliens, he hoped they would be his old friends.

# Chapter Four

## Out of this World

The rusted old car barely held together as it sailed over the deeply rutted dirt road. The rear bumper, held onto the car with wire, bounced up and down as did the passengers inside.

"There!" Stanley shouted, pointing to the left side of the front windshield.

Roger and Rick leaned forward from the back seat to get a better look. Across a large field of dried cornhusks and through a line of tall oak trees, the four boys spotted an object, flying low and close to the ground.

"Oh, man! A U.F.O! A real unidentified flying object! I told you so," Roger shouted excitedly.

"I don't know," Stanley responded with a question in his voice. Something didn't seem right.

"Drive faster, Rick," Roger urged. "We can't let it get away!"

"I'm driving as fast as I can on this road," Rick exclaimed. "If I go any faster, I'll lose my bumper and the muffler." Still, he pressed down a little harder on the gas pedal. Hold it together, girl, he thought. Aloud he said, "A real U.F.O.! I can't believe it!"

The excited boys babbled, shouted, and encouraged the car to hold together. Roger hanging precariously out the back window, they raced toward the gleaming object of both their dreams and their nightmares.

"I wish I had an eight-cylinder instead of six. I could drive a lot faster," Rick said.

Fearing the U.F.O. Might take off at any minute, he felt like he would never catch up with it. He sighed with relief as the dirt road, though still in the woods, turned back into asphalt, and the ride smoothed out. Seconds later, the roar of an engine startled them as Mark Whitfield's Corvette pulled up behind, and then alongside them.

Both cars raced down the narrow asphalt. All three boys in the Bel Air looked over, but as soon as Stanley spotted Mary and the quarterback, he ducked down under the dashboard. Rick rolled down the windows, Roger's body still halfway out his window on the other side.

"What's the rush?" Mark called out.

"We spotted a U.F.O," Roger yelled over the top of the car. "Look!"

He pointed in the right direction, but as everyone turned to look, the U.F.O. was gone.

"It's there," Roger insisted. "It just moved out of sight. We've got to hurry before we lose it completely!"

Mark's expression turned sarcastic, but before he could open his mouth to mock them, Mary spoke up.

"A real U.F.O? That's fab!" She turned to the Corvette's driver. "Mark, this is so cool! We have to find it!

Mark swallowed the smart remark he was about to make. He didn't want to upset Mary, because he was still hoping for a kiss from her. He decided to play along, even though he didn't believe in aliens any more than he believed in Big Foot or The Loch Ness Monster.

Although Mark would rather have led the procession, he didn't know which way to go, so he slowed down and pulled in behind Rick's car. The two vehicles sped along for another mile before they spotted the U.F.O. Once more.

"It must be over there!" Rick shouted, pointing out the still open window.

"That'll show him," Roger said, triumphantly, as he clumsily pulled his body back inside the car.

Rick looked at him. "What do you mean?"

"Mark didn't believe us. You could see it on his face. If Mary hadn't wanted to chase it, he would've made fun of us," Roger replied.

Rick looked down at Stanley, who was still crouched on the floor. "What are you doing down there?"

"Nothing," Stanley replied, sliding up onto the seat.

"Your hiding, so they don't see you with us nerds, aren't you?" Roger accused him.

"No, I'm not!"

"Yes, you are. That's why you don't come to our U.F.O. Club meetings. That's why you walk behind us in the hallway!"

"You imagine things, Roger," Stanley replied, but his voice held little conviction.

"Am I?"

With those words, Stanley sat up and said, "I dropped something."

Rick and Roger only rolled their eyes.

The two cars raced down the road. When they reached the tree line, they turned right onto a wider paved road. The object veered off to the left and slowed, disappearing behind a set of trees.

"I know one thing, airplanes can't do that," Roger yelled.

Now that they were on a better road, Rick floored it. They traveled a half-mile, the Corvette right on their tail, slowing down a bit when they came upon a group of houses.

"Look!" Stanley yelled. "The street lights are out."

"So are the lights in those houses," Roger added. "This is getting hairy."

"It must be over there!" Mary shouted, pointing out the passenger side window of the car. Mary's car took the lead, and the other cars followed behind.

As the three cars reached the knoll, Mary stopped. The cars would get stuck in the dirt, and so they all climbed out of the vehicles.

"I think it is over near those trees," Roger declared.

"I agree," said Mary.

"Come on, guys. We'll have to hoof it." Rick was determined to get a closer look at that flying saucer.

"Isn't that your grandpa's farm over there, Stanley?" Roger asked.

Stanley turned red with embarrassment. Why did Roger have to bring the old man up at a time like this?

"No," he mumbled.

"Yes, it is?" Mary said, "that's my house next to his."

"Come on," Rick said, running into the field.

"Coming?" Roger asked Stanley when he didn't move.

"Yeah, I guess," Stanley replied. What choice do I have?

Roger took off after Rick. A moment later, Mary started to run after them, Mark grabbed her arm and held her back, "There's nothing there."

Mary took off running after the boys. Roger, huffing, and puffing quickly fell behind. The smell of freshly turned soil-filled their nostrils from a neighboring farm. With the moon shining brightly overhead, their running feet made one of the few sounds in the now quiet evening. Rick was taking the lead, shining his flashlight on the ground so they could see where they were running. Occasionally, the wind would gust, but with most of the leaves on the ground, the tree branches waved back and forth like skeletal hands.

As they got closer to their destination, a prick of fear touched each of them.

"You hear that?" Rick asked.

"Hear what? I don't hear anything," Roger replied.

"That's just it," Rick said. "Something has spooked the crickets and frogs."

"What if they landed? What if the aliens have left their ship?" Roger asked. "They probably have big black eyes just like the ones we've seen in pictures."

"Those are fake pictures," Stanley said.

"Just because no one has taken a photo of one, doesn't mean they don't look like that," Roger said. "The pictures are made from eyewitness descriptions!"

The boys slowed their pace.

"Do you think they'll beam us up to their ship and experiment on us?" Rick asked.

"Why would they do that?" Stanley asked.

"According to the reports I've seen on U.F.O. Encounters, that's what they do," Rick replied.

The boys and Mary came to a halt, their hearts pounding with a mixture of fear, excitement, and anticipation.

"We'd better sneak up on them, just in case," Roger said.

Beyond a grouping of evergreen trees, strange lights lit the darkness, casting a vast saucer-shaped shadow over the field.

"It's just over the knoll," Mary said.

They kept moving, with more fear than excitement.

"What are we getting ourselves into?" Stanley asked.

When they reached the top of the knoll, the boys came to a dead halt. The U.F.O. was right in front of them. A huge helium balloon in the shape of a flying saucer lit from inside. Written in large black letters on the side of the ship were the words, "Come to Beckman's Used Cars, where the prices are Out of this World!"

"That can't be it! There's no way that's what we saw," Rick said. "That bright light that looked like a crashing vessel didn't come from this thing. Besides, a balloon wouldn't cause a blackout or make a car stop working."

"I feel like an idiot," Stanley said.

"Don't sweat it," Roger consoled him. "It's no big whoop."

"Not for you," responded Stanley.

"What's that mean?" Roger questioned.

"It means your grandfather isn't the town's crazy scientist."

"Oh wow, a real flying saucer," Mark said mockingly. "Save me, save me. The big bad aliens are going to take me away and eat me!"

"Cut it out, Mark," Mary said, defending the boys. "We all thought it was an alien, even you."

"Oh, no, Mary, not me, I never said I thought it was a U.F.O. I just came along for a lark," Mark snorted. "I'm not crazy like these guys."

Rick moved in front of him. "Cut it out. These are my friends, you stupid jock. You got a problem with them. Take it up with me."

"Ooooooooooo," Mark sang eerily.

"Stop it, Mark," Mary said.

"Now can we go get the burger you promised," Mark said.

Everyone walked back to their cars with no one really saying anything.

For Stanley and his friends, disappointment enveloping them like a low-hanging rain cloud. The boys were depressed because it wasn't a U.F.O; Stanley because Space Boy was going to start all over again, Mark would be sure of that.

"We should have stayed home," Stanley said.

The others nodded in agreement. Thanks to Mark, they would never hear the end of it at school.

# Chapter Five

## Artificial Intelligence

In one of the hundred-plus hallways in the Pentagon Building, Lieutenant Stone walked briskly toward Brigadier General Allen Mitchell's office. He had collected as much data as he could for his presentation to the general. Now it was time to deliver the bad news.

Stone turned quickly into Mitchell's outer office, his demeanor serious. The message he carried was so urgent that he walked past several people waiting to see the general. As he started past the secretary, she tried to stop him.

"Hold it, Lieutenant. The general is on the phone."

"I have a Code Green," Stone replied quietly, so the others wouldn't hear.

Now she understood the look on his face and the sweat on his temples. She said nothing more as he moved past her, causing the men who had been waiting, to exchange looks as he continued to the general's door, opened it, and went inside, closing it behind him.

The general raised his hand to make sure Stone didn't say anything. "Yes, sir, Mr. President. I think we understand what the Russians can do," he said.

Having no choice but to wait until Mitchell was off the phone, Stone looked around the familiar office, trying to calm his racing heart. The general sat behind a massive mahogany desk in a brown leather executive chair. Two visitor's chairs of the same leather were placed squarely in front of the desk. Books filled several shelves, and on the deep blue carpeting, hundreds of white boxes lined the walls. They contained files labeled Project Vengeance and Operation Trojan Horse. They were contingency plans should the planet ever be invaded by space aliens. Even though the government denied the plausibility of visitors from outer space to the general public, they knew better and took the alien visitations very seriously.

Knowing that the lieutenant would not have barged into his office unless it was important, Mitchell cut his telephone call short.

"Thank you, Mr. President."

The lieutenant saluted. "I'm sorry to interrupt, General, but two visitors have entered our atmosphere."

"You sure they aren't Russian jets?"

"They entered over Kansas, sir."

Mitchell's eyes widened, and he stood up. He knew that the visitors the lieutenant was referring to were not from this world. Straightening the jacket of his uniform, the general's expression became stoic. "Two of them? Then it has happened again. We're going to war."

"They hit our airspace at 2115 hours, sir," Stone informed him. "And sir, I don't think they're from the same planet."

"Why?"

"There are indications that they were firing at each other."

"Not good."

"Then again, they could be from the same planet, and they're fighting over which faction gets to make contact or take over the planet or something."

"I don't like either scenario, but why come here?" the general asked. "Where did they land?"

"I'm sorry, sir, we haven't been able to ascertain that yet."

"You don't know?"

"No, sir, they disappeared off the grid shortly after our sighting. We don't know if they're cloaking, or if they've landed.

The general had no doubt that aliens existed. He believed that anyone traveling across the galaxy to our planet had only one agenda. They were out to conquer Earth, and he would do whatever it took to stop them.

"I want a full debriefing at 2300 hours."

"I'll set it up, sir," Stone said

\*\*\*

Early the next morning, the paperboy rode his bike down, well-kept simple streets, delivering the morning news. Occasionally, a vehicle would pass, and the paperboy would wave at the driver. The air was crisp and cold, and as he whistled, he could see his breath as it left his mouth.

Habsburg was a small farming community that was usually quiet, nothing exciting happened there. Everyone knew everyone else's business. The downtown consisted of a single street of mostly brick shops with glass fronts.

In Stanley Adam's home, his mother fixed breakfast for Stanley and herself. From the small kitchen, Caroline watched the morning news on a television set in the adjacent living room.

It was a tradition for them to have breakfast and talk about the day before she headed to work at a metal company, the town's largest employer, as a welder. After the death of her husband, Caroline took her experience of welding equipment on her father's farm and turned it into a job that would take care of the two of them. Stanley admired his mom, who worked so hard in what was considered a man's job. He knew his mother was strong and could hold her own. Drinking the last of her coffee, she rinsed the cup and placed it in the sink. Then she looked at her watch.

"Stanley, are you up yet?" she shouted. When she heard no reply, she went to her son's bedroom. "Wake up, Stanley. You're going to miss the bus."

Stanley's eyes popped open. He yawned. Then as her words sank in, he vaulted out of bed and ran around the room, snatching up clean clothing before heading into the bathroom across the hall. "Thanks, mom. I slept through the alarm again."

Caroline headed back to the kitchen. After a quick shower, Stanley entered the kitchen wearing dress pants and a light blue button-down dress shirt and headed straight for the kitchen table. Twenty years of growing up on a farm had conditioned his mother to start the day with a big breakfast. She placed two plates on the table with eggs and bacon and a side of toast. They both sat down to start their daily routine together. The two were very close.

"How did the tee-peeing go last night? Did you have fun?"

"Yea, it was great. We ran into Mary."

Stanley hadn't lied. He figured he was answering the second part of the question first. He and the boys had had a big night, and he knew that if he threw in Mary's name, his mom wouldn't ask any more questions about his outing and focus on Mary.

"She's so sweet. Does she still live next to your grandpa?

"Yeah."

"Why don't you take Mary out?"

"Maybe because she's the most popular girl at school, and I'm not even in her league."

"What time did you get home last night?"

"After ten."

"How late after ten?"

Stanley stood up and went over to the refrigerator to get orange juice and to stall for time so that he could come up with the right answer. He was tempted to lie, but he didn't, he never did to his mom.

"Maybe an hour and a half."

"That's way too late for a school night."

What stopped their conversation was a local special bulletin on television came on the air where local reporter, Mike Crenshaw made an announcement.

We interrupt this program to bring you a special news bulletin live from the Anderson Farm outside Habsburg, Kansas.

The camera switched from the reporter at the TV studio to one in the field.

Good morning. I'm Doug Myers for KLEP News, coming to you live from Charles Anderson's farm.

As he spoke, the camera panned the farm, showing dead grass, cows, pigs, and chickens running loose, and an old car up on cinder blocks.

As you can see, the Anderson Farm is unlike any ordinary farm you're likely to see. You won't find any sign of corn or other crops usually grown in this area. Instead, the fields are littered with homemade satellite dishes, linked together and connected to a powerful telescope located in the barn behind me. Unlike the rest of the buildings, the owner keeps this building in good repair. With me this morning is Charles Anderson, the owner of this unusual farm.

The camera pulled back, revealing Stanley's grandfather, dressed in blue denim bib overalls and a blue and black checked flannel shirt.

Stanley and his mom stopped eating and looked at each other.

Besides housing the telescope and other equipment used to study the stars, I understand that you also run a little store. What kind of merchandise do you sell? The reporter asked.

Never mind that, Anderson said. We need to talk about the aliens.

Stanley rolled his eyes and sighed deeply. "Here, we go again."

"Be quiet!" His mother's words came out a bit louder than she had wanted them to.

Yes, I understand that once more, you have been visited by aliens, Myers said.

His head turned from the farmer to face the camera, giving the viewing audience a wink and a look that clearly stated how he felt about Anderson's aliens. He turned back.

Didn't this happen once before, five years ago?

Yes, but no one believed me, except the military. They denied it, but then why did they make such a stink about it?

So, where are these so-called aliens?

In their spaceship on the other side of the trees, Anderson replied.

The reporter's grin widened. Where?

The other side of the trees, Anderson repeated.

Can we speak to them?

Nope, ain't seen them yet myself. They'll come to see us when they're ready.

It seems as though your visitors are a bit shy, Myers said to the camera.

What do you say we walk over there and see if they're willing to grant us an interview?

Before they took a step, the owner of Beckman Used Cars walked around the building with three other men, pulling the gigantic helium balloon of a spaceship.

Is this what you saw? The reporter asked.

I'm not daft, son, Anderson asked. I didn't see a balloon. I saw a real flying saucer.

The reporter turned to Beckman and asked him when his balloon took flight. Anderson grew agitated. He could see what was happening – the same thing that had happened five years earlier.

It seems like someone's hitting their 'special medication' a little early. Still, there's nothing like some local humor to liven up the morning news.

Behind him, Anderson's face turned red with anger, but the reporter didn't give him a chance to respond.

There you go, folks. It appears that all the hubbub about a flying saucer has turned out to be nothing more than an advertising prank.

It's real! Anderson yelled in the background. You think what you want, but I did not see an advertising balloon. I saw a real, bona fide flying saucer!

As the camera prepared to return to the news studio, the last thing viewers saw was the car salesman pointing to the hot air balloon and shouting.

Come to Beckman's Used Autos for deals that are 'Out of this world!'

Stanley turned off the television with an angry click. "School's going to be a nightmare," he groaned.

"It won't be any better at work."

Stanley grabbed his books and headed for the front door.

"Stanley, I love you all the way to heaven and back."

"Me, too, Mom."

"We'll get through this, son. I promise."

Stanley was already out the front door and never heard her last few words. She knew he didn't believe it. Stanley reached the street just as the bus stopped. As he climbed on board, he faced everyone on the bus and the day with dread. His grandfather's latest escapade meant trouble. There would be no end to the teasing he'd have to endure.

Today was not going to be a good day.

# Chapter Six

## Space Boy

When Stanley arrived at school, he headed straight for his locker. Taped to the door was a drawing of a flying saucer with bug-eyed aliens looking through the windows. Their ships were blasting the local farms to bits. Stanley ripped it off and opening the combination lock, threw open the metal locker.

Pulling out the stuff he would need for his morning classes, Stanley slammed the locker door, put the combination lock on it, and whirled the dial. Laughter erupted behind him, he turned around. Mark Whitfield and several of his football cronies stood across the hallway, laughing and joking. He tried to ignore them, but that was impossible since they all wore strange hats made of aluminum foil on their heads. One boy held a balloon with a picture of a spaceship crudely sketched on it.

"Look, aliens! Stanley's grandfather is right," one of the boys joked loudly. "They're coming to get us. Argh!"

Seeing the commotion, more kids crowded around, joining in the laughter. Then Roger and Rick pushed through the crowd and surrounded their friend in support. It was the last thing Stanley wanted, especially when he saw Roger wearing a t-shirt with a picture of a U.F.O. Stanley gave Roger an exasperated look. More and more students joined in with Mark and the other football players' antics. As Stanley walked down the hall, they mocked him.

"Take me to your leader!" One boy shouted.

"Wait! Isn't your leader a flaky old farmer?" Another boy yelled.

More and more kids played off the jokes.

44

Mark pushed his way through the crowd and tapped Stanley on the shoulder. "Can we catch a ride with your grandfather tonight? We'd like to visit Mars. Who knows? Maybe we'll find some good looking alien chicks there."

A cute girl stepped in front of Stanley and batted her eyelashes. "I would love a date that is out of this world. Can you make that happen, Stanley?"

"Make way!" Someone shouted.

Stanley stepped back just in time to avoid a collision with four boys making eerie noises while carrying a fifth over their heads.

"Look! I'm flying!" The boy being carried said.

Stanley's face turned beet red. He put a book in front of his face, wondering if this torment would ever stop. Finally, a teacher stepped into the hallway in front of the crowd.

"That's enough!" he shouted.

"Mars to Stanley. . . Mars to Stanley. . . this is your grandpa."

"Everyone get to your class," one of the teachers ordered.

In physics class, the teacher wrote on the blackboard:

Types of motion: linear, circular, parabolic, and periodic

When he turned around, he called the class to order. "All right, class, let's quiet down."

Once he had everyone's attention, he began to teach. "Using Newton's Law of Universal Gravitation, we have learned how to distinguish between inertia and gravitational mass. Today, we are going to talk about the types of motion: linear, circular, parabolic, and periodic." As he pronounced a word, he unlined each one on the blackboard.

Seated behind Stanley, Mark raised his hand.

"Yes, Mark, do you have a question?"

"Would the movement of a spacecraft, say a flying saucer, be linear or circular?"

"If the spaceship is flying in a straight line, its movement would be linear," the teacher replied. "Why do you ask?"

"I just thought that Stanley could tell the class about his discovery of the alien ship last night. I think its trajectory was more circular than linear."

Everyone in the class laughed as they turned in their seats to look at Stanley, who slid down in his chair, trying to hide his embarrassment.

Roger turned to Mark with a lop-sided grin, "well, Mark, you should know. You were right there with us last night, following the flying saucer balloon."

Several students snickered.

Mr. Stuart knew what Mark was doing, but chose to ignore him. Raising his voice to gain the class's attention, he described the difference between the four types of motion.

As he continued speaking, the girl sitting next to Stanley passed him a note. He opened it and discovered that it was from Mary.

It read: Don't let them get you down!

Stanley looked at her, and she smiled.

Mark saw the exchange, and when the teacher turned his back to write on the blackboard, he slapped the back of Stanley's head.

"Stay away from my girl," he whispered fiercely.

***

Things continued as badly as Stanley had feared. Mark and his cronies tormented him unceasingly, as did many of the other students. At one point, things got so out of hand that Rick stepped between Stanley and Mark. The confrontation nearly came to blows until the school secretary, Mrs. Habersham, called them out.

"Break it up, you two. This ends right now! Get to your next class, and don't let me hear this has gone any further, or you'll be in the principal's office quicker than stink on a pig!"

Rick and Mark glared at each other until Mark shot Stanley a nasty look.

Stanley dropped his head and stared down at his scuffed black and white saddle shoes. He swallowed hard. Mark would retaliate.

Everyone watching knew this incident was far from settled. As the crowd broke up and headed for their different classes, the secretary reached out and touched Stanley's shoulder.

"I need you to follow me, Mr. Adams."

A flash of anger shot through the young man's body. *It figures. I'm going to get into trouble, while Mr. Star Quarterback walks away free and clear. It's not fair!* Making an effort to keep the anger from his voice, Stanley asked, "Is something wrong, Mrs. Habersham?"

"Not out here, Stanley. Your mother will explain when we get to the office."

*My Mother? What's going on? Why was she dragged into this?*

Stanley fumed inwardly until he arrived in the office and found his mother worriedly pacing the polished tile floor.

"What's going on, mom?"

She stopped pacing and turned to face her son. Her expression was strained, and deep worry lines made her seem years older.

Stanley still believed this was about his confrontation with Mark until he saw the tears in her eyes.

"It's your grandfather," she replied with a shaky voice. She and her father may have been at odds for the past five years, but she still loved him. "He was so angry after that noisy, rude reporter interviewed him that he had a heart attack. I thought you'd want to go with me to the hospital."

They exchanged looks, fighting back the fear threatening them both.

"I'll notify Stanley's teachers," the secretary told Mrs. Adams. She turned to Stanley. "Is there someone who can get your class assignments?"

"Yeah, Rick Turner can bring them to me, but I won't be gone long." Stanley hesitated. "Will I, Mom?"

"We have to go. We'll talk about it in the car," Caroline replied.

"Let me write down your classes and teachers, so we don't miss anything," the secretary said.

Stanley gave her the information, then went to his locker to retrieve the rest of his books. Heading to the front of the school and outside, where his mom was waiting. He dumped his stuff in the back seat and joined her in the front. She had already started the engine. Neither he nor his mother said anything as they headed for the hospital. Both lost in their own thoughts and feelings.

Upon arrival, they took an elevator to the second floor. They then walked down a series of seemingly endless hallways, following the signs that led to the Coronary Care Unit. Caroline led her son to the nurses' station and approached one of the duty nurses.

Stanley tried not to wrinkle his nose. He hated the sterile, antiseptic smell of hospitals. It reminded him of when his grandmother had been so sick and died of cancer.

"We're here to see my father, Charles Anderson. I'm his daughter, and this is his grandson. How is he?"

"He's resting comfortably at the moment. The heart attack was a mild one, but the doctor wants to keep an eye on him for the next forty-eight hours."

"Can we see him?" Caroline asked.

"Yes. You can stay with him for fifteen-minute intervals. For now, visitors are restricted to family only."

"We're the only family he has, so that won't be a problem," Caroline replied.

The nurse-led them to a private room filled with equipment. Medical personnel had hooked Charles up to machines that monitored his cardiac rhythm, blood pressure, and pulse, among other things. An IV tube fed a saline solution into his left arm, along with IV medications. A tube fed oxygen into his nostrils.

Caroline approached one side of the bed. Stanley stood next to her. As she looked at her father's drawn, ashen features, a mixture of emotions filled her: love, regret, anger, confusion, and fear. He seemed so helpless and vulnerable. Several questions assaulted her mind, but only one word escaped her lips. "Why?"

Stanley looked up at his mother, took her hand, and squeezed it. She squeezed back, grateful for his support. Returning his gaze to the man on the bed, he was surprised to realize that although his grandfather's condition did little to ease the anger. It reminded him that despite everything, there was still love and compassion in his heart for the old man. He felt conflicted. Stanley watched as his mother took his grandfather's hand and gave it a little squeeze. There was no response. She looked almost upset and guilty as he felt. They stayed for what seemed like a long time, just looking at him, not saying a word.

"Excuse me." A woman's voice startled them both. A nurse stood behind them. "I'm sorry, Mrs. Adams, you have to leave for now. You can come back in an hour. The more rest he gets, the sooner he will recover."

"Of course," Stanley's mom responded, turning toward the nurse. "Please call me any time if there's any change."

"Leave your name and phone number with the nurse at the desk. The doctor will be making his rounds at about five o'clock. That might be a good time to come back. We'll call you if anything happens."

"Thank you, I may just stay and wait for the doctor. I haven't decided. Where is the waiting room?"

"Just take a left. It's right across from the nurses' station on this floor."

"Thank you." Following his mother to the waiting area, Stanley was thinking about how he did not want to stay here for the next three hours. They made their way to an ugly green room filled with old magazines, several straight back chairs, two beat-up couches, and a vending machine. There was a small TV with the sound turned down in the corner. They sat together at the other end of the room. Four or five people looked up when they entered but quickly turned back to their own thoughts and fears.

"Why can't he be like other people's fathers and grandfathers? Why is he so flipped out over aliens and spaceships? Why does he have to be the laughing stock of the town and make our lives so complicated?" Stanley looked at his mom, hoping she had an answer.

"I don't know," his mother replied. As she thought, the beeps of the monitors and the sound of the inflating blood pressure cuffs were the only noise inside her head. "He changed so much after Grandma died. I know he misses her terribly, but to let the farm go to ruin. I just don't understand it."

"Do you think they messed up Grandpa's brain because he used to be a world-famous astrologer with the government? I mean, maybe they brainwashed or hypnotized him or something. Could that be the reason he has these crazy ideas about aliens?"

Despite the seriousness of the situation, Stanley's mom started to laugh. "Oh Stanley, you read too many of those Sci-Fi comic books. Really? You think the government hypnotized him?" She smiled at him. "No, I don't think that's what happened."

"If he dies, I don't want to remember him as kinda crazy. I'm afraid I'll forget the good times we had before he started talking about aliens. I really want him to get better, mom, even though he's sort of ruining my life."

Caroline looked at her son and felt a lot of empathy for his situation. She knew how difficult it was. "Not just yours," she told him. "When this alien thing started five years ago, people wouldn't leave me alone. Complete strangers would ask me the most bizarre questions. Others made fun of him: people on the street, my friends at the metal shop. Everyone thought it was just the funniest thing. It's not when you think your dad is losing his mind. So many people wanted me to have him committed, even Doctor Frankel."

"Why didn't you?"

"That's a good question." She paused. "I just couldn't. He's my dad. I remembered all the good times and how he took care of me. When I was sick with the mumps, he brought me ice cream every day. When I broke my leg, he made this kind of sling or saddle and carried me around on his back. He told me he didn't want me to stay in bed and get lazy, but I knew it was because he felt sorry that I was isolated. How could I put him in a home? He's not dangerous, he's just…I don't know, obsessed, I guess, with aliens and spaceships."

"So, why did we leave? Why didn't we stay at the farmhouse?"

"Maybe we shouldn't have. I guess I was worried about you. I didn't want you to turn into a weird kid, living in his make-believe world." She looked at him sideways.

"I hope I made the right decision. Sometimes I wonder."

Stanley didn't dare look at her directly, he just nodded his head. She would freak if she knew about all the space comics, books, and stuff I've collected, and hide from her, he thought.

To change the subject, and also because he had always wanted to ask, he said, "Is that why you never go out? A lot of women your age got married again, or at least they're dating someone."

"Hmm, listen to you. I think maybe you're off the subject. You don't need to worry about me. I'm very happy."

"But mom…."

52

"Listen, we've got to make some plans. All right? You're going to have to stay at the farm, feed the animals, take care of the place."

"What? You're joking, right?"

"You heard me. We can't leave it empty. I'm afraid someone will vandalize the house or, I don't know, break into the shop, do something to the satellite dishes. Someone needs to be there."

"Why can't you and I do it together?"

"I wish I could, but I have a large, expensive piece of art commissioned. I have to work on it in the shop; I can't do it from the farm. I'll need to spend five or six hours every night just to meet the deadline."

"I'm sorry, Stanley. There's no one else.

"When the kids at school find out I'm staying there, it'll ruin me. I'll never live it down."

"You'll just be taking care of the farm. Lots of your classmates help on their family's farm every day."

"Yeah, but they live on actual farms that grow crops or raise animals," Stanley argued. "Grandpa's farm looks like a nightmare out of some horror flick. You don't know how bad it will be."

"I do know. Besides, it won't be forever. Once he's better…"

A frightening thought provoked his next question. "What if he doesn't get better? Then what?"

"I can't think about that right now, Stanley. We'll just have to take it one day at a time."

Resigned, Stanley slumped in his seat. He could not believe this was happening.

"We'll stop at the grocery store on the way home and pick up some food to take with you."

"Can I pick out what I want to eat?" Stanley asked hopefully.

"Within reason," Caroline replied. "When we get home, pack a suitcase, and I'll order pizza. How does that sound?"

"Okay, I guess."

Stanley loved pizza, but right now, he didn't feel very hungry.

If I thought today was bad, tomorrow is going to be even worse.

# Chapter Seven

## Home Base

The 1960 green and white Ford Fairlane turned up the gravel drive of Charles Anderson's farm, leaving a trail of whitish dust chasing after the car. Six inches longer, five inches wider, and 200 pounds heavier than the previous models, the Fairlane had a smooth sloped hood. As the car bumped along the long rutted gravel drive, Stanley looked out the window. What he saw was nothing short of total chaos. It had been five years since he'd visited his grandfather's farm. Although he had seen some of the satellite dishes, decrepit buildings, and farm animals on the TV news that morning, seeing the overall decay in person shocked him.

The once lush fields Stanley remembered from his childhood were gone. Formerly neat, well cared for animal enclosures were broken down, rusty, splintered, and worthless. The beautiful thick lawn had gone to weeds, overgrown in places, dried and yellowed in others, and speckled with patches of bare dirt. The farmhouse his grandmother had been so proud of looked abandoned and badly in need of repairs and a coat of fresh paint. The outbuildings weren't any better, except for the barn, which housed a laboratory and looked like someone had purchased it new and dropped it in the middle of the devastation.

The garage was in slightly better repair than the house as it had been converted into a small shop where his grandfather sold U.F.O. And alien paraphernalia. The place looked sad and abandoned.

Caroline stopped next to the large front porch and got out of the vehicle. Stanley stayed inside the car, hoping his mother would change her mind about making him stay there. His cherished memories of the wonderful times he'd spent living on the farm began to fade in his mind. He feared the inside of the house might be as bad or even worse, and he just couldn't face that.

"Stanley, let's hurry up and get you settled. I have to get back to work."

The boy slowly opened the car door and slid out, trying to hide from anyone who might drive down the street and see them. Crouching beside the car, he opened the rear passenger door, reached into the backseat, and grabbed a beat-up green travel bag. He set it down in the driveway and followed his mom across the expansive front yard, where they stopped and surveyed the most horrifying aspect of the property. Fifteen large homemade satellite dishes dotted the landscape like weird metal machines from another planet.

"If I didn't know better, I'd swear I was standing on the film lot of the next low budget space invasion movie," Caroline said in a voice filled with dismay.

"This is a nightmare," Stanley agreed. "No wonder everyone thinks he's crazy. Can you blame them? This looks like something H. G. Wells might have written about in his next sci-fi book."

A spattering of animals completed the scene. Over the years, straw and dried grass had blown into the bottom curve of the satellite dishes. Many of them now held nests for various birds. Even the chickens roosted and lay their eggs there.

Hearing a noise behind him, Stanley whirled around, fearing Anubis, the goat, was about to attack. It turned out to be the neighbor's dog, a black and white sheltie. The animal wagged its tail questioningly until Stanley called him over.

"Hey, fella, where did you come from?" He asked.

The dog yipped, and its tail went into overdrive in response to some vigorous petting. When Stanley straightened up, he remembered the foul-tempered goat and searched the area for it. He finally saw it standing on the roof of the old doghouse like a pharaoh surveying his domain.

Caroline walked back to the car to grab two bags of groceries. Stanley grabbed his suitcase and one bag, and together they made their way to the steps of the wide front porch.

"Careful, Stanley," Caroline warned. "There's a loose board on the top step that needs to be nailed down. It might trip you."

Setting her bags on the bottom step, his mom retrieved the house key from beneath a large green ceramic frog in what had once been a flower bed filled with sweet peas, petunias, and hosta plants. Retrieving the groceries, they went up the steps. Opening the door, she led her son inside. Stanley dropped his suitcase on the floor next to the staircase that led to the second floor and followed his mother into the kitchen. Where they placed the groceries on a round table in front of a double window that looked outside on the equally dismal backyard.

"This should keep you fed for a few days. I don't know how long your grandfather will be in the hospital," Caroline said. "I'll swing by after work." She turned to leave. "Don't try to cook. I get off early, so I'll bring burgers from Bill's tonight," she smiled. "Just get situated, and Stanley..." Caroline gently brushed a lock of hair off his forehead. "You know, I love you."

"To heaven and back, Mom, I know."

"To heaven and back," she responded. It was something they always did to remind each other they were family.

"You're sure no one else in the universe can do this for grandpa?" Stanley asked, this time with a teasing grin.

"You're the only one in the entire universe who can save us from this situation," she laughed back as she went out the front door.

Stanley followed her outside and stood on the porch as she got into the car and backed out of the driveway. He stood there alone for several minutes, wondering how long he would have to babysit the farm, and hoping that no one would discover he was there.

He went back inside and looked around as half-forgotten memories washed over him, visions of a happier time, before his grandmother's passing. Scenes of life before his grandfather became convinced aliens were invading their planet. To this day, he didn't know what had set Grandpa Charles off. Had it been the result of his grandmother's death? He wasn't sure.

Stanley laid his suitcase on the twin bed and emptied the contents into the drawers of his old wooden dresser. Except for a thick layer of dust on the furniture, the room looked just like it had when he and his mother had left that fateful day. I guess I ought to clean it, he thought. Maybe later. With nothing more to do, he went outside to look around. In the barren backyard, he found his grandfather's old Ford pickup truck parked next to the garage. Then his eyes went to the sign hanging over the garage. It read: The U.F.O. and Alien Invasion Preparation Store

Curiosity got the better of him, and he went inside. It was no longer a garage. He flipped on the light. His grandfather had painstakingly built shelves and counters around the perimeter. One counter near the door held a completely restored old cash register that still said Woolworths on it. Inside, he found a five, six one-dollar bills, and miscellaneous change.

Shaking his head, he examined the merchandise displayed throughout the shop. Unlike his old room, everything was neat and clean. The variety of items he discovered amazed him. They included: plastic flying saucers, both models and kits, small plastic alien men, keyrings handmade posters, movie posters, playing cards, and t-shirts – all made with the U.F.O. And/or alien theme. Moving to the shelves in the back, he found six alien survival kits, a very convincing alien costume that was perhaps used for Halloween, a gas mask, and two handwritten books by Charles Anderson. They were titled, How to Defeat a Bad Alien, and The Day I Met Two Aliens From Another Planet.

"This is worse than I thought," Stanley muttered. Picking up one of the many alien comic books, he was startled by a sudden noise. Dropping the comic back on the shelf, he spun around, hoping the intruder wasn't Anubis or someone he knew. A stab of fear churned his stomach. What if it was a stranger? Everyone in town knew his grandfather was in the hospital, thanks to that nosy reporter. Stanley swallowed hard. Believing the farm was deserted, someone might decide to break in and steal stuff.

Stanley looked around for something he could use as a weapon. He saw nothing until he looked under the counter that held the cash register and spotted a baseball bat. Snatching it up, he held it over his shoulder, flipped off the light, and flattened his body against the shelves behind him. He didn't see her at first, but then a chicken let out a squawk and ran through the open door.

Sighing with relief, Stanley flipped on the light and set down the bat to continue his exploration. In one corner, he found an alien-themed pinball machine. "Well, if I get bored," he mused, "I can always play this."

In one corner, he discovered some old tarps, which he used to cover up as much of the merchandise as he could. The only thing left in the open was the pinball machine. He didn't want the kids from school to see any of this stuff. The pinball machine, however, was cool. Most of the kids loved playing pinball, but no one actually owned one. They were found in public places like bowling alleys and restaurants.

Leaving the garage, he wandered over to the barn. He knew something significant had to be inside because of the care the building had received. Pulling back the latch, he slid the huge door open. It was too dark inside to see much further than a few feet. Still, a ray of light from the setting sun illuminated a huge set of lights on tall poles connected to a large generator not far from the door. Curious as to why his grandfather would have the barn so well lit, Stanley went to the generator and checked the gas level. It was full, so he started it.

The lights came on all at once, nearly blinding him until he shut the generator off. Stanley found the light switch for the normal barn lights, flipped it on, and explored the building. The centerpiece was a massive telescope that poked through a hole in the roof. Scattered around were several half-finished projects, including the hull of a full-size partially constructed model spaceship. He touched the surface, with respect. It was amazing.

"I wish I could have helped grandpa built this. This is better than any model you can buy in a store." He sighed with longing and turned to leave. The setting sun reminded him he had better feed the animals before it got dark.

He found the feed in the far corner and went outside to coax the chickens over to the barn. Scattering the oats and dried corn kernels on the ground, he called, "Chick, chick, chick. Come on, you crazy birds, time to eat."

They weren't the only animals to come running. Anubis climbed down from the doghouse roof and lowering his head, made a beeline for the young man's posterior, knocking him to the ground. The crazy goat then tore a piece of cloth from Stanley's jeans and chewed contentedly.

He jumped to his feet. "Stupid, ornery goat!"

He was about to say more when he realized he wasn't alone. Spinning around to hide the embarrassing hole, he found Mary Guthrie trying to hide a smile.

She stifled a giggle, and her expression turned serious. "I'm sorry to hear about your grandfather. Is he going to be all right?"

"The doctors said it was a mild heart attack. I think he'll be okay," he replied, blushing furiously. Swallowing his embarrassment, he tried to play it cool. "I have to feed the goat before he eats everything in sight."

"Mind if I tag along?" She asked sweetly.

"Me? Mind? Ah…no, I mean, sure, why not?"

As Stanley fed the rest of the animals, Mary talked about the various unfinished projects inside the barn. It was obvious she had spent a lot of time with his grandfather.

"Most of these are inventions. Your grandfather is so smart. At first, he tried to look at the stars with only a single satellite dish, but he couldn't see much. Then he got the brilliant idea of adding another. When he did, he was able to see more, and he realized that the more dishes he linked together, the further out in space he could see."

"Really?"

Even though he hid it from everyone, he realized at that moment that he was proud of his smart grandfather. He still didn't believe Charles Anderson had met any aliens, but he saw the telescope as an opportunity to explore the stars like never before.

"See this machine here?" Mary grabbed his hand and pulled him over to an unknown contraption. "This makes fuel for the spaceships, but it's broken."

"Uh-huh." The old doubt began to creep in Stanley.

"No, really, I'm sure your grandfather can figure out how to fix it."

"So, do you believe he really met a couple aliens?"

Mary gazed into his eyes, a serious look on her face. "Of course I do. Don't you? I come here a lot, and your grandfather teaches me about the stars and constellations. He even lets me look through the telescope and help with his experiments."

At this point, it didn't really matter what Mary Guthrie said. Stanley was in love. Just walking next to her, made life great.

"Well, I'd better go home. See you around," she called as she walked across the yard toward her family's farm next door.

Stanley just stood there watching her walk home. Mary was beautiful and really kind. He had always thought she was the prettiest girl he'd ever met, but he never had the courage to ask her out. Once Mark claimed her as his girlfriend, Stanley figured he didn't have a chance. Now that he knew Mary lived next door to his grandfather, things might change for the better.

Maybe moving into Grandpa's isn't the worst thing that could happen, he thought. But he was wrong.

# Chapter Eight

## Greetings, Earthling

His stomach grumbling, Stanley realized he hadn't eaten since breakfast, and it was now nine o'clock at night. He entered the house and closed the door, making a beeline for the kitchen. Right about now, a couple ham and cheese sandwiches and some chips sounded good to him. Taking a plate from the cupboard, he grabbed a loaf of Italian bread, pulled out four slices, and headed for the refrigerator. As he reached inside for the ham and cheese, he heard a knock on the front door.

Thinking Mary might have returned for some reason, he walked into the living room but stopped to make sure he looked okay in the vestibule mirror. He brushed back a lock of errant brown hair with his fingers. Satisfied, he opened the door. The greeting on his lips disintegrated like smoke in the wind before he spoke a word.

A man and a teenage boy stood on the porch. They had thick black hair and eyes so blue they were violet in color. Although alike in coloring, the similarities stopped there, as their features were quite different. The man was average height with well-toned muscles, a long straight nose, and a jutting chin with a dimple. The teenage boy was tall and slender with a short, turned-up nose and freckles. His muscle tone had not quite reached the bulkiness that comes with maturity. Both wore a tan jumpsuit with a utility belt and had black boots on their feet. Their expressions were pleasant yet devoid of emotion.

"Could we talk to Charles Anderson, please?" The older man asked.

When he spoke, Stanley felt a wave of strange sensation pass through him. He not only heard the words, but he also saw, smelled, and tasted them, and in his mind, he

64

touched them as well. The feeling stunned him. He had no idea how this was happening. He opened his mouth to say something but closed it again without speaking a word.

The older alien cocked his head to the side and thought for a moment. If memory serves me, there was a woman, Charles Anderson's daughter, I believe, the last time we visited. She had a young son, who would be the age of the one standing before us. Although we did not meet them, I was aware of their presence.

Indeed. I believe you are correct, the younger alien agreed, having read the former's mind.

"We must speak to Charles Anderson," the elder alien said aloud. "Please announce us."

Stanley blinked and shook off the feeling that had momentarily overwhelmed him. He wondered if they were foreigners because of the strange way they spoke. "Uh, he's not here, and the shop is closed."

"You must be his…" the younger alien stopped, searching for the right word. "…his grandson. What are you called?"

"What? Oh, you mean my name? I'm Stanley Adams."

The younger alien reached out and vigorously pumped Stanley's hand. "I am Mourda. This is my father, Lutsik."

Although the greeting seemed enthusiastic, both aliens remained expressionless. It was almost as though they were imitating the actions of someone they had seen in a movie without understanding the emotions behind the words.

"Nice to meet you," Stanley said hesitantly. "Uh, my grandfather isn't here. He's in the hospital. Would you like me to give him a message?"

Both aliens nodded solemnly.

"We need the Core back," Lutsik said.

"The Core? What's that?" Stanley asked.

"Please take us to Charles. He will know of what we speak," Mourda replied. "It is of the utmost urgency that we obtain the crystal."

"You're not from around here, are you?" Stanley asked, wondering what country they were from and how they knew his grandfather.

"Our planet is located in the southeast section of the constellation Cetus named Tau Ceti, twelve light-years from Earth. We crash-landed not far from here and were knocked out. When we woke up, it was light, so we waited until now to come. The last time we visited, your grandfather said that if we ever needed a hand, he would help us," Lutsik said.

"Five years ago?" Stanley asked, stunned. "Okay, who put you up to this? Was it Roger or Rick? Mark? Mark probably did this, the stupid jerk."

"I'm sorry. We are not acquainted with the persons you have mentioned. Do they know where the Core is hidden?" Lutsik asked.

"Listen, if you're trying to make me look as crazy as my Grandfather, it's not going to work."

Lutsik and Mourda exchanged glances, their expressions still deadpan.

"Your grandfather is not crazy," Lutsik assured him. His tone of voice remained even and unemotional as before.

Stanley looked disgusted. "You're not very good actors, are you?"

"We are not actors. We are from Tau Ceti."

"You want me to believe the two of you are aliens from some star system…"

"Tau Ceti," Lutsik said with a nod.

"…twelve light-years away…"

"That is correct," Mourda replied.

"…who came here five years ago and gave my grandfather, Charles Anderson, a present."

"A crystal," Lutsik said, "a significant crystal."

"And now you need it back?"

"That is correct. Do you have it?" Mourda asked.

"No, no, no! I am not falling for this. You can just go back to Rick or Roger or whoever sent you and tell them it won't work." Stanley was nearly shouting by the time he finished the sentence. He walked out on the porch and looked around. "I don't know where you guys are hiding, but you're not fooling me."

He continued to squint, studying the darkness for any movement and listening for the sound of laughter. Nothing but the sound of crickets could be heard. Then Stanley had another terrible idea.

"Who's Mark," Mourda asked.

Stanley looked at him, "Did he set you up."

"That was the name you were thinking right then," Mourda responded.

"Mark, I know you put these two guys up to this," Stanley yelled.

Mourda and Lutsik turned and faced each other.

He does not believe us, Lutsik said mentally.

He thinks we are playing a trick on him, Mourda agreed. He believes someone has put us up to it.

Then we must convince him otherwise, Lutsik said.

Show him the ship. Both aliens thought at the same time.

"Come," Mourda said. "We will take you to our ship."

"Oh. Ha. Ha. Don't you mean, take me to your leader? That's what they always say in the movies."

He must be confused, Mourda told his father.

We must unconfuse him then, Lutsik replied. "Please, Stanley-Grandson, we will show you our ship. Then you will understand."

Stanley was still reluctant, but he knew the only way to end this farce was to go with them and play it out. He was about to step out when a feeling of caution stopped him. Wait a minute. These guys are complete strangers. How do I know I can trust them?

You can trust us, Stanley-Grandson. Lutsik's thoughts entered his mind, once more nearly overwhelming him again.

Stop calling me Stanley-Grandson!

"Very well, Stanley," Lutsik said aloud. "You do not have to shout when you speak to us telepathically."

"We can hear your thoughts loud and clear," Mourda explained.

Turning on the outside lights, they left the house and headed into the field of satellite dishes. Once they passed beyond the pool of outside light, Lutsik and Mourda touched a button on their left sleeves. Within seconds, a small device, four inches long and the width of a AAA battery, materialized in each of their right hands. Stanley was stunned, and for the first time, he began to wonder if these two really were aliens.

Seeing his expression, Mourda explained. "It is what you would call a flashlight." Their flashlight, however, emitted enough power to light the next twenty feet as brightly as daylight.

"Wow, that's some flashlight," Stanley said in awe. "I wouldn't mind having one of those."

They maneuvered through the eerie forest of satellite dishes like rats in a maze, walking toward the very spot where the U.F.O. balloon had passed over the previous evening. Even though Stanley's mind told him those so-called flashlights were something unknown to the people of Earth, his doubts loomed up once more like ghostly apparitions.

"I know all about that stupid balloon," Stanley warned them. "You can't trick me into believing it's a real spaceship, not after last night. Fool me once, shame on you. Fool me twice, shame on me."

"What balloon?" Lutsik asked. "We don't know anything about a balloon."

"Our ship is real," Mourda insisted.

"Yeah, right."

Stanley was about to say more until Mourda grabbed his arm and turned him around. Pressing a different button on his sleeve, his spaceship, hidden by a cloaking device, materialized.

Stanley blinked and blinked again. He opened his mouth to speak, but no words came out. Extending his arm, he reached out and touched its metallic surface. At first, he jerked his hand back. Then he touched it again, this time gently caressing the metallic surface in wonder.

"Mark sure went to a lot of trouble trying to make me look bad," Stanley said. "I know his family's rich, but having this made must have been expensive."

"Mark had nothing to do with making this," Lutsik said.

"Would you like to see the inside?" Mourda asked.

Stanley nodded. "I'll go along with this prank."

Mourda pressed his hand to a small panel on the side of the ship that read his DNA. A moment later, the hatch opened, revealing the interior of the silver-colored flying saucer. Grabbing his arm once more, Mourda led Stanley inside and gave him the tour. It was large enough to hold four people comfortably with two pilot seats in front and two seats set at a station on each side. It also included a small sleeping compartment.

Stanley walked through the ship in a daze. The words, This isn't real, swam around his mind like little fish. When they left the ship, and Lutsik turned the cloak back on, he was still coming to terms with what he'd just witnessed.

Grandpa isn't crazy. The aliens are real!

At first, he grew excited, but doubts crashed down upon him. This will completely turn my life upside down. I can't deal with it. It's too much.

"Will you help us?" Mourda asked.

"What?"

"Will you help us retrieve the crystal?" Lutsik asked.

Stanley backed up and thrust out his hands toward them as if to push them away. "No. No! Go away." Then he ran blindly back to the house and slammed and locked the door. He slumped with his back against the door. "This can't be happening," he said aloud.

***

Lutsik and Mourda did not intend to go away. They couldn't. There was too much at stake. They needed that crystal if they were ever going to save their planet. Although he heard nothing, a strange feeling that he was not alone made Stanley look up from his position on the floor. He nearly jumped out of his skin. The two aliens stood in the living room, not more than five feet away.

"How did you get in here? How do you keep doing that?"

"We teleported," Mourda replied in a matter of fact tone. "We can do that over short distances."

There was a knock at the door. Panic overwhelmed him, and he ran around the room, trying to push the aliens toward the back of the house.

"Run. Get out of here. Hide!" He whispered.

"Why?" Lutsik asked.

"It's probably the sheriff or the military looking for you."

Lutsik shook his head no. "It is your neighbor, Mary."

Stanley stopped short and wrinkled his brow. "Do you read everyone's mind?"

"Yes," Mourda replied. "On our planet, no one speaks aloud as you do."

The knock sounded again, a little louder this time.

"At least hide in one of the bedrooms. We need to talk before you meet anyone else." Stanley said, running to the door. He stopped, squared his shoulders, and took a deep breath. You can do this. Make something up. Lie if you have to. His expression went from panic to calm as he opened the door.

Mary stood on the porch with a covered plate in her hands. "Hi," she said as she brushed past him on her way to the kitchen. "I usually bring your grandfather dinner on Thursdays, so I thought I would do the same for you. I'll just put this on the table…." Her words stopped in mid-sentence when she noticed the two aliens standing near the hallway. "Oh! I'm sorry. I didn't know there would be three of you."

"Three?" Stanley asked, whirling around to see Lutsik and Mourda still standing there. "No, not three, there's only me. My friends were just leaving."

"Don't be silly." She hurried into the kitchen and set down the plate, then turning, she said. "I'll be right back. There's plenty more where this came from."

"No, you don't have to do that."

As he finished his sentence, he realized she had already gone out the door. Turning to the aliens, he said, "Why didn't you leave?"

"We cannot leave until we get the Core back," Lutsik said.

Stanley's shoulders slumped, and he sighed. "Okay then, listen. Don't tell her who you are."

Lutsik and Mourda cocked their heads sideways, but their expressions were bland.

"Why not?" They asked in unison.

"Because you can't!"

Lutsik's brow wrinkled. "Of course, we can. We told you."

"No, no, no. You don't understand. If you start telling everyone you're from another planet, someone will notify the military. Or at the very least, the police, and

72

they'll call the Army, or the Air Force, maybe even the Marines. Anyway, if they get their hands on you, they'll take you away somewhere, lock you up, and interrogate you and maybe even dissect or experiment on you."

Lutsik and Mourda exchanged glances again.

"We have been monitoring your planet for some time, and I believe that what you say is correct," Mourda said in his moderate tone. "That would be unfortunate."

"Mary will keep our secret," Mourda said, sending a soothing wave of calm into the young man's mind.

"What makes you think she'd... No, don't tell me. You read her mind," Stanley said in a disgusted voice. "You really have to stop doing that. It isn't cool."

"We do not wish to be invasive or rude, but you must understand that we do it for our own safety," Lutsik said. "Humans often say one thing while thinking about something else entirely. We discovered this the last time we visited. Those in positions of power often do this. They say one thing, but in their minds, they are thinking about something entirely different."

"Still, the fewer people who know you're here, the better," Stanley insisted.

As he finished speaking, Mary returned with two more heaping plates of food. "Here we go," she said, setting the plates on the kitchen table. "Come on now. Don't let it get cold."

# Chapter Nine

## Galactic Cuisine

Stanley and the aliens entered the kitchen and sat down. Mary uncovered the plates, revealing fried chicken, mashed potatoes, peas and carrots, and biscuits. She placed the covers in the sink and retrieved three forks and knives, which she handed to each of them. Then she went to the refrigerator and took out the butter and a gallon jug of milk.

"Milk, everyone?"

"Yes, please," Mourda replied.

The other two nodded.

After giving each a glass of milk, she grabbed some napkins and sat down.

Stanley picked up a chicken leg from his plate and took a healthy bite. "Mmm," he said after chewing and swallowing. "This is great!" He looked at the two aliens. "Eat up. It's delicious."

"Yes, do," Mary said. "By the way, what are your names?"

"I am Mourda. He is Lutsik," the younger alien replied.

Each took a piece of chicken in their right hands but made no effort to bring the food up to their mouths.

"What unusual names," Mary said with a smile. "Where are you from?"

Stanley looked up in a panic. He chewed furiously. He wanted to break into the conversation with a made-up reply, but Mourda opened his mouth to speak, so he thought of an answer and prayed the aliens would read his mind.

Make something up! Don't tell her anything about your planet!

Mourda nodded, and Stanley sighed with relief until he noticed the chicken the aliens held in their hands. It was disappearing – bones and all! Stanley choked on a mouthful of mashed potatoes, which drew Mary's attention. Sitting next to him, she reached over and slapped his back.

"Must have gone down the wrong pipe. Are you okay?"

Stanley nodded, but continued coughing, his face turning red from the effort. Glancing over at the aliens, he saw that the chicken they had held had completely disappeared. Mary also noticed.

"Wow, I guess you like the chicken, huh? I never even saw you eat it."

"It is delicious," Lutsik replied.

"To answer your earlier question," Mourda said, "our names are quite common where we come from."

Stanley thought furiously. Don't tell her where you're from. Make up something. Lie!

"And where is that?" Mary asked brightly.

"Our home planet is called Tau Ceti. It is located in the Cetus constellation," Lutsik said. He looked at Stanley with an apologetic look. We always tell the truth. We cannot lie.

No! Stanley thought back.

We are incapable of lying.

Stanley swallowed some milk and cleared his throat to break the silence. "Ha, ha, what a joker you are, Lutsik." He turned to Mary. "Always fooling around."

Mary frowned, her expression making it clear she was confused and wasn't sure who to believe.

Stanley thought she was convinced and felt relieved until he looked down at Lutsik's place and saw something that made his eyes pop. The older alien held his hand over the mashed potatoes and sucked them up through his palm. He quickly finished the rest of his meal in the same way. When he turned his hand sideways and delicately patted it with a napkin, Stanley saw a mouth. A small, smiling mouth in the palm of his hand!

Turning to Mourda, he saw him absorb the remainder of his food and do the same. As he finished wiping his hand, the mouth closed and disappeared, looking like nothing more than an ordinary line across the palm. Both aliens looked up at him as his eyes darted from one to the other.

While this was happening, Lutsik and Mourda kept up a conversation with Mary. She never noticed a thing. At one point, she realized their plates were empty.

"The meal was delicious," Mourda said. "Thank you. We were famished."

"You're welcome," she said, then looked at them both carefully. "I read a lot about space travel. According to the scientists, any habitable planets in the galaxy are so far away that it would be impossible to travel to them unless the astronauts used generational ships. They said that even if traveling to the closest star, it would be the future great grandchildren who would actually reach the planet, not the people who had initially set off."

"That would be a languid way to travel indeed," Mourda said. "It would be much quicker to use a…."

"Say, what do you think of all those homemade satellite dishes my grandfather has strewn around his property?" Stanley cut in. "Kinda crazy, don't ya think?" Stanley was trying to change the subject, but the looks the other three gave him, told him he had said the wrong thing.

"Actually, those satellite dishes are quite impressive," Lutsik said. "With a little fine-tuning, Charles Anderson would be able to see a great distance. He might even be able to spot our...."

Before he could finish, Stanley jumped up and grabbed Mary by the arm.

"Supper was great, Mary. Thanks for thinking of us. I'll do up those dishes and get them back to you tomorrow."

"But I...."

"Gee, look at the time," he said, pushing her toward the door. "I'd better get busy. Gotta big test tomorrow I still need to study for."

"I should like to talk to Mary. Perhaps she could...."

Stanley closed the door on her.

Puzzled, she knocked, but he did not answer. She knocked again.

"Stanley, you cut Lutsik off in the middle of his sentence," she yelled from outside.

"It's okay. I'll see you at school tomorrow, Mary. Thanks again."

When he said nothing more, Mary left and went home, wondering why he was acting so weird.

"That seemed rude, according to your cultural codes, Stanley," Lutsik said. His expression was deadpan.

"Don't you guys have any emotions at all?" Stanley asked in exasperation.

"No," they both replied.

"It's something you're going to need to work on. Listen, I told you. You can't tell anyone who you really are, especially Mary. Her dad is the sheriff. We're going to have to come up with some kind of cover story and figure out a way you can use it without lying, or something." Then his mind returned to the way they ate. "And for heaven's sake, don't eat in front of anyone but me. You hear me? It's a dead giveaway."

"We told you, Stanley. We cannot lie," Mourda insisted.

The aliens looked confused. Although highly intelligent, they were a bit naïve when it came to why humans acted the way they did.

Stanley was torn. With Mary gone, his mind whirled with conflicting thoughts. *Maybe I should have trusted her. The aliens do, and they can read her mind. No, no, that's not the problem. No one can find out they're here.*

"What am I going to do with you?"

Although he spoke aloud, he didn't direct his question to Lutsik or Mourda. They understood his dilemma and remained silent.

"You're aliens. I get that. Since you are, you could prove to the world that my grandfather isn't crazy, and you really did visit him five years ago."

"Your grandfather is quite sane," Lutsik replied in a soft voice. "I'm sorry we caused him so much trouble. It was not our intent."

"If only he had kept his mouth shut about you. Then none of this would have happened. Mom and I could have remained here and been a family. We wouldn't have had to suffer so much torment and ridicule from everyone." He stood still, lost in thought of what might have been.

"We are truly sorry for your pain," Mourda said. "However, I believe your grandfather would still have built his telescope and satellite dishes. The end result would have been the same."

Stanley looked up and gave him a blank stare. It was almost as though he wasn't connecting the events he spoke of with the aliens. Then his eyes focused, and anger filled his next words.

"Sorry? Sorry, it doesn't cover it. Sorry doesn't fix it. You have no idea what my mother and I have been through because of you guys! This is why you can't go around telling people who you are. Even if you manage to evade capture, the military won't leave us alone. They made my grandfather out to be a crazy old codger. It was all over the news. We became the laughing stock of the whole town."

"They did that out of fear," Lutsik explained.

"Who?"

"Your country's military. They did it out of fear. We are an unknown entity to them, and because we can travel across vast distances of space in very little time, and have better technology, they fear us. They do not need to fear us. Our goal is not to capture and enslave."

"They'd never believe that. The government is paranoid, and not just my country's government, but every government around the world. They're all afraid of someone more powerful coming along and taking over their country."

"That's because the people of this planet have not yet learned how to embrace each other's differences. Anything that veers from the norm is suspect. Many examples fill your history," Lutsik explained.

Stanley shook his head." No, we won't. We're not like you. We're selfish and paranoid. It's never going to be any different, and that's why I can't help you. You can spend the night in the barn. The hay in the loft is fresh."

He went to the closet in his mother's old room and pulled out two thick quilts and two pillows. Returning to the living room, he handed them the bedding. "I'm sorry. This is the best I can do. After tonight, you're on your own."

"Please look inside your domicile for the Core," Mourda said.

"Okay, okay, I will, now good night."

Lutsik and Mourda exchanged glances. Stanley's emotions had run the gamut from hopeful to helpless to angry. The aliens were thoroughly confused. Lacking emotion themselves, they did not understand why he wouldn't help them. Taking the proffered bedding, they turned and left the house, heading for the barn.

Lutsik spoke telepathically. Why didn't Stanley allow us to sleep in the extra bedrooms?

I think I understand why Mourda replied. Being younger and closer in age to Stanley, he was better able to relate to the young man's thoughts. Had he done so, he would have taken a step closer to making friends with us. He is too conflicted right now with taking that step. We must be patient.

Stanley stood in the doorway and watched them go. His thoughts were somewhat similar to theirs. If they were human, would I still have sent them to the barn?

He didn't have an answer, and that saddened him. Closing the door, he drifted over to the television and turned it on, switching the channels with the tuner until he came to the show, The Fugitive, he walked over to the faded flower couch and slumped down to watch.

Eventually, he fell asleep, his dreams a crazy mixture of the TV show and aliens. He was on the run for siding with his grandfather, but instead of the military pursuing him, the aliens were chasing him. They were eating buckets of fried chicken through their hands, and shouting. "Help us. Help us. Help us!"

\* \* \*

# Chapter Ten

## The Greys

Two towns over, other aliens in gray space suits walked down a dark, one-lane back road, searching for the Tau Ceti's ship, their enemy. Those humans, who knew of their existence, called these aliens the Greys. Their appearance was very different. They stood between three and four feet tall. Their bodies, arms, and legs were so thin they looked gaunt. Their heads, however, were just the opposite, large and turnip shaped with huge eyes that could not tolerate bright light, a tiny mouth, and slits for a nose and ears.

After a fierce battle in space with the aliens from Tau Ceti, their ship crashed outside town sixty miles from Habsburg at around 10:30 p.m. the night before. The Greys spent the next several hours repairing their ship. When they finished, they searched for Lutsik and Mourda's ship, using a tracking device. Because Lutsik and Mourda's ship from Tau Ceti was concealed under a cloaking device, their hunt was in vain. When the sky lightened in the predawn, The Greys set their ship down in a wooded clearing to wait for evening.

They spent the day sleeping, eating, and making adjustments to their instruments.

"Have you checked the tracking device yet?" Drees, the alien in charge asked, like the sunset.

"Several times," Jeet replied. "Nothing shows, except the humans' worthless aircraft. What if the Tau Cetis don't remove their cloaking device? We'll never find them."

"The exterior of their ship is damaged. They will have to remove it for repairs at some point," Drees pointed out.

Jeet walked over to view the screen to check once more. "Drees! There it is! I found it!"

"Where?" Drees hurried over for a look.

"No! It's gone again," Jeet moaned as the blip disappeared from the screen.

"Pull up an overlay map of that area and show me what you saw," Drees commanded.

Jeet obeyed.

Generation after generation of Greys had been visiting Earth since ancient times, so they already had a complete map of the world in their computer, waiting for the day they would come as an invading army to take over the planet.

"There," Jeet said, pointing to the spot where he had seen the blip. "They must have removed the cloak for a brief period, then turned it on again."

They were right. Lutsik and Mourda had removed the cloaking device when they showed their flying saucer to Stanley.

"Now that we have a general idea of where it is, we should move our ship closer," Drees said.

"No," Jeet said. "Last night, during our search, our computer warned that the U.S. military was tracking us. We must stay off the grid until we find and steal the crystal."

"Then, we will have to go on foot until we find a suitable mode of transportation, which means we will have to use our holo disguises."

"I hate those disguises," Jeet complained. "Can we not leave them off until we actually approach a human?"

"I suppose so. However, if one shows up unexpectedly, we can always eliminate them. It's dark. Time to go. We will have to find the Tau Ceti's before morning."

The earth seemed very strange to them. Long ago, they had used up the natural resources of their own planet, Xylanthia, located in the Sirius binary star system approximately 8.7 light-years from Earth. Things like trees, plants, animals, even insects no longer existed in their world. They had destroyed their ecosystem centuries ago and everything along with it.

"This place is strange. I never liked coming here," the alien named Drees said.

"That is so, yet it is filled with valuable resources just waiting for us to plunder," Jeet replied.

They walked at a steady pace, serenaded by the song of insects, frogs, and an occasional barking dog. The sounds unsettled them so much that when an owl hooted from its perch overhead, Jeet drew his phaser and fired at it. Fortunately, the owl spotted a field mouse and had left the branch before the weapon could incinerate it. Jeet fired twice more, but sensing the danger, the owl snatched up its meal and soared off into the darkness.

"After we take care of Tau Cetis, we will come back and eradicate that creature along with the humans," Drees said.

They continued walking.

"The Tau Cetis' tricked us with their last maneuver," Jeet said. "Now, we must find where they have hidden their ship."

"Who would have thought they had enough imagination to pull that off?" Drees said.

"Certainly not I. However, I view their lack of emotion as a good quality in this case," Jeet said thoughtfully.

"Why is that?" Drees asked.

"They are so droll. They will not complain when we conquer their world and enslave them. They will just consider their plight to be highly illogical and improbable.

"That maybe, but I do not think we should underestimate them," Drees warned. "They may not have a single emotional cell, but they are very clever, and they will use that cleverness to try to outwit us, and then to overthrow us."

"Bah. They are insipid weaklings. Once we get our hands on that crystal, they will have no way to defend themselves. The Tau Cetis will be ours to do with as we please," Jeet bragged.

Drees was about to continue arguing the subject when he stopped walking, practically freezing in place. "Listen," he said quietly.

"What is it?" Then Jeet heard it, too. "Quick, make the change."

They touched a spot on the cuff of their spacesuits. At first, the aliens appeared to pixel out of focus. When their bodies settled, they no longer looked like a couple of aliens. They had completely transformed into middle-aged humans, dressed in blue jeans, navy pullover sweaters, and black boots. Their large black eyes were now human-sized but were still black. Their almost non-existent noses became elongated and flared but were still on the small side. Their mouths were larger, but still thin-lipped, and they now had tiny visible ears. They were, however, still somewhat short and bald.

The transformation took only seconds. A moment later, the headlights of an oncoming vehicle came into view. The aliens flinched at the light and turned away but remained standing firm in the middle of the road. When the driver finally spotted them, he slammed on the brakes, threw the truck into park, and hopped out.

"What's the matter with you two goofballs? Why are you standing in the middle of the road? You got that deer caught in the headlights to look on your ugly faces."

When they remained silent, he went on. "Cat got yer tongue?" He marched closer, ready to drag them off the road and out of the way if necessary. "Turn around and look at me," he grumbled. He was about five feet away from them, blocking the glare of one headlight and clearly bent on violence when Jeet turned and pulled out his phaser.

"Hey, wait just a minute," the driver said, coming to a halt. He peered closer at the phaser and then grinned. "What kinda cockamamie peashooter you got there, boy? It looks like a toy. Whatcha gonna do with that, squirt me?" He guffawed and took another step.

Changing the setting on his phaser, Jeet fired, hitting the man point-blank in the chest. The human's eyes went wide with pain and surprise. Smoke poured out of his ears, nostrils, and mouth, and his hair stood on end. He tried to speak, but no words came out. He just stood there, twitching.

"Good one," Drees chuckled, "but you should have killed him."

"No. Better that I knocked the gruff right out of him," Jeet laughed. "Everyone will think he is a blubbering idiot."

Slipping on a pair of sunglasses, they walked right past the driver and climbed inside his rusty white truck. Drees sat behind the steering wheel. It took some time to figure how to operate it, but soon, they drove past the still frozen driver, knocking over mailboxes, trash cans, and part of a white picket fence. Since the vehicle had a manual stick shift, the truck jerked and backfired, making the neighborhood dogs bark, and scaring away a stray cat that hissed and flew across a yard into the bushes. Eventually, Drees got the hang of it, and they drove straight down the middle of the street.

In the morning, when the driver of a passing car found the man still standing in the middle of the road, he rushed him to the hospital. None of the medical staff could figure out what had happened to him. When he was finally capable of speaking, he couldn't stop talking.

"I'm tellin' you, it was two little bald men with strange guns that shot out beams of light." He held up his right hand with his index finger and thumb a quarter-inch apart. "I swear. They came this close to killing me. I stole my truck, too. You gotta let me call the sheriff."

Shaking his head, the doctor assured the man they would report the incident to the sheriff, then placed him in the psychiatric ward.

"Must be having a breakdown," he told the staff.

# Chapter Eleven

## Star Struck

Having spent the night on the couch, Stanley awoke the next morning with a stiff neck. As he headed into the kitchen, he glanced at the apple-shaped clock hanging on the wall over the sink and panicked.

"I'm going to be late!"

Running to his bedroom, he hurriedly shed his clothing from the day before and replaced them with a somewhat fresher pair of jeans and a green flannel shirt. Gathering his books and supplies for the day, he laid them on the kitchen table and stepped out onto the front porch. He was about to pull the door shut behind him when he spotted some of the chickens in the front yard.

He darted back to the kitchen and grabbed a basket from the kitchen. He raced around gathering the eggs and put them in the refrigerator. Feeding the animals didn't go any better than it had the day before. As he worked, he had to keep from stepping on them, as they were always underfoot.

Looking up at the loft, he saw the aliens peering down in sympathy. They descended to the floor of the barn

"Did you get a chance to search for the Core?" Asked Lutsik.

"I'm sorry, but I forgot."

Lutsik and Mourda exchanged glances.

"This is most unfortunate. Do you not understand the urgency of our request? The fate of the entire universe lies in the balance," Lutsik said.

"Indeed, we must find the Core," Mourda replied. "It is critical."

"Nevertheless, we must find that crystal with all due haste," Mourda said.

"Why?" Stanley asked. "What's so important about it?"

"If we can return it to our planet, it will save the universe Stanley," Lutsik replied.

Stanley thought that if the crystal saved the universe, it would be crazy for him to spend the day at school. If he didn't go, his mom would get a call that he was truant. Then life would really get crazy if it wasn't already.

"Listen, I will go to my first class, and then I will pretend to be sick and get sent home early. I'll look for it as soon as I return. Is that all right?"" Stanley told them.

"It will have to do," Mourda said.

Please don't let anyone see you," begged Stanley.

"We will hide for you."

As he finished speaking, he heard the bus coming down the street. Stanley grabbed his school stuff, slipped on his dress shoes, and ran outside, heading toward the road. He made it to the end of the driveway, just as the bus drove past. A deep sigh escaped his lips.

Stanley stood alone in the street, watching as the back of the yellow school bus grew smaller as it continued down the road without him. He stood there stunned, not knowing what to do but knowing that nothing had gone right for him since the aliens had landed.

Suddenly, behind him, he heard a car horn. It was Mary in her blue 1960 Volkswagen Beetle, leaned across the seat, and rolled down the window. "Need a ride?"

"Thanks," Stanley replied. "You're a lifesaver."

Climbing into the car next to Mary did make him think that maybe not everything had gone wrong.

He looked out the passenger window back at the house, seeing Mourda and Lutsik standing on the porch, waving goodbye and mimicking some of his actions. Stanley shook his head and turned to stare straight forward.

"Did you sleep well last night?" Mary asked as Stanley settled onto the seat next to her.

"Okay, I guess."

"How are your friends?"

Stanley stifled the sigh that wanted to escape his lips. "Fine, they're fine."

"Where are they from originally? They did not get a chance to say that last night. They have such unusual names," Mary asked.

"Canada…California."

She glanced sideways at him. "Which is it? Canada or California?"

He hesitated then answered, "Canada. Look, can we change the subject? I don't want to talk about them right now."

Mary blushed. "I'm sorry. I don't want you to think I'm nosy. They just seem interesting, but if you want to talk about something else, we can. How's your grandfather doing?"

"Besides being crazy, he's fine."

Mary's expression clouded. "He's a wonderful man with an insatiable curiosity. Unlike some people, he's not satisfied with the government's typical lies."

"If you say so."

"I do. He's a smart man, and he taught me all about the stars," she said. "I like learning about the stars. Do you?"

"No," Stanley lied.

He didn't want to shut Mary down, but he'd never told anyone how much he loved studying the sky.

"Every Saturday night, your grandfather and I watched The Outer Limits together. He has really missed you and your mom. He often talked about how proud he is of you and your mom. I remember when he bought your telescope and left it on your front porch. I was with him, and I can tell you how proud he was," Mary said. The expression on her face dared him to deny the gift.

"Why are you looking at me like that?" Stanley asked. Mary's words made him uncomfortable. "Okay, I admit it. I love the telescope. I use it all the time, but it's not something I go around talking about."

"Why? Are you ashamed of your curiosity? I don't care who knows about my love of the stars. In fact, I'd rather spend time with your grandfather learning about the universe then doing anything else."

* * *

Across the street, Margaret Webber, the neighbor lady came out to retrieve her newspaper. She leaned over to pick it up, and as she straightened up, she spotted Mourda and Lutsik. She wondered who they were and what they were doing at Charles Anderson's house. About to turn and go back inside her home, she studied the two strange men who left the porch and head for the satellite dishes. Realizing they were ignoring her, she slid behind the wide trunk of an oak tree. Taking a deep breath, she peeked around it. After examining the exterior of the old tractor, Lutsik lifted up the front end with one hand. He inspected the ground beneath and then set it down. Walking around to the rear of the tractor, he repeated the process.

The younger alien was busy examining each of the satellite dishes, cobbled together using bits and pieces of whatever Charles could get his hands on. He carefully examined each piece, making sure the crystal was not within. Afterward, using nothing more than his thoughts, he lifted the satellite dish three feet into the air and examined the ground beneath it, before setting it back down and moving on to the next one.

Margaret had seen enough. She ran into the house, looking for her husband. "Jack! Jack! Where are you?"

"In the kitchen, finishing my coffee," Jack replied.

Margaret found him sitting at the breakfast table in front of a large bow window that looked out over their backyard. Looking up from the newspaper, he realized she was highly agitated.

"Jack, aliens."

The emphasis she placed on the word 'aliens' nearly made him laugh. "You've been watching too many flying saucer movies, Margaret."

"There are two men over at Charles's house, and they aren't human."

"If you don't believe me, come see for yourself."

After forty-two years, Jack knew his wife. She would continue to go on about those supposed aliens until he looked for himself. Pushing back his chair, he stood up and followed her to their large living room window.

"I don't see anybody," Jack said.

Margaret looked around frantically, hoping the men had not left. She finally spotted them walking toward the rear of Charles's home. "There," she said, pointing. "They're over there."

Lutsik and Mourda, however, weren't doing anything unusual.

"They look like a couple ordinary guys to me," Jack said.

"I'm telling you. There's something not right about those two."

Jack put his arm around her and steered her back to the house. "Now Margaret, you just have an overactive imagination. Charles's grandson, Stanley, is looking after the place until his grandfather comes home from the hospital."

Jack headed back to the kitchen when Margaret looked back just in time to see the aliens walking toward the tree line when right before her eyes, Lutsik and Mourda disappeared.

"See," Margaret shouted.

Jack continues to sit down at the kitchen table and read his newspaper.

* * *

Stanley sat at his desk, utterly bored. He was in his first class of the day, Mr. Stewart's physics class, and as soon as it was over, he would go to the office complaining of a stomach ache.

Mr. Stewart stood in the back of the class by a school film projector.

"Because of Mary's interest in life in outer space, I have a short reel from an Army General about aliens."

He reached over, turned off the lights, and started the projector.

General Alan Mitchell was sitting at his desk in Washington, D.C.

"Let me repeat to my fellow Americans there is no life in outer space. We have followed every lead since 1942 when flying saucers first reported by…"

The class watched for fifteen minutes the general talk about the fact that no aliens had ever been spotted or had ever landed on the earth.

Mr. Stewart turned off the projector.

"Hey, Stanley, did you hear that?" Mark Whitfield asked. "If the Air Force says there are no aliens, then there aren't, which just goes to show. Your family is crazy."

The class laughed.

Mary rounded on him. "Why don't you just leave him alone? The government isn't going to tell you the truth about U.F.O.s one way or the other. The existence of aliens threatens national security."

Mark gave Stanley a dirty look. He didn't like Mary standing up for the nerd.

"Yeah," Roger added. "If an alien was standing right in front of that general, he would still deny its existence. He'd probably tell us the alien was in a Halloween outfit."

Mary spoke up again. "I think the government is wrong to treat aliens that way. After all, they're probably a lot smarter than we are. They could teach us a lot, but our government just wants to lock them up. That's terrible!"

It was turning into a lively discussion, but the bell rang, and the students headed toward their next class. Mr. Stewart yelled over their exit.

"We'll continue this tomorrow!"

# Chapter Twelve

## Search Your Feelings

Outside the classroom, Stanley hurried to catch up with his friends. He needed Rick to give him a ride home.

"Hey, guys," Stanley said as he hurried after them.

The two boys turned their heads and glanced at him before turning their backs and walking away, ignoring him. They didn't slow down, just kept walking down the crowded hallway.

"Rick, I need a favor," Stanley said.

"Did you hear something?" Rick asked no one in particular.

"Not me," Roger replied. "I didn't hear a thing."

"I thought somebody said something, but I must've been mistaken," Rick concluded.

"Aw, come on, guys," Stanley pleaded. "I'm sorry I acted the way I did in the field, but you know how much guff I have to put up with, thanks to my grandfather."

"All the more reason why you shouldn't turn on your friends," Rick replied.

"You got that right," Roger said.

Stanley hung his head. "No, you guys have always been there for me. Come on, you have to forgive me. I'm sorry. I'll never do it again."

Rick wanted more than a quick apology. "That was really lame," he commented.

"You're right. I really was a jerk."

The two boys stopped walking and turned to face Stanley, forcing their classmates in the hallway to stream around them.

"You want us to forgive you?" Rick asked.

"Please, I'll do anything you ask," Stanley begged.

"Anything," Roger said.

Stanley swallowed. "Well, I think so."

"Do you want us to forgive you or not?" Rick asked.

They stared at him with very serious expressions on their faces.

Stanley sighed. "Okay, okay. What do I have to do?"

"First of all, you have to stop blaming your grandfather for everything," Rick said. "He believes in aliens, and we think that makes him pretty cool." Looking around the hallway, he spotted Mary. "Next, you have to walk over to Mary and tell her that you love the stars, and you absolutely believe in aliens."

"Yeah," Roger agreed. "However, you gotta say it loud enough so that everyone can hear you."

"Can't it be something else?" Stanley protested.

The boys spoke at once. "No!"

"All right! Guess I deserve this."

"You do," Roger said. "Now, promise you'll stop blaming your grandfather for being picked on. We all get picked on, not just you."

"Promise," Stanley said with a sigh, realizing they were right.

"Well, what are you waiting for?" Rick asked when Stanley hadn't moved toward Mary. "There she is, walking behind Mark and his Neanderthals."

Stanley would have preferred to do this anywhere else, but he was stuck, and he couldn't blame his friends for pushing him. After all, he had really finked out on them the other night. Taking a deep breath, he worked his way through the crowded hallway until he reached Mary's side.

"Hey, Mary."

"Stanley, wasn't that cool in class? The film and the discussion we were getting into? I know I made a good point about cooperating with aliens."

Stanley just stared at her. She realized she was insensitive. "Oh, I'm sorry those guys picked on you again. They can be such bozos."

"Well, uh, yes. I just wanted to say that…you're right."

"About what?" Her curiosity was aroused.

"I told you this morning," he said quietly," that one of the best things that ever happened to me was when my grandfather bought me that telescope." He looked over her shoulder at the guys. Rick mouthed the words "Louder."

Stanley raised his voice a little, "I love looking at the stars, and I believe that somewhere out there, aliens do exist. I should have said that the other night, out in the field."

Her grin almost made his heart stop. "I know, I remember," she said quietly. "You're smart, Stanley, so it only makes sense that you believe!"

"Well, I'm not ashamed, and I wanted to say it out loud."

Roger and Rick had moved closer and were now right behind Mary and heard the last part of their conversation. They were surprised at his sincere admission. They weren't the only ones.

Mark Whitfield turned on his heel to look at Stanley and began to hoot and holler. "Hey guys, you hear that? Old Stanley believes in aliens. I guess that makes him as nutty as his grandfather."

"Do-do-do-doo, do-do-do-doo," one of the other jocks started doing the theme song from The Twilight Zone television show, then quoted part of the opening. "This is the dimension of imagination. It is an area which we call the Twilight Zone. Do-do-do-doo, the aliens, starring Stanley Adams."

One of the other jocks put his arms out straight and walked stiffly toward Stanley, "Take me to your leader."

"That's Frankenstein, stupid," another one of Mark's cronies called out. The kids in the hallway started laughing as they headed for their next class, leaving Stanley, his two friends, and Mary behind.

"Just ignore them," Mary said, referring to Mark and his gang. She laid a gentle hand on his shoulder. "They're nothing but a bunch of immature jerks, and they don't know what we know, do they."

Mary quickly walked off to her next class, and Stanley watched her. That was not a question, that was a statement. Did she know about Lutsik and Mourda? He thought they had fooled her. Why did she say that? That jogged his memory. He had to get back.

He turned to Rick, "you need to take me home. Now!"

"I can't leave school now, it isn't over, and I have perfect class attendance," Rick whined.

"This is more important than perfect attendance." He paused. Rick still wasn't convinced. "You'll want to see what's at my grandfather's farm."

"What?"

Stanley looked around as kids passed them, trying to get to class.

"I can't say now with this many people around."

"Man, if it's that important, tell me."

Stanley cut him off. "I'm trying to get you to see something…out of this world."

Rick still didn't get it.

"Rick, trust me. You will never forgive yourself if you don't meet the guests that showed up at my grandfather's farm."

"You mean…."

Before Rick could finish his sentence, Stanley gave him the stink eye, which made Rick stop mid-stride and nod in understanding. The two made their way to the school office with Stanley practicing his fake 'I'm sick' routine.

The school nurse bought the whole act. Rick even added he thought Stanley looked a little 'green around the gills,' and that although he wasn't happy about taking him home since he might upchuck in his car, he would be willing to do it anyway. The nurse said Rick was a good friend, and she gave him a white mask to wear over his mouth. "We don't want you sick too," she said. "Get him home quickly, so he can go right to bed. And then you come back right away. Don't want you to miss too much school."

# Chapter Thirteen

## Abduction

In a nearby county, miles away from Stanley's grandfather's farm, the Greys, stood alongside a road, waiting for the next vehicle to approach. They had abandoned the truck when it ran out of gas. A 1963 Chevy Fleetside pickup truck flew down the highway toward them. When it got within fifty feet of the aliens, the engine suddenly died. Puzzled, the driver, Willy Atwood, grumbled under his breath and tried to restart his vehicle without success. Camouflaged in their human disguises, Drees and Jeet approached him. The driver did not see them until they stood right next to his window.

When he saw them in his peripheral vision, his head jerked around to look at them, and he jumped. "You guys scared the living daylights out of me."

"Is something wrong with your truck?" Drees asked.

"The thing just stopped running. I can't figure it out. It's barely a year old. If you two will step back, I better take a look under the hood."

"That won't be necessary," Jeet said.

He raised his hand, which held a small, slender device with a small window that showed a digital readout, and four buttons, one red, one blue, one green, and one yellow. He pressed the red one, and Willy's eyes glazed over.

"I don't know how any advanced species can possibly consider them sentient beings. Their heads are too small to hold a large enough brain," Drees said.

Jeet scooted around the front of the vehicle, opened the passenger door, and hopped inside. Grabbing the helpless driver by an arm and a leg, he pulled him to the center of the seat so that Drees could get in on the driver's side. Jeet then pointed his mechanism at the truck's ignition and started the vehicle. Before they drove away, he stuck his hand out the window and pressed the yellow button. The little mechanism acted as a tracking device and began to beep quietly for a second or two, but fizzled out.

"What's your reading?" Drees asked.

"Nothing. It acts as if it's in a holding pattern. I think it was damaged upon landing."

"We must fix it. We must seize that power crystal," Drees said. He turned to the human sitting next to him and placed his hand on his head. "You will direct me to the nearest reverberation modulator recalibration specialist."

Willy gave him a puzzled look.

"I do not believe the human understands what you're asking for." Jeet looked at Willy. "We need a shop with tools."

Still, in a trance-like state, Willy raised his right arm and pointed his index finger down the long road toward a large red barn. Nodding, Drees headed that way, but instead of following the road, he cut through the fields, making a beeline for the building. As the truck left the concrete, it hit a bump, and a large TV antenna in the back bounced partially out of the truck bed. It dragged along the ground behind them.

"Once we fix the modulator, we should be able to discover the whereabouts of the Ceti's ship as soon as they turn off their cloaking device," Drees said.

"They won't be far from their spaceship," Jeet suggested.

"Once we find their ship, we will destroy it, and eliminate our adversaries with extreme prejudice," Drees said.

Jeet grinned. "Then we take the crystal, return to their planet with the fleet, and destroy their planetary defense grid."

"And that will put us that much closer to taking over the universe," Dress said.

As the vehicle came within a quarter-mile of the barn, the aliens realized they would need to return to the road as a large fence blocked their direct access to the building. The farm was used for raising horses and had several large sections fenced off. Drees had to backtrack before he found an open area that would allow him access to the road. As they moved closer to their destination, another street came in from the right side, forming a three-way stop. Not knowing or caring anything about traffic laws, Drees drove straight through the stop sign.

He did not see a sheriff's car coming up on that same intersection. When the sheriff saw the truck drive through without stopping, he hit the lights in his vehicle and raced after them. The aliens paid no attention to what was going on. They continued along at the same rate of speed with a stoic look on their faces. When the police car was nearly on top of them, the sheriff hit the siren, giving off two loud blasts.

Drees turned his head to see what was causing this annoyance. Confused, he turned to Willy and placed his hand on the human's forehead. "What is happening?"

"They're gonna arrest you, man," Willy replied.

"They seek to detain us?" Drees asked. "Who are they?"

"The law."

"Are they authority figures?"

"Yup!"

Drees turned Jeet. "We must avoid detainment at all costs. We have no time to waste. We must find the Core."

"Then you'd better step on it," Willy said. When Drees gave him a confused look, he clarified. "Floor the gas pedal, unless you want to be caught."

The alien did so and sped down the street with the Sheriff tearing after them. When they came to the next side street, the truck flew around the corner and cut through a farm. Drees drove through the cornfield until he came upon another street, which he took. He drove another mile, crossing a bridge in the process. The sheriff was hot on their tail, his vehicle's siren wailing like a banshee.

"The sheriff following us is good," Drees said.

Jeet nodded, reached into a carrying case about the size of a briefcase, he pulled out a phaser.

Turning back around, Jeet adjusted the setting on his weapon and fired a laser beam that sent a pulse wave through the vehicle. The siren abruptly went quiet, the red flashing lights died, and the engine began to smoke as the car slowly rolled to a stop.

Confused, the sheriff reached for his radio to call for help, but it, too, was dead. Not even static issued from the speaker. He threw up his hands in frustration and got out of the car to walk to the nearest house and call for help.

Even though the police were no longer chasing them, and not knowing that the radio in the sheriff's vehicle had died before he could get off a call for help, Willy advised Drees to keep going. The alien continued driving at a high rate of speed and return on another road to the red barn.

The Greys climbed out of the truck, Drees placed his hand on Willy's head.

"Go home and forget all about us."

Nodding, Willy slid into the driver's seat and drove away. Jeet and Drees entered the barn and finding where the tools were stored, began searching for what they needed to recalibrate their reverberation modulator.

"These tools are crude in comparison to our technology," Jeet said. "It's going to take a while to complete the recalibration."

"Nevertheless, it must be done," Drees said.

As Jeet worked, the horses, locked in their stalls for the night, began to stomp and whiny in fear. At first, the Greys ignored them, but as the animals' agitation grew, Drees realized they were making so much noise, it could draw unwanted visitors.

Inside the house, the elderly farmer, dressed in pajamas and half-asleep in front of the television, shook himself awake and stood up. Putting on a coat and a pair of tall rubber boots, he grabbed a flashlight and his shotgun and headed outside. When he reached the partially open door of the barn, he realized that the critter alarming his horses were the two-legged kind. He opened the door wider. Spotting Jeet, who was still in his human disguise, he aimed his shotgun at him.

"Just what in Sam Hill are you doing in here?" the farmer punctuated the question by spitting on the floor.

Jeet turned and looked at him, studying the situation.

The farmer wasted no time, "Put down the tools and get your hands in the air before I blow a hole in you a mile wide."

Drees was in another part of the barn, calming the horses. He quietly moved through the shadows and approached the farmer, who didn't see him until it was too late. Placing his hand on the farmer's head, he took control.

"Go back in the house and continued doing whatever you were doing before."

The farmer lowered his shotgun and nodded. He turned to leave, but Drees stopped him.

"We need the keys to your vehicle."

Still in his trance, the farmer pulled the keys from his coat pocket and handed them over to the alien. "Trucks in the garage. Help yourself."

Jeet continued his repairs, but the farmer was oblivious to everything except the television screen. He wouldn't snap out of the trance for several more hours. In the morning, he would discover that his truck and keys were gone and call the sheriff to report a theft.

"That should do it," Jeet said after forty-five minutes had passed.

He and Drees left the barn, and the device began to beep.

"We've got a signal. Let's go find that ship," Jeet said.

"I'm hungry," Drees said as they climbed into the truck.

"Me, too, but what do they have on this planet that we can eat?"

"A friend of mine works with one of the ships abducting humans and experimenting on them. He told me that the bread is good," Drees said.

"Where do we find this bread?"

Drees thought a moment, then a smile crossed his face. "We passed a place earlier today. The humans call them restaurants. It's where they go to eat."

"Then we must go there, too."

# Chapter Fourteen

## The Search

When they reached the farm, Rick scanned the front of the house looking for the aliens, his eyes wide with anticipation.

"They're inside. I told them to stay out of sight. Look, you don't have time now to meet Mourda and Lutsik. You'll get in trouble for taking too long to bring me home, but tomorrow, you and the guys can come in the morning. I promise. You'll get to meet them both. We'll spend the whole morning together."

Rick started to protest but realized Stanley was right. He had to get back, pronto. If he got into trouble at school, his dad would take the car away, and then they would all be in a pickle. "Okay, Stanley. We'll be here first thing tomorrow."

Stanley ran into the living room, Anubis, the goat, had already chewed a good-sized hole in one of the cushions on the couch. Mourda sat in a recliner, fascinated by the goat's actions.

"Get away from there, you stupid goat!" Stanley shouted. He turned toward Mourda. "How could you just sit there and let him do that?"

"I'm sorry. I was so fascinated by the animal's actions, I didn't stop to realize that he was destroying the furniture," Mourda said.

Stanley led the goat outside and returned and said, "Man, my mom is going to have a fit when she sees this."

"I can repair it," Lutsik said.

Stanley looked skeptical. "You'd have to re-upholster the whole couch."

"Not so."

Lutsik programmed the buttons on his left cuff. Then he closed his fist, bent his wrist down. Pointing at the damaged portion of the couch, a beam shot out from a tiny hole in the cuff, which he passed back and forth over the damaged area. Stanley's mouth dropped in astonishment as he watched the beam re-create the missing portion of the cushion perfectly. When Lutsik shut off the beam, the couch looked better than ever.

Lutsik turned to Stanley. "Now, we must continue our search for the Core."

"What does it look like?"

"It is four meggards in diameter with a seven joshar configuration," Lutsik replied.

Stanley looked confused.

"You need to translate that into earth terms," Mourda told Lutsik.

"It is the size of an American football and has seven prisms of the light spectrum," Mourda said.

"Okay," Stanley said, scratching his head in wonder. "Let's split up. It'll go faster that way. I'll start with the bedroom, you guys look in the living room. Just be careful, and don't break anything!"

Stanley, Lutsik, and Mourda began a methodical search.

On his way to his grandfather's bedroom, Stanley noticed the pictures on the walls and wondered if one of them might be covering a safe or hidey-hole. He examined each painting and then turned to the photographs. As he looked behind them, he found himself returning to the front of each picture and gazing at them.

One was a photo of his grandparents sitting on a glider on the front porch. There were a few pictures of his mother at various ages, from childhood to adulthood. The last one showed his mother and grandmother shortly before his grandmother had passed away. There were also pictures of Stanley. One showed him at age six, seated in his grandfather's lap and grinning from ear to ear with a popsicle in one hand. In the last photo, he and his grandpa knelt on the garage floor, repairing his bicycle. He was eleven at the time.

The love and happiness in his grandfather's eyes were easy to see even in the photograph. Stanley thought back to that day. They had been a family then. They had been happy. As his mind returned to the present, he caught his reflection in the glass of the picture. He sighed. Moments passed before he was able to shake himself from his reverie. Sighing again, he moved on to his grandfather's bedroom.

As soon as Stanley walked through the door and switched on the light, his eyes traveled around the room in astonishment. Weird things filled every available space. The handmade doilies his grandmother had used on the furniture were gone, as were the knick-knacks that once covered the chest of drawers, dresser, and bookshelves.

In their place, the corner on the nightstand next to the bed held a radio with an extra antenna. A small bookcase on one wall held endless stacks of comic books. The latest was the same one he had read a couple days ago. He picked it up and held it in his hands. As he did, he whispered, "Grandpa?"

He realized then that he needed to talk to him. He had questions, lots of them. Returning the magazine to the shelf, he remembered why he was in the room and scoured it. Although he found many unique things, he didn't find anything resembling a crystal.

As Stanley worked, he heard loud noises, glass breaking, and loud thumping, coming from the living room where the aliens were searching.

When the noise continued, Stanley hurried to the living room just in time to see Lutsik mentally lifting the couch and placing it on the coffee table. There was a loud crack. The table splintered and crashed to the floor. At the same time, Mourda lifted the TV and took it apart piece by piece.

Glancing around, the coffee table and television weren't the only things broken. "I told you not to break anything," Stanley exclaimed with a sigh.

"You said to be careful," Lutsik corrected him.

"We were not injured," Mourda added as he lifted the couch from the broken table and set it back into position. "Don't worry. We will make them as good as new."

"Let's try the basement," Stanley said.

Mourda and Lutsik followed him down the steps into the dark, damp cellar. Consisting of one large area and a twelve foot by twelve foot, windowless room with a solid metal door. Stanley remembered this room. It was a safe place to go should a tornado touchdown. While the two aliens searched the rest of the basement, Stanley focused on this room. They shouted back and forth to each other as they worked.

"We gave it to Mister Anderson," Mourda replied. "He said he would hide it in a safe place."

"Well, this is the safest place in the whole house, but it's not here. He is kind of crazy, you know. This house is a mess," Stanley said. But as the words left his mouth, for the first time in his life, Stanley didn't feel right saying them.

"Charles Anderson is a good neighbor," Lutsik said.

"He's a good grandpa, too," Stanley admitted.

When they finished searching the basement and becoming discouraged, all three sat on the couch to talk.

"If this Core is so important, why did you leave it when you were here last time?" Stanley asked.

"It was a gift to your grandfather," Mourda said.

"But if you needed it, why would you give it away?"

"We had to hide it from our enemies from another planet. We had another crystal, but an unforeseen incident has damaged it," Lutsik said. "That is why we need the one we gave to your grandfather for safekeeping five years ago."

"But why would you give it to him of all people?" Stanley wondered.

"Mister Anderson believed in us, he was our friend," Lutsik explained.

"He is a kind and extraordinary man," Mourda added.

Stanley decided to question the aliens further. "I know you said the one you have was damaged, but what does it do? Why is it so important that you find the other?"

"It is a crystal, capable of providing more power than all of your energy-producing systems on Earth combined," Lutsik explained. "This is why it must be kept out of the hands of not only our enemies."

"So why wouldn't you hide it closer to home?"

"We wanted to place it on a planet where it could not be found. Most of the worlds in our universe are unaware of your planet's existence," Lutsik said. "Should it fall into the wrong hands, it would destroy my people's freedom."

"How so?" Stanley asked.

"In part, it operates a shield that encircles our planet, keeping us safe from invasion. Nothing can harm us as long as the shield remains. Occasionally, it has to be re-charged. We need the crystal to do that."

Stanley said, "so what you're telling me is that you need this crystal to save your planet."

"Not only our planet but the universe." Mourda's expression was grave. "The Greys, as your people have nicknamed them, want it. They would not only use it to destroy my people but yours and everyone else."

"So, I guess they want it pretty bad." Then a thought occurred to him. "Are they here? On Earth? Right now?"

"Yes, Stanley, even now, they are searching for our ship, hoping it will lead them to us and the crystal," Mourda said. "That is why we must speak to your grandfather. He will know where the crystal is."

"He wasn't awake the last time I saw him." Stanley became teary-eyed. "I've been wrong about him this whole time. I feel terrible."

Lutsik was aware of the emotional problems that this conversation was having on Stanley. He hoped to resolve things by telling him the truth. "You are strong, Stanley, like your grandfather," he said. "And you are truthful, like him. You will do the right thing."

"I'm like him?"

"Yes, very much so. We all have strengths," Lutsik said. "We just need to discover what they are."

"I think it's better than cool to be like my grandfather."

"I have heard this term, 'cool' several times," Lutsik commented. "It is not related to temperature, as I first thought. It means having done something significantly good, being admired, elevated in popularity, or societal standards. Am I correct?"

"Uh, yeah, I think that might describe cool. I really never thought of it. We just say it and understand what it means."

"Then, I would tell you that strength and truthfulness are cool. You and your grandfather both possess them. We would say they are great attributes. Gifts that when you use them, you will develop even more cool attributes."

"Well, then I better use them, so I can be the coolest cat on the planet!"

"Cat?" Like the small feline animal? I am confused."

"Later. I'll explain later. Right now, we'd better hurry and find that crystal before the Greys find us, or the crystal. I sure don't like their plan."

"Yes," Mourda said. "According to our tracking device, they are getting closer. If they find us, they will not hesitate to put their evil plan into action.

"I need to get to my grandfather quickly," Stanley said. It was after 3:00 p.m. The day was going fast, and they still hadn't found the Core.

Stanley walked over to the phone, knowing the one person who could help him.

***

# Chapter Fifteen

## Does Not Compute

Mary and Stanley rode the elevator up to the sixth floor of St. Bart's General Hospital of Habsburg, Kansas.

Earlier that day, his mother had phoned to tell him that the doctor had transferred his grandfather out of intensive care and into a regular room in the coronary unit. As they walked down the corridor looking for the room number, a nurse approached.

"Excuse me, but who are you looking for?" A voice said from behind them. They turned to look into the stern eyes of a nurse.

"I'm here to see my grandfather Charles Anderson. It's urgent," Stanley said.

She turned to Mary and asked, "Is he your grandfather, too?"

"No, just Stanley's," Mary replied. "I live next door. We're very close friends."

"I'm sorry. I can only allow family members to see Mr. Anderson. There is a waiting room down the hall past the nurse's station where you can wait until your friend is finished."

Stanley was about to protest, but Mary placed a hand on his arm.

"It's okay. You're the one who needs to see him."

Stanley passed two more doors before he came to his grandfather's private room. When he walked inside, Charles was awake. Stanley approached the bed and smiled. His grandfather smiled back.

"It's good to see you, Stanley. How's your momma?"

"Good. Grandpa, I'm sorry."

"For what, Stanley?"

114

"For losing track, for not believing in you, for thinking that you were…"

"Crazy?"

"Yeah."

During the ride to the hospital, Stanley thought about what he would say. Since his grandfather was recovering from a heart attack, he wasn't sure it would be a good idea to tell him about the aliens' return. Although he was more interested in rebuilding his relationship with his grandfather, he now understood the importance of finding the crystal. He just had to figure out a way to ask about its location, without exciting the old man.

"Hey, grandpa, I'm watching your house, and I have something significant to me that I have to hide while I'm at school."

"How important?"

"A matter of life and death."

"How did you come across something so important?"

"It would take too long to tell you this late."

Grandpa smiled. "They're back, and they want the Core," His blue eyes twinkled, "It's stored in the false pantry."

"Where?"

"It under the false door…"

Whatever else he was going to say did not come out. His heart rate increased, setting off an alarm, which brought a nurse running. She checked the monitors and spoke to Charles to calm him down. Then she left and returned moments later with a needle, which she injected into the IV attached to his left arm. During this, although worried about his grandfather's condition, Stanley could not let the question slide. If heaven forbid, his grandfather got worse and was unable to speak, he would not be able to find out where the crystal was. Conversation, however, was awkward. He tried to question his grandfather between the nurse's questions.

"I'm sorry, but you'll have to leave," the nurse told Stanley.

Stanley's grandfather began to slide into shock. Stanley didn't want to leave. He didn't have all the information he needed yet, but she forced him from the room. Still, he remained in the doorway, hoping things would calm down, so he could speak to his grandfather awhile longer.

"Where is the false door?"

"That's my grandson," Charles told the nurse. "He is twenty-five, no thirty-two. No wait, he's eighteen." He winked at Stanley.

"Go now, Stanley, and help them," his grandpa said before he passed out.

Stanley nodded. "I love you, grandpa. I'll come back tomorrow."

He walked down the hall to find Mary sitting in one of the chairs, paging through a copy of Life Magazine.

"That was quick," Mary said. "Is everything alright?"

"Grandpa's heart rate picked up. The nurse said I had to leave."

"Oh no! Will he be okay?

"She said he would and to come back tomorrow,"

"Did he tell you what you wanted to know?"

"He started to, but before he could finish, he…." Suddenly, his face lit up. "Come on. I think I know what he was trying to tell me."

Stanley grabbed Mary's hand, and they ran out of the hospital to her car.

As they drove through town, heading back to the farm, they passed a caravan of black vehicles going in the opposite direction.

Curious, Stanley examined the ominous parade and spotted the military license plates. Panic rose in his throat like bile. He couldn't see them but seated in the first car were General Alan Mitchell and his aide, Lieutenant Stone, who was driving.

"They know," said Stanley.

"Who knows, Stanley?"

"Step on it."

Although the Air Force personnel were using special instruments to locate the downed spaceship, it soon became apparent that they didn't know exactly where it was.

Arriving at the farmhouse, Stanley hurried inside with Mary following on his heels. His mind was abuzz. With the military searching for Mourda and Lutsik, he had to keep them hidden. He also had to keep Mary from discovering who they really were, since her dad was the sheriff. Worse yet, he had to keep the aliens from saying anything that would give them away.

He was trying to figure out how to handle it all, at the same time, wondering where the two aliens were. It was tranquil. No Lutsik or Mourda, at least not downstairs.

"Are your friends still visiting?" Mary asked as she filled a glass of water from the kitchen faucet and drank it."

"You know, they talked about going to see some other friends. I'm looking to see if they left a note," he replied as he started up the stairs. "Those guys, always on the go."

Before he got to the third step, he heard a car pull up. Fearing it was the military, he held his breath and rushed to the front window to see out. No military. The car belonged to Rick. He was so relieved to see Roger with him as well.

Racing to the door, Stanley opened it and rushed outside to meet them.

"Hey, Stanley, we got here as soon as we could," Rick said. "The military is all over the place. They're looking for the aliens."

"Quiet down," Stanley whispered. "They're inside."

"The aliens are inside? Really?" Roger asked. "Why didn't you tell us sooner?"

"The fewer people who know they're here, the better, especially with the government looking for them."

"Aw, man, that ain't right," Roger said.

"You know you can trust us," said Rick.

"I know," Stanley replied, although he wasn't sure Roger was capable of keeping such a secret. "Anyway, you got to promise me you won't let on that they're aliens. Mary's inside. I don't want her to know who they are."

"Mary Guthrie? She's inside? With you?" Roger asked.

"Yeah, she took me to the hospital so I could ask grandpa where the crystal is hidden."

"Now, what are you talking about?" Rick asked quietly.

"I'll explain everything. Right now, Mary's inside, and...."

"Fabulicious!" Roger broke in.

"Come on, guys," Rick said, starting toward the door.

"Guys, seriously, she doesn't know, and I don't want her to find out."

"Don't worry, she won't find out from us," Rick said.

Although his friends really wanted to meet the talked-about aliens, a beautiful girl, especially Mary, at your friend's house, was also worth checking out. As soon as they got inside, Roger walked up to Mary, smiling.

Stanley was fairly certain Roger would do something stupid as he was already sweating profusely under his arms.

"What's wrong, Stanley?" Dave asked, watching him watch Roger.

"Nothing," Stanley replied, trying to hide his anxiety.

"Is something wrong?" Mary asked.

"Stanley's embarrassed by us, afraid you'll think he's a nerd," Roger said.

"No, I'm not," Stanley replied vehemently.

Mary, however, knew what Roger said was true. She turned to Stanley. "I happen to like these guys, and I'll bet they'd do anything for you. You shouldn't be embarrassed about who or what you are. You have to be true to yourself. Otherwise, how will anyone know the real you?"

Stanley didn't know what to say in response. He stood there.

"And, the real, you are a great guy."

Now, all four of them stood there, unable to say a word. Forgetting the aliens, they were blown away by her compliment to Stanley.

"All of you…."

They stared at her.

"All of you are okay. Just because you're smart doesn't make you a dork or a nerd. You guys are actually kinda cool."

Roger found his voice first, "Gee, Mary, you want to be in our…"

Nooo, Stanley thought, interrupting Roger just in time. "Hey, Mary's gotta go. She was just dropping me off. She can't really stay.

"Yeah, I'd better get going," Mary said, heading toward the door. "Gee, Stanley, I'm sorry I did not get a chance to say goodbye to your friends from Canada."

The boys looked at each other. Canada?

"Yeah, I don't know where they are. Maybe they walked into town," Stanley quickly interjected.

Stanley walked Mary out to her car.

Once the dust from her car disappeared over the hill. The guys all snapped back to the present and rushed into the house. It took Stanley about twenty minutes to fill them in. Revealing what Lutsik and Mourda had shared, to convince them that there were two aliens, they were here and needed their help; desperately needed their help.

***

# Chapter Sixteen

## Take Me To Your Leader

That same morning, the motorcade of black cars and military vehicles drove down the middle of a dirt road outside a nearby town. Two Air Force helicopters circled overhead, searching for the alien spacecraft.

"It should be around here somewhere," the pilot in one of the helicopters said.

"Keep looking," General Mitchell ordered. "Any sign of trouble, start shooting. That thing will have advanced weaponry, so don't take any chances."

"Yes, sir," the pilot replied.

"Copy that, sir," the gunner in the back replied.

The line of vehicles continued moving forward toward a large corn farm. Behind them, a bevy of news vans followed closely.

"Get rid of the press," Mitchell ordered. "We can't let them know we're looking for U.F.O.'s."

Several of the vehicles came to a halt, and Air Force personnel piled out, cordoning off the area and blocking the road. Since they had no choice, the media also stopped. Doug Myers and his camera operator jumped from their van and were the first to reach the barricade. Rushing up to a beefy, stern-looking sergeant, the reporter made sure the camera was rolling as he thrust a microphone at the man's face.

"Doug Myers reporting for KLEP News. Excuse me, Lieutenant, can you tell me what's going on?"

Several more reporters hurried forward, rolling their cameras and crowding the line of Air Force personnel, trying to get a better look at what was ahead.

Lieutenant Stone scanned the crowd of reporters and raised his voice. "You all need to return to your vehicles and leave the area."

"Why are you here?" A reporter asked. "What can you tell us?

"We were testing a new top-secret aircraft, and the pilot had to land due to mechanical failure. Once the aircraft is repaired and takes off, we'll be gone," Stone replied

"We'd like to get a look at this new craft," Doug Myers said.

"That's not possible. It requires a high-security clearance, which you don't have. If you don't leave now, you will be arrested and charged with interfering in official military business," the sergeant warned.

The reporters met his response with groans and complaints.

"I thought you only did that kind of testing in Area 51," Myers said.

Stone gave him a stony stare. "There is no such thing as Area 51."

"Yeah, sure, typical government denial," Myers responded sarcastically. "I've seen Area 51 with my own eyes. I know it exists."

Lieutenant Stone did not take the bait. "Gentlemen, ladies, please leave the area immediately." He then turned his back on them and walked away. With nothing to report and banned from the area, the press dispersed, disappointed, but they did not want to be arrested.

One hundred military men swarmed the field, looking for anything that would indicate that a U.F.O. had landed there. The discovered a few pieces of a strange-looking metal on the ground. Several men pulled out metal detectors. The bits and pieces were small and few and far between. The detectors allowed them to follow a flimsy trail, which led straight to the corn farm. As they approached, a thin woman with mousy brown hair rushed out of a small house adjacent to the field. She seemed distraught, waving her arms at the men.

"Stop right there, ma'am," one of the soldiers said. "I can't allow you to go any further."

"I need to speak to someone in charge," she said, her voice filled with desperation.

"I'm sorry, ma'am, but we have a situation, and I can't allow you to come any closer."

The woman wasn't ready to give up yet, and when the general approached, she stood her ground.

"What's going on?" General Mitchell asked the soldier.

Before the officer could say a word, the woman spoke up. "My husband got home very late last night, and when he did, he couldn't remember where he had been or what he had been doing. That's never happened before. Something's wrong."

Mitchell shook his head. "Perhaps he had a fall. Have your doctor check him out. I don't think it has anything to do with why we're here." He started to turn away, but she grabbed his arm.

"Well, I think it does have something to do with whatever's going on here. She waved her hands toward the field. Just exactly, why are you here? "

"Official military business, ma'am. Did you see or hear anything last night?"

"I didn't, no, but, the sheriff saw my husband. That's what I'm trying to tell you. He saw Willy in his truck with two strange individuals, not from here, and Willy wasn't driving, just sitting in the truck."

"Thinking that was odd," she continued, "the sheriff gave chase until the man on the passenger side pulled out some type of weapon and aimed it at his car. Sheriff said some sort of beam came from it, and everything just died in his patrol car: the siren, the flashing lights, even the engine."

Mitchell turned to his aide. "I want to see that sheriff. Now." Stone nodded. Calling another man over, he explained the situation and sent him to locate the sheriff. The general turned and smiled at the farm woman, then he gently took her arm and led her away from the other men. The woman squinted her eyes slightly.

"I'll be frank, ma'am. What's your name?"

"Bradley, Marilyn Bradley."

"Mrs. Bradley...may I call you Marilyn?"

The woman nodded but kept her arms folded, still suspicious.

"You seem to be a real patriot, a real American. Can I trust you with this information?"

Marilyn Bradley unfolded her arms and looked in the general's eyes. "I swear on a stack of Bibles, you have my word. What you tell me will go no further."

"Good, good. I knew I could trust you...we could trust you."

"Someone stole a new experimental weapon from the military base last night, and we just received a lead on the perpetrators."

"That must be it! Those men stole the weapon and forced my husband to use his truck to take them somewhere, but why doesn't he remember?" She persisted.

"I don't know, Marilyn. We'll be talking to the sheriff, and of course, we'd like to talk to your husband."

"I told you. He doesn't remember," she said again.

"That's all right. There may be some little thing. You never know, but more importantly, we need you to keep this information quiet. Just you and the sheriff…and me. That's the only ones who should know about this. Would you help your government by doing that?"

"Yes, of course. Is there anything else?"

"I believe we have it under control, but I'm going to give you my phone number. If you see anything else unusual or odd, call me. You'll get my aide, but he'll find me. I want to know if anything, or anyone, shows up suspicious. Okay?"

She nodded and stuck out her hand. "For the U.S. of A."

"Thanks, Marilyn. Now, we're going to keep searching the cornfield for clues." The general motioned for his aide, who immediately appeared by his side. "Give Mrs. Bradley the phone number. She may need to get in touch with me." The soldier jotted down a number and gave the slip of paper to the woman.

"You go on inside now. We don't want to disturb you." Mitchell guided her firmly toward her front porch. One of my staff will call you so we can talk to your husband in the next couple of days."

As soon as she stepped inside the house, two men ran up to the general. "We found it, sir."

"Any aliens nearby?" General Mitchell asked.

"No sign of them, sir."

The officers took him across the cornfield, behind a large red barn with the local cola drink advertisement painted on one side. Mitchell walked up and inspected the space ship. It looked the way he thought it would. It was a small round saucer-shaped ship made from a black metallic substance with silver trim. The top was a dome made of see-through material, strong enough to withstand the external pressures of space.

"Is the truck on the way?" General Mitchell asked Lieutenant Stone.

"It should be here any minute, sir."

"Climb up there and take a look," Mitchell said. "Tell me what you see."

The lieutenant did so, using the silver hand grips on the side of the saucer. Looking inside, he shrugged. "Can't make anything out, sir, the dome is opaque, and I don't see a way to get inside. The hatch is probably controlled remotely."

As he finished speaking, a large semi with a flatbed trailer pulled up next to the ship. Two men got out, and using a crane attached to the trailer, they lifted the saucer onto the bed of the truck. Next, they unfolded a large canvas tarp. They draped it over the alien vessel, tying it securely to several rings fastened to the floor of the trailer, hiding it. The vehicle then pulled away at a good clip, escorted by several military jeeps. The only thing left was to remove all traces of the U.F.O.

"Has all the debris and unidentified objects been gathered and bagged and tagged?" The general asked.

"Yes, sir. We've contained it all."

Using small torches, the remaining Air Force personnel started a controlled burn to eliminate the damage caused when the ship landed. By the time they were finished, no traces of its former presence had remained, just a large rectangular scorched area of grass and earth.

As they packed up their gear to leave, a sergeant spotted one of the neighbors, hiding in the nearby woods, taking pictures with his Polaroid camera. He quickly arrested the man and confiscated his camera and the photos, then handcuffed him and placed him in one of the military jeeps. Wondering how he got through the barricades, the sergeant sent several soldiers into the woods to search for more curious citizens. Finally, the last of the military personnel were gone, leaving only the vehicles belonging to the general and his aides.

Looking around to be sure no one else was watching, the general pulled out a small detection device and adjusted it to zoom in on the area. Hoping to pick up the Greys' essence. After the Roswell incident, scientists took years to develop this apparatus. They used reverse engineering on a similar alien device. They calibrated it to the remains of the two aliens that had died in the crash. Its existence was classified as top secret. The device immediately started beeping.

"We've got a reading," General Mitchell exclaimed excitedly. "Let's pack it up here." Walking back to the car, he smiled, murmuring to himself, "After five long years, I finally have you."

The caravan of black cars left town the same way they had entered. Only this time, the general was following the flashing device that would lead him to the aliens. The farther they drove, the faster it flashed. He still wasn't sure how precise it would be, but the little flashing light must mean he was getting close.

The detector had never been used for any other species, so he didn't know if it would help him locate the other aliens or their craft. Once he found the Greys, he would broaden the hunt. The other aliens had to be around here somewhere. He was determined to capture both species and do whatever was necessary to prevent their kind from invading his planet.

# Chapter Seventeen

## The Core

The boys scurried to the kitchen, and Stanley poked his head out of the pantry, then walked out, followed by Mourda and Lutsik, who still looked very human.

The boys gaped. These were the aliens? They sure didn't look like aliens, not like all the pictures they had seen.

"I'm glad you're all here. Grandpa told me where to look for that missing item. At least, he gave me a general idea. Want to help me search?"

"Sure," Rick said, "but...."

"Oh! Sorry guys," he turned toward his two new friends. "This is Mourda, and this is his dad, Lutsik," he said, smiling brightly.

The two aliens put their hands out, and the boys, grinning from ear to ear, shook hands enthusiastically, hardly believing that this was actually happening.

Lutsik spoke first. "We are very pleased to meet Stanley's friends."

Mourda then spoke, "He believes in his mind that you are his very best friends, you and Mary."

"We are!" Roger said, still pumping Mourda's hand.

Lutsik suggested that the boys spend the night. Tomorrow, they would continue to search for the crystal.

***

The next morning was a Saturday, and Stanley was back in the pantry early, trying to find the hiding place his grandfather told him about. Mourda and Lutsik were there also, anxious to help in any way they could. It was a good-sized room. Stanley's grandmother had used it to store the jars of food she canned each year, as well as kitchen appliances, pots, and pans, and dishes she used when entertaining. The homemade goodies were gone, except for a few jars of jelly. Canned goods purchased at the grocery store now stood in their place. Even though his grandfather lived alone, the shelves were far from empty. In the years since Stanley and his mother had moved out, Charles Anderson had become a packrat. Besides the food and kitchen items, the room also held the extra merchandise from his alien store.

Rick and Roger kept asking questions to the aliens, which infuriated Stanley.

"Enough talk, guys, we have to find that Core," Stanley cut in, a little embarrassed.

"Yes, if we are to save the universe, it is our only hope," Lutsik added.

"Where do we start?" Roger asked.

"Grandpa said it was a secret compartment hidden in the pantry, but I can't seem to find it," Stanley replied.

What's up?" Mary asked.

The boys spun around, totally surprised.

"Mary!" Stanley sputtered

"What are you doing here?" Rick asked.

Roger began to sweat.

"I saw your car out front Rick and thought you'd be up to something interesting, so I came over. Is that okay?"

All three boys stared at her without saying a word. The silence was awkward until Stanley found enough air in his lungs. "Sure, we're just looking for something."

"Hello, Mary," Mourda greeted her.

"Hi, Mourda, Lutsik, I'm glad you're here. I missed seeing you yesterday. Mary looked around at all the boys, "Well if you're looking in the pantry, I can help. I've been there many times to get something for your grandfather. There's a ton of stuff in there. What are you looking for?"

Stanley waved them all in. "A secret panel, a fake door somewhere. Grampa said it was in the pantry."

"Shoot! Look at this mess," Roger said. "It'll take forever!"

"Is it on the wall or on the floor?" Rick asked.

"I don't know. Grampa didn't have time to tell me."

"If we just move everything out to the center of the next room, we should be able to find it," Mary said.

***

They cleaned off the floor of the pantry, piling everything into the kitchen. Once it was clear, Stanley and the others examined the floor, looking for loose boards or possibly a hatch. They found nothing.

They all sat silently on the floor.

"It's not here," Stanley said, exasperated. "But he seemed so sure."

"Then it must be under one of the shelves," Mary said.

Everyone looked up and saw Mary standing with a tray with five glasses of ice tea.

"I thought I would bring something fun for you guys to drink."

"Thanks, Mary," they all responded, and with a sip of iced tea, they began thinking again.

"Maybe not under the shelves, but behind them," Rick said.

"That would make a lot more sense. If it were under the floorboards, it would be too easy to locate," Mary said.

They dropped-down onto their hands and knees and carefully examined each board. Moments later, Stanley shouted, "I found it! The hatch is perfectly concealed along the board seams, and it's irregular."

"What a great hiding place," Mary said. "We were looking for a square patch."

"The Core crystal must be located there," Mourda said.

Mary turned to Stanley. "A crystal? What kind of crystal? What did he mean by Core? Is it valuable?"

"Very," Lutsik said. "Without it, our homeworld will be destroyed."

"Ha, ha," Stanley said. "You're such a joker, Lutsik."

Mary put her hands on her hips, narrowed her eyes, and turned to Stanley. "No, he's not. You've been trying to hide this from me since the very beginning." She turned to Lutsik and Mourda. "You're the aliens that everyone's looking for, aren't you?"

"Yes, we are," Mourda said.

"I knew it!"

Then Mary turned to Rick and Roger and asked, "Did Stanley tell you?"

They nodded solemnly.

Mary turned back to Stanley, her expression angry. "Why didn't you tell me? I thought we were friends. Do you think you can't trust me?"

"It's not that, Mary," Stanley stammered. "I just don't think we should go around telling everyone. The more people who know, the harder it will be to keep their existence a secret."

"The military is already looking for them. I would say the secret is out," Mary said. She turned to the aliens. "So everything you said…"

"Is the truth," Lutsik said.

"How refreshing," Mary said, giving Stanley a dirty look. "It's nice to know there is a whole race of people who don't lie, unlike some people."

Stanley hung his head. "I'm sorry, Mary. Trust had nothing to do with it."

"Really? Then how come your friends knew?"

"Because I've known them longer," Stanley replied. "I'm sorry, really. Can you ever forgive me?"

"Only if you promise never to lie to me again," Mary said.

"I promise."

"Now that we have that out of the way, let's get this hatch opened up," Roger said.

It took everyone's effort to pry open the hatch, but once they did, they discovered disappointment. Only darkness could be seen in the trap door. Nothing else.

Frustrated, Stanley threw a can of food in the hidden space in a dark corner of the hole, making a metallic sound when it landed.

All of them exchanged looks.

Stanley dropped to his knees and stuck his head inside the hole. Pulling out his head, he said, "I need a flashlight."

Mary ran out to the kitchen and retrieved the flashlight. She brought it back and handed it to Stanley, who stuck it inside the hole and turned it on.

"It's safe! That's where it is. It has to be," Stanley said excitedly.

"Do you know the code?" Lutsik asked.

"Did Charles Anderson give you any passwords?" Mourda asked.

Stanley looked at the lock, it was a similar type of lock he used on his own locker at school. He just needed the right combination.

"Well, I don't know what his code could be," Stanley admitted.

"Maybe he used birthdates," Roger suggested.

"It's worth a try," Stanley said. He wasn't convinced, but he tried his mother's birthday and then his own on the safe dial.

Nothing.

"Did your grandpa mention anything while you visited him at the hospital?" Mary ventured.

Stanley pondered, trying to remember the conversation he had with his grandfather.

"Right before his vital signs went crazy, he mentioned some numbers. What were they?"

"Think, Stanley, try to remember," Rick said.

Lutsik walked over to Stanley and sat facing him. "Concentrate on the conversation with your grandfather. I will use my abilities to boost your memory."

Stanley closed his eyes, and in his mind, he saw the hospital bed with his grandfather swirl into focus.

"He said a lot of numbers when he introduced me to the nurse. He kept getting my age wrong. Maybe that was the code?"

"Can you visualize them?" Lutsik asked.

Stanley concentrated on the conversation he had with his grandfather.

"25...32...18, that's it!" He shouted aloud.

The atmosphere in the room grew tense with anticipation as Stanley leaned into the hole once more and spun the dial. When he stopped on the final number, he reached for the handle, and the safe opened.

"Eureka!"

When he came back up, he had the Core in his hands. Lutsik stepped forward, and Stanley handed it to him while everyone else stared in awe at the crystal.

"Let's get to the ship," Lutsik said. "There is no time to lose."

* * *

In the woods near Charles Anderson's home, Stanley and his friends watched as Lutsik turned off the cloaking device that hid their spaceship.

"Wow!" Mary said. "It looks just like your grandfather described it."

Roger and Rick walked around the ship, reverently touching and admiring every curve and its sleekness.

"Now that you have the Core, you can go home and save your planet," Stanley said to Mourda.

"They have to leave now? Roger asked, disappointed.

"We're just getting to know you guys. I mean…We have a lot of questions. Can't you stay for a little while?" Rick asked, hopefully.

"It is critical that we return immediately to Tau Ceti. Every moment jeopardizes our mission and possible discovery by the Greys. We must leave. I am sorry. Perhaps we can return in the future," Mourda said.

"If we are welcome," Lutsik added. "We have brought you much anxiety."

Stanley walked over to the two aliens, followed by the others. "You had better come back and as soon as you can!" He stuck out his hand, but Mourda ignored it and stepped in to give Stanley a hug. Soon, they were all hugging and wishing each other well, the boys asking them to return. Both aliens assuring their earth friends that as soon as their planet and the universe were secure, they would return for an Earth vacation.

"We can all go to Disneyland!" Roger exclaimed.

"Oh! I think that's a wonderful idea," Mary said with a smile towards Roger.

"Thank you, friends, for everything. Now, you need to stand back so we can take off," Lutsik said.

Everyone backed away, with Stanley and Mary ending up together, separated from the others. When they realized this, they looked at each other. A powerful feeling of friendship overwhelmed them. And for the second time in his life, Stanley reached for Mary's hand, holding it tight as they watched the fantastic spaceship.

As soon as Lutsik and Mourda entered the ship, they placed the Core into a slot on their instrument board. It fit perfectly. Satisfied, they started the ship and rose vertically into the sky. The boys cheered, jumped up and down, and hugged each other. Stanley squeezed Mary's hand, then placed his arm around her shoulders as they watched the ship ascend into the sky. They all ran and joined them on that side of the field, formed a semi-circle, their arms around each other now, staring up at the hovering ship. The universe would be safe now.

Suddenly the ship began spinning. The swirling silver sphere seemed out of control one moment, then in control the next. Mary gasped and put her hand over her mouth. What was happening?

Inside, Mourda and Lutsik did everything possible to gain control of the ship and keep it in the air. It went up, then down, almost hitting the ground and then straight up again, to the horror of Stanley and the others watching below. The saucer looked like it was doing some kinda crazy dance. Their hearts beat faster with every dip. Roger crouched and put both hands over his eyes, watching through the slits in his finger. The others stood paralyzed.

Stanley was praying. No, No, No! Please, God, no!

Something was terribly wrong!

Within moments it was over, they crash-landed in Charles Anderson's field, destroying one of his satellite dishes and causing additional damage to the ship.

Inside, one of the instrument panels blew, making it sizzle and spark. Mourda and Lutsik looked at each other. They would have to fix the damage before they could return home. Given Earth's current technology, that could take a very long time.

Time, they did not have

# Chapter Eighteen

## Necessary Repairs

The boys and Mary ran over to the spaceship. As they approached the side where the hatch was, the aliens came out, a little beaten up, but without serious injury.

"What happened?" Stanley asked.

At first, neither Mourda nor Lutsik said a word. Although their expressions didn't show it, they were upset as they walked around the ship and inspected the damage.

"I should have inspected the ship more carefully before we attempted to take off," Lutsik said. "Any more damage, and we will never get home."

"What are you going to do?" Mary asked.

"We have to fix it," Stanley said, matter-of-factly.

Stanley looked at his four friends. Unsure but wanting to help, they shrugged their shoulders.

Lutsik completed his inspection, stopping at the metal fin that had been bent and nearly broken off earlier.

"We cannot get home without fixing this and the damage to our panels inside," Lutsik stated.

"The panels will be easier, but the exterior damage presents a much bigger problem," Mourda added.

They all exchanged glances. One-by-one, then all together, they tried to bend the metal back into shape, but it was impossible.

"Let's check my grandfather's barn. He's got lots of tools. After all, he built all these satellite dishes," Stanley said.

They ran back to the barn, grabbing a car jack, a sledgehammer, a clamp, and a few other odds and ends. Returning to the ship, they tried each tool, but nothing worked. In fact, they made it worse. The bent and sheared piece of metal broke off the ship entirely. With nothing else left, Roger picked up the car jack.

"What are you going to do with that?" Stanley asked.

"Jack up the ship?" Roger replied.

"And do what? Change a tire? It doesn't have any. That's not going to work," Stanley said.

"We need a welder," Rick advised. He turned and looked at Stanley. "Your mom could weld the piece back on."

"Oh no, not my Mom," Stanley said, shaking his head. "We can't get her involved."

"Who else then?" Rick asked.

No one said a word.

"We have to do something. We're running out of time," Mary said worriedly. "If we can't fix it, the whole universe will be affected forever.

"You don't understand," Stanley said. "I can't tell my Mom that grandpa really met aliens. She'll think I'm crazy, too."

"Tell her we snapped something off Rick's car," Roger said.

"Tell her you to need it for Mr. Stewart's physics class," Rick suggested.

"Tell her the truth." Mary insisted.

"If there is anything you can do to help us fix our ship, you must do it," Mourda said. "Our situation is dire. We must stop our enemies back home, or your planet will be next."

Stanley looked at Mary and nodded. Then he turned to Roger and Rick. Everyone nodded in turn, making a silent pact. With everyone in agreement, they ran to Rick's car, but as they did, Rick's foot went into a gopher hole, and he twisted his ankle painfully.

"Ow. Ow. Ow!"

"What's wrong?" Mary asked.

"I twisted my ankle," Rick replied.

"We'd better take you to the hospital," Mary said.

"No time." He tossed his keys to Stanley. "You drive."

"What about your ankle?" Mary asked.

"As long as someone helps me walk, I'll be fine," Rick replied.

"But…." Mary started to protest.

"The ankle can wait!" Rick insisted. "We have to save the universe!"

"Wait," Stanley said. "We'll take my grandfather's truck."

As he ran into the house to retrieve the keys, Roger hurried over to Rick and helped him climb in the front seat next to Mary. The others jumped into the truck bed. Keys in hand, Stanley got in the driver's side, slid the back window open so they could hear each other talk and headed toward home and his mom as fast as he could.

"Somehow, we do manage to convince my mom to weld it," Stanley said. "Then Mourda and Lutsik can leave, save their planet, our planet, and the rest of the universe."

"Do you really think it's going to be that easy?" Mary asked.

"Why not?" Roger wanted to know.

Mary's question made Stanley stop and think. He turned toward his friends, to make sure those in the back could hear him. "The truth is, the whole universe hangs in the balance, waiting for some high school kids to save it." As he spoke, the reality of what he said hit them all.

Stanley turned back around just as the truck hit a pothole. Losing control, he swerved wide, missing a tree by inches, then pulled the steering wheel sharply, bringing it back onto the pavement and crossing the centerline. Everyone was quiet, their eyes bulging in fear. The kids in the truck bed held on to the sides as he swung the wheel to the right, back into the correct lane.

An oncoming car passed them, horn blaring. "Watch where you're going! Stupid kid!"

"Weird!" Roger said. His expression bewildered. "We're going to save the universe!"

Everyone turned to look at him, thankful they had survived the last forty seconds.

"Get a grip, Roger," Rick said.

Suddenly, the car slowed down, sputtered, and jerked. Stanley pumped the gas, but there was no response. It rolled to a stop. The engine had quit. Stanley looked at the gas gauge. Empty. "I don't understand it. I just put gas in it the other day."

"How much?" Rick asked.

"Three dollars."

"That should have given you at least half a tank," Rick said. "How much gas was left before you filled it?"

"Almost empty. I couldn't fill it up. That's all the cash I had," Stanley said.

Everyone groaned. They had run out of gas.

"Wonderful, here we are in the middle of saving the world, and we have to stop to find gas!" Roger said.

"There's a gas station down the road," Rick said. "We better walk down there and see if they have a gas can, we can borrow."

***

As soon as they arrived, Stanley ran inside and approached the attendant. The attendant was working under the hood of an old car. "Do you have a fuel can we can borrow? My truck ran out of gas. It's just down the street from here."

"Sorry, kid, I don't have any extra cans."

"Look, I need to buy enough gas to get my car here so that I can fill it up," Stanley pleaded.

The attendant was an older man with dirty hands and grease smudges on his face and clothing. "I'd like to help you, but I'm out of gas containers."

They were stuck.

Stanley looked at Rick. "What are we gonna do? We can't push the truck that far."

"Mind if we look around and see if there is something else we can put it in?" Rick asked the attendant.

"Go ahead."

Everyone headed in a different direction. After several minutes, they gathered in the garage, disappointment on their faces.

"Nothing," Mary said.

Everyone nodded, wondering what to do next.

"Hey, where's Rick?" Stanley asked.

"Over here by the trash barrel," Rick called out. He walked over to the attendant with something in his hand. It was an empty plastic gallon milk jug. "Could we use this?"

"You can't do that," the man replied and squinted. "That's not an approved container."

"We have to," Stanley replied. "The fate of the universe hangs in the balance."

"The what? What does a gallon of gas have to do with the universe?"

"Trust me," Stanley urged. "It does."

The attendant looked at the assembly before him. They certainly were serious. Even if it wasn't true, they seemed to believe it. "Oh, what the heck. I guess it won't hurt this once, but you'll have to be careful how you put the gas in. The nozzle won't fit through that opening, so you'll have to pump it real slow."

"Don't you have a funnel we could use?" Rick asked.

The man scratched his head. "I suppose you could use the one I use to put oil in the cars. As long as you clean it out afterward. Don't want any gas getting into the wrong part of someone's engine."

"Great!" Rick said. "Is this it?" he asked, pointing at a gray metal funnel on the shelf at the back of the station.

The man nodded.

Rick took the funnel and the empty milk jug and filled it with a gallon of gas. Returning to the attendant, he reached into his pocket, pulled out thirty cents, and handed it to him. "We'll be right back."

***

Using the funnel, Stanley poured the fuel into the truck's gas tank.

"Rick, please, come sit down so I can repair your ankle," Mourda told Rick.

"You can do that?" Rick asked.

"Yes." Mourda pulled a small device, the size of a cigarette lighter, out of his pocket, and passed it back and forth over the injury.

"That's it?" Rick was not convinced. Standing up, he gingerly tested the ankle. "Wow, it's good as new. Thank you! Hey guys, look! Mourda fixed my ankle!"

Ten minutes later, the truck's tank was full, and they headed for Stanley's house. When the truck pulled into the driveway, everyone piled out. As usual, Caroline was working in the barn, welding large pieces of metal into beautiful, serene expressions of art. Sweaty from their run to and from the car, the seven friends ran to the barn. Piling into one another as they came to a halt beside her.

Turning off the welder, she straightened and flipped up the faceplate of the welding mask. "What's going on? Has something happened?" She looked at Mourda and Lutsik and wondered who they were.

"We need your help, mom," Stanley said, out of breath.

"Why?"

"Well, you see, Rick had a little accident with his car, and something needs to be welded back on."

"Something? You mean like his bumper or something like that?" Caroline asked.

"No, there's nothing wrong with Rick's car," Mary said as she pushed through the others to stand next to Stanley. "We need you to fix something else…a spaceship."

Caroline looked at Mary and then at Stanley. He had never lied to her before. That he might be lying now upset her. She was about to say something when she looked again at the pretty girl standing next to him who had made such an outlandish statement. It was Mary, the sheriff's daughter, who lived next to her father's farm.

"Mary? I haven't seen you since we moved from the farm." She noticed how close Mary stood to her son. "Stanley is Mary, your girlfriend?"

"I wish," Stanley said. "Did I just say that out loud?"

Everyone nodded. Mary smiled and took Stanley's hand.

"Please, Mrs. Adams, you must help us," Lutsik pleaded.

Caroline ignored him. She wanted to know more about Stanley and Mary.

Seeing that he had no choice and encouraged by the gentle pressure of Mary's hand, Stanley decided to tell her the truth. "Mom, this is Mourda, and Lutsik, they are from Tau Ceti. The guys and I, and Mary, have been helping them get back home.

"Well, that's very nice of you. And you need my help? What an odd name for a city. Is it nearby?" Caroline asked.

"Not a city, Mrs. Adams," Lutsik replied. "It is a planet in the Cetus Constellation."

Caroline looked at him, and his younger companion, like they might be dangerous.

"It's true, Mom."

She was about to interrupt him, but Stanley pressed on. "Please, mom, hear me, hear us out," Stanley told her the short version of how the aliens had met her father and all the things that had happened since their return. The others all nodded in agreement.

She didn't believe him, not one word. Had they all been hypnotized? Had they been given some kind of drug? She thought Mary was a fairly straight-up girl from a good family. She didn't know which she felt most, fear or anger. She turned on Stanley, her eyes boring into his.

"Obviously, your grandfather has more influence on you than I realized. I knew I should never have let you read those comics and put those posters up in your room. I'd have put a stop to it sooner, but you always acted like you agreed with me that he was crazy! And I believed you, but all along, you've been lying to me. I'm a terrible mother. I've failed you somehow."

"No, you're not! You're the best mom ever! You allowed me to discover my passion and to find the truth!" Stanley insisted.

"Passion? Truth? A passion for aliens who don't exist, except in the minds of crazy people?" she said, her voice getting higher. "I tried so hard to raise an intelligent, rational son. Instead, I end up with a crazy boy!"

"I'm not crazy. It is the truth, and we really need your help. Otherwise, the evil, destructive Greys will take over Mourda and Lutsik's planet, and after they do, they'll take over ours. You have to come with us and fix their ship!"

Caroline shook her head. "What? The more you talk, the crazier you sound! No, I'm not going anywhere. You sound just like your grandfather! There is no such thing as an alien! That craziness ruined my life, and it will ruin yours. Enough is enough. Come back down to earth, Stanley, and I suggest the rest of you do, as well." She turned to Lutsik and Mourda. "Whoever you two are, leave my son alone. He doesn't need any more friends, like you."

She took a step back and turned the welder on, pointing the flame in the air, as if waiting for someone to attack her. Roger slipped around the others and turned off the gas that fed the welder.

"Sorry, Mrs. Adams, but you have to come with us," he apologized.

"I guess we'll just have to kidnap you," Stanley said as Rick and Roger grabbed her from behind.

She kicked and screamed. Caroline was a fighter. Going to the shelves where supplies were stored, Stanley grabbed a rope and a roll of duct tape. Together, the boys tied her up and taped her mouth.

"I'm sorry, mom," Stanley said, shaking his head. "We don't have a choice. There is too much at stake here. Soon, you will understand. I promise."

Caroline gave her son a furious look. She couldn't believe they were actually kidnapping her. And for the first time in her life, fear crept through her body. She was afraid of her own son.

# Chapter Nineteen

## The Truth

Stanley and his friends picked up his mom, now tied securely with her mouth taped, and carried her in a horizontal position to the truck. When they reached the back of the truck, Mary noticed it was filthy.

"You can't lay her down on that dirty floor," she protested.

The boys exchanged looks.

"Wait a minute," Stanley said. "I have an idea. Mourda, take my place."

The alien did so, and Stanley ran into the house. He returned a moment later with a sleeping bag and blanket, which he laid down in the truck bed. Mourda and the boys eased Caroline's body on top and climbed inside.

"Lutsik, will you help me get her welding equipment?" Stanley asked.

"I will do that," the alien replied.

When they returned with everything she would need, the boys put it in the back of the truck and closed the tailgate.

Mary, Lutsik, and Stanley jumped into the front seat. Backing out of the drive, Stanley drove down a rutted dirt road. The truck's suspension system was in bad shape, and his mother, who felt every bump they hit, squeezed her eyes shut and grumbled from behind the tape. Knowing the ride could not be comfortable for her, Caroline's son looked through the back window and sighed.

"I'm going to be grounded for the rest of my life," he told Mary.

"I'll slip food under the door," Mary teased, and then added, "Once she sees and understands, you'll be her hero, not her crazy son."

When they finally reached his grandfather's farm, Stanley turned into the driveway, and then continued on through the fields, weaving a convoluted path between the satellite dishes, until he came to what appeared to be an open area. Everyone piled out of the truck. Then they pulled Caroline out and stood her on her feet. Mourda gently removed the tape from her mouth.

She immediately started screaming, yelling at everyone, and then started to rip into Stanley.

"Before you say another word," Stanley said. "Look."

Mourda and Rick turned her around toward the field.

Lutsik removed the cloak from the ship.

A round, silver spaceship appeared out of nowhere, in the empty air before her. She nearly fainted. Her mouth flew open, but nothing came out. To say she was overwhelmed was a huge understatement. A myriad of emotions battled for supremacy. Finally, one thought overruled all the others, and she spoke.

"All these years, I thought he was crazy," she said in a voice barely above a whisper. "All these years, we didn't talk." She tried to swallow the lump in her throat. "All these years, I turned my back on him." She began to cry.

"There will be plenty of time to cry later, mom," Stanley said as he gently rubbed her back. "Right now, it's welding time."

Lutsik engaged the cloaking device again, and the ship disappeared. Caroline was almost as amazed as when it had first appeared.

She turned to Stanley and hugged him fiercely. "I'm so sorry, Stanley, so sorry!"

"I'm not grounded, then?" He teased.

She smiled at her son and released him. "We'll talk about that later. Right now, better get the welder fired up. What do you need first?"

"I'll get the stuff set up, Mrs. A," Rick said as he headed toward the truck and the welding equipment.

Then she walked over to Lutsik and Mourda. "I am sorry for my previous comments to you. I didn't understand. I didn't believe it. Can you forgive me?"

"We understand. You had to see it for yourself."

"Yes, I did. Did you come here five years ago?"

"Yes, your father was very kind to us," Lutsik said. "He is a good man."

"Yes, he is." She shook their hands. "I never dreamed. No, that isn't entirely right. I thought there might be other life somewhere out in space, but I always believed it was too far away to ever come here."

"If we were using the technology you currently have, your assumption would be correct," Lutsik said. "Our technology is far more advanced than yours, as are our people. In comparison, your world is still in its infancy."

Caroline nodded. "Well, I had better take a look at what needs welding. It sounds like getting back to your planet is the most important thing on the agenda."

"I think it would be best if we move the ship into the barn first," Lutsik said. "We won't be able to turn the cloak off, and it will be too dangerous to work out here in the open."

"Good idea," Stanley said. "How will you do that?"

"It will not be so difficult," Lutsik said.

Entering the ship, the alien started it up. Although it was too damaged to fly very high, Lutsik was able to go high enough to pass over the top of the satellite dishes. Then he brought the ship closer to the ground. Stanley and the others ran to the barn and threw wide the doors. Rushing inside, the boys moved a few things out of the way to make room. Once they were finished, Lutsik slowly guided the ship inside, lowered it to the barn floor, and shut it down.

Exiting the ship, he nodded to Mourda, who showed Caroline the damage. The others followed, carrying her welding equipment. Mary brought the light over and turned it on so that Caroline could see better, while the boys quickly closed the barn doors.

"I don't know. Are you sure a weld would hold while traveling through space?" Caroline asked Mourda.

"The most dangerous time will be when we leave your atmosphere, and eventually enter our own," Mourda said. As he finished speaking, Lutsik, who had gone inside the ship, returned with a small piece of metal in his hands.

"You'll need this to make the welds," he said, handing her the metal.

Caroline set up her equipment and started working. As she did, Mary moved closer to watch.

"He's really a good kid," Caroline told Mary.

"I know," Mary replied.

"My father isn't crazy. You'll see."

"I never thought he was. How did you learn how to do that?" Mary asked.

"The same way everyone else does, I guess. Welding is my main source of income. I don't make a lot of money at my waitressing job. Still, it helps pay the bills."

"I didn't know women could do this kind of work," Mary said.

Caroline gave her a strange look.

"Oh, it's not that I don't think a woman could do it. I just didn't think any company would hire a female welder."

"Many wouldn't, and while it's true that women have a difficult time being hired to do a man's job, some of us do make it. In the future, I hope the line between what is considered a man's work and a woman's work will disappear."

While they talked, Caroline wasn't paying close enough attention to what she was doing. She didn't realize the weld wasn't holding.

"Mom, you're not paying attention," Stanley said.

Looking closer, she realized her son was correct. She focused on the welding but continued talking to Mary.

"Mom, I need you to stop talking and fix this. It's important that our new friends return home as soon as possible."

"Oh, I'm sorry, Stanley." She looked at Mary.

"We'll talk more once you're finished," Mary promised with a smile.

Caroline worked for ten minutes but stopped and turned off the torch and walked over to the others. "Excuse me, boys, but I need to talk to your friends."

"Is something wrong?" Lutsik asked.

"I'm going to need more metal. That piece you gave me just isn't enough," Caroline said.

"What metal?" Stanley had been talking to Mary when Lutsik gave his mother the small piece of metal.

"I'm sorry," Lutsik said. "That's the only piece we can spare. I took it from a damaged panel inside, but if I take any more, I won't be able to finish my repairs."

"We will need to find something to do the job," Mourda said.

"Does that metal even exist on Earth?" Dave asked.

"Not specifically," Lutsik said. "We must find something similar that can withstand the heat of takeoff and reentry."

"Our only hope is N.A.S.A," Roger said.

"Our only hope is a metal shop," Mary countered, being realistic. "There's one just outside of town, Whitfield's Metal Shop."

"Doesn't Mark's father own that?" Roger asked frowning.

"Yes, he does," Mary replied.

"Great," Stanley moaned.

"Then we have a problem," Roger said. "When it comes to his dad, Mark is just like him."

"Maybe I can help," Mary said. "Can I use your phone, Stanley?"

"Sure. I'll show you where it is."

"That's okay. It's in the kitchen, right?"

Mary ran into the house and dialed the Whitfield's number. Fortunately, Mark answered the phone.

"Hello."

"Mark, we have to talk."

"Sure, Mary, what do you want to talk about?"

"Not on the phone. We have to talk at your dad's shop."

Mark was definitely curious. "Why?"

"I'll tell you when I see you there," Mary said, turning on the charm.

Now he was really intrigued. Maybe she had finally gotten sick of her nerdy friends and was ready to come back to a real man. "Is this about us?" he asked hopefully.

"Kind of."

Hope brimmed anew in Mark's heart. Was Mary coming to her senses? "Okay, I'll meet you there tomorrow morning."

Hanging up the phone, she sighed. Mary knew it would be tricky. Should she go alone or have Stanley hide in the back seat of her car? She would have to come up with a reason for wanting the metal. Even then, Mark might not want to give it to her, and if he knew who really needed the favor, he might not be willing to oblige, since Mark believed that Stanley had stolen his girlfriend.

When she returned to the others, Mary told them her plan.

"Maybe we should ask him," Lutsik said.

"No!" Stanley shouted. "We can't let him know who you are. He'll tell his father, who will take the information right to General Mitchell. We'll just have to get the metal ourselves."

"In the meantime," Lutsik said, "we are putting up a force field around the property for your safety."

"Our safety?" Roger asked.

"There are people searching for us," Lutsik said.

"Yes, we know, General Mitchell and his men," Stanley said.

"Yes, but not just them."

"Who else?" Roger asked.

"Do you remember the bad aliens we told you about?"

"What about them?" Rick asked.

"They're here on this planet searching for us," Lutsik said. "They will allow nothing and no one to get in their way."

"And they don't leave witnesses," Mourda added.

Lutsik's words sent a chill through everyone, even Stanley's mom, who, up until that point, was unaware of any other aliens on the planet.

The color drained from their faces as they realized their situation was life-threatening. Now everyone was terrified.

## Chapter Twenty

### Heavy Metal

Mary walked up to the door of Whitfield's Metal Factory. The building and grounds were huge, with carefully landscaped facing the street. The company specialized in cold and hot rolled steel. As well as aluminum, galvanized steel, and stainless steel, which were formed into alloy bars, plates, sheet, coil, steel bars, tubing, and pipe. Mark's father also had a laboratory on the premises, where he and another scientist experimented, trying to develop a new type of more reliable, more durable aluminum. The largest employer in this little town, Whitfield's business, was a rich, powerful, and successful company. It literally smelled of money, and the family's influence was felt by everyone in the area.

This afternoon, Mark was working at the front counter when Mary walked in alone. He walked over, smiled, and hugged her, thinking they were getting back together again. Her return smile was awkward, and her hug unenthusiastic. Taking a step back, he caught her nervously, glancing out the big front window toward her car.

"I thought you wanted to tell me you wanted to go steady," he said.

"I need a sheet of metal," she replied.

Mark raised an eyebrow. "What for?"

Mary hesitated before plunging into the story she had made up. "I looked at some of the metal art the other day. It's interesting how a welder can come up with such intricate pieces of art. So I decided to try it, just for fun."

"Doesn't Stanley's mom do metal art?" He narrowed his eyes and folded his arms over his chest. "Are you getting close to the crazy family?"

"Can you please just show me some metal sheets?"

"No, you're here to get back together with me," Mark insisted.

"I'm here because I need several pieces of sheet metal, something that will tolerate a lot of heat. Do you have any?"

"I might. What's in it for me?" As he spoke, his gaze went from Mary to her car outside. He was about to say more when he spotted something. Mark moved closer to the window and saw Stanley inside her vehicle, peaking over the front seat. Mark's complexion turned red with anger. "Is this for him?"

Mary would've been better off had she said the metal was for Stanley's mother, but she couldn't continue the lie.

"Yes," she admitted.

"Sorry, can't help you. See you later." He turned and headed back to the counter.

"Come on, Mark," Mary pleaded, following him. "Don't be such a jerk."

"There's nothing you can say or do that would make me give him anything but a black eye and a split lip."

The two argued until the front door opened, and Stanley walked in.

"I need your help," Stanley told Mark.

"Why me?" Mark asked.

"Let's just say, it's for the universe."

"Yeah, some project you and your nerdy, stargazing friends are working on, right?"

"Yes," Stanley stated simply.

"Then, the answer is no. Capital N capital O, no. Now get lost, creep."

"Please, Mark, we really need that metal," Mary pleaded.

Mark was about to repeat no, but his anger grew. "You guys can spend all day here, but I'm not giving you anything."

Just then, Mark's father, who had overheard the argument, walked through the door that led to the shop. "Hi, Mary."

"Hi, Mr. Whitfield."

"Stanley."

"Mr. Whitfield."

"It sounds like you're looking for some costly metal, Mary. Now, why would you need metal of that caliber?"

Mary blinked and opened her mouth, but she had no idea what to tell him.

Stanley came to her rescue. "I'm working on a science project."

"My son will help you. I have to go to a meeting now. I'm working on a new type of metal that just might catch NASA's interest." He turned to Mark. "Give them whatever they need, son."

As he walked out the door, Mary and Stanley smiled, but as soon as he was out of sight, Mark turned on them.

"No! Never! Now get out of here and take your nerdy friend with you."

Crestfallen, Mary, and Stanley walked out and got into her car.

As they drove through the parking lot toward the street, Stanley got an idea. "Slow down a minute."

"What are you thinking?" Mary asked.

"We need metal. Drive down the road some distance and pull over. Let's find someplace inconspicuous to park the car. I have an idea."

Mary did as he asked. She spotted a dirt road, not much more than a path really with a stand of trees alongside. Pulling on the berm, she backed up the dirt path until the car was hidden from view by the trees.

"I'm going to sneak back to the factory," Stanley said.

"We're going to sneak back," Mary corrected him.

Cutting across a field that lay between the little inlet and the warehouse, they made their way to the rear of the building and looked for a way in. Naturally, there was a back door, but going through it would be too obvious. Someone would surely spot them.

"Let's see if there's a window we can climb through," Stanley suggested.

"Wait a minute," Mary said. "Maybe there's something in the dumpster." She pointed to a large open container.

"Good idea," Stanley agreed. Hauling himself over the top, he dropped inside. "There are all kinds of scrap metal pieces in here."

A sense of urgency made him want to search quickly, but at the same time, he needed to be quiet. If he made too much noise, someone might hear and come to investigate. He routed around for several minutes.

"Did you find anything?" Mary asked in a loud whisper.

"I think I found some of the stuff Mr. Whitfield was working on. I'm no expert, but I've never seen anything like it. If I could just find a large enough piece… Wait! I think I found it." Standing on a mound of scrap metal, Stanley looked over the edge of the container. "Here, take this so I can climb out."

Mary took the metal and looked at it, while Stanley pulled himself up and jumped out of the bin. Reaching out to steady him as he hopped down, Mary dropped the metal. Fortunately, Stanley caught it before it hit the ground. They smiled at each other.

Mary took the sheet of metal back and examined it. "You know, this does look strange. In fact, it looks a lot like the metal your mom used when she was welding the ship." Excited, she looked into Stanley's eyes. "This might be just what we need."

They were about to leave when a worker came out of the door. They scurried behind the container and dropped down. The man approached and dumped a cardboard box full of metal filings into the container. As soon as he went back inside, the two friends looked at each other and sighed. Standing up, they moved along the back of the building, heading for the field and Mary's parked car. They rounded the corner of the fence around the factory grounds and ran right into Mark.

"We have video cameras all around the building to stop thieves like you," he snarled. He looked at Mary. "I'm calling the sheriff, who, guess what, just happens to be your old man. I can see the story in the newspaper now: Sheriff's Daughter Caught Stealing."

"Please don't," Mary begged.

"We have to save the universe," Stanley insisted.

"Yeah, right."

"Look, it's just a piece of trash," Mary said. "If it really had any value, it wouldn't have been tossed out."

"Just goes to show how much you know about metal," Mark sneered. "We sell that to a scrap yard, who sells it to a factory that recycles it."

160

"Even so," Stanley said. "It couldn't be worth much."

"Look, we will pay for it," Mary said. "Whatever it costs, we'll give you the money."

"We'll give you the scrap value," Stanley corrected her, "because that's all it's worth."

"I don't know. This looks like the new stuff my dad's been experimenting with. That means it is worth quite a bit more." Various prices ran through Mark's head, all of them way above the actual value of the piece. Then he got a better idea. "I'll tell you what. I'll give it to you on one condition."

"What kind of condition," Stanley asked suspiciously.

"You and I will race tonight. If I win, I get to keep your car, and you don't get the metal." Mark grinned. "If you win, you get the metal and my car, which I gotta tell you, ain't gonna happen."

"I don't have a car," Stanley said.

"You can use mine, Stanley," Mary said.

"No, Mary, I can't allow you to lose your car. Your father would never understand, and it wouldn't be right."

"No race. No metal," Mark said a smart-aleck grin on his face.

"I am not racing Mary's car. Period!"

Mark thought for a moment. "Say, your grandfather has that classic truck. I've always wanted it."

"Why would you want my grandfather's old truck?" Stanley asked.

"It's an antique. I figure I can fix it up to add to my collection."

"That truck wouldn't stand a chance against your Corvette, and you know it," Mary said, staring angrily at Mark.

"He loves that truck. My grandfather would have fit if I lost it in a race."

Mark reached out and grabbed the scrap out of Mary's hand. "Sorry. No race. No metal."

Mary was right, and Stanley knew it, but what choice did he have? They had to get that metal to repair the spaceship.

"Okay, we'll race later tonight; I'll let everyone at school know."

"Let's just make it between you and me."

"And have everyone at school miss out on me at the finish line with you still at the starting line? Perish the thought," Mark said, laughing as he went back inside the building.

Stanley and Mary returned to her car.

"You can't do it, Stanley. Your grandfather loves that truck."

"What choice do I have?"

"But you know you can't win. You'll just lose the truck, and we still won't have the metal," she insisted.

"Maybe once he gets the truck, he'll have a change of heart and give us the metal anyway. It's worth a try."

"We should just come back after dark and take another piece," Mary suggested.

"Knowing Mark, he'll have some of his buddies guard that container. And if we got caught, he'll go straight to your father. I know it's hopeless," Stanley said with a shake of his head. "But we have to try winning the race."

# Chapter Twenty-One

## The Race

When Mary and Stanley arrived back at the farm, they found everyone inside the barn working on the spaceship.

"Did you get the metal?" Stanley's mother asked.

"No, we didn't," Stanley replied,

"But we found some we think will do the job," Mary added enthusiastically.

"Well, where is it?" Caroline asked.

"There was some in a dumpster outside the building. But Mark caught us just as we were leaving, and made us put it back," Mary replied.

"It gets worse," Stanley said. "Mark was going threatened to call Mary's father and accuse us of stealing."

Everyone looked at Mary

"That's when he came up with an even better rotten idea," said Stanley

"What kind of rotten idea?" Rick asked.

Everyone again focused on Stanley.

"He wants to race me for it."

"Race you?" Rick asked. "How can you race him? You don't even own a car."

"That's stupid . . . and rotten," Roger added.

"That's where it gets worse. I have to race him in grandfather's truck. If we win, we not only get the metal but also his Corvette."

"What's wrong with that?" Rick asked.

"If he wins, he takes grandfather's truck. And, we don't get the metal."

163

"There's no way your grandfather's old truck could beat his Corvette," Roger said.

"Unless we modified it," Rick said thoughtfully.

"We don't have time to make all the right modifications," Stanley responded.

"Maybe we can help with that," Lutsik added.

* * *

Outside, Stanley and Rick and Mourda stood before the open hood of the truck.

"It's old, rusted, and it doesn't run. I don't see why Mark even wants it."

"I do," said Rick, "his father collects antique cars. This is a vintage year and design. With a little improvement, they could sell this for a fortune a lot of money."

"Stanley must win - to obtain the metal," Lutsik said, as he peered thoughtfully at the engine. "Therefore, let us determine a way to fix the truck."

After discussing the competition and what kind of power the Corvette engine had, Mourda ran some tests, while the others looked on. It didn't take him long to figure out what was wrong.

The boys looked around the barn and found the tools they needed. Carting the stuff over to the truck, Stanley looked skeptical. The truck wouldn't even start.

Mourda brought all the tools up to eye level by levitating them. Using his telepathic mind, he chose a large wrench and quickly positioned it inside the engine.

"Even if we do get it working, we can't we can never soup it up enough to outrun Mark's car," Stanley said. "I'm going to lose the race and my grandfather's truck."

"Not if you don't believe," Lutsik said as he gave Mourda a hand. Slight nod.

While they worked side by side, tools floating around their heads, Stanley kept glancing at his watch. Time was running out. "If we don't get this thing started soon, we'll have to forfeit the race."

Stanley was about to give up when suddenly, the truck's engine roared to life. Mourda made a few more adjustments and soon had cocked his head to one side, and the engine started purring like a kitten.

I have an idea that would help him win the race, Mourda told Lutsik telepathically. With a few modifications, we can use some of the fuel from our ship.

Good idea, Lutsik thought back. Aloud he said, "Is there a fuel can around here that we can use?"

"I saw one back with the rest of the tools," Rick said. "I'll get it for you, but I don't think we have time to get gas."

"That will not be a problem," Lutsik said. Taking the can from Rick, he went to the barn.

He quickly returned with the fuel can and poured its contents into the truck's gas tank. Restarting the engine, it sputtered for a moment before settling down.

"It's time to leave," Mourda said. "Go out there and..." He looked at Rick.

"Force Mark to eat your dust," Rick shouted.

"Eat your dust," Mourda repeated

"Leave them in the dust," Rick said.

"Leave them in the dust," Mourda repeated.

Stanley, Mary, and Mourda piled in the truck and headed off to the race.

* * *

When they arrived at the cornfield where the race was to be held, it looked like the whole student body of their high school had shown up to watch. Mark sat on the hood of his Corvette, a cocky grin on his face.

On both sides of the makeshift straight track, kids had lined up their cars with their headlights on,

"Oh man," Stanley moaned. His nerves were about to go through the roof.

"Listen, Stanley, you can do this," Mourda said, giving his new friend a pep talk.

"I didn't know the whole school would be here to watch," Stanley groaned. "This is a disaster. I will never live it down. We'd better go. Let's get out of here. Maybe we could just ask Mark's father for what we want."

"Perhaps his father would simply tell his son to give it to you again, which he won't do again." Mourda countered. "We cannot take that chance. You have to race, Stanley. If you are fearful that you won't win. Don't be. Stanley, he "will eat your dust." If you lose, we can try your way."

Stanley looked turned to look at Mary, who smiled and nodded encouragement.

"Let's do this," Stanley sighed. said with determination.

He pulled the truck up alongside the Corvette. Mourda stayed inside, while Stanley and Mary got out.

The kids crowd pointed at the old truck and laughed, as Mary walked over to Stanley from the passenger side, she and laid her hand on his arm. She smiled and looked into his eyes. And smiled sweetly.

"Mourda's right, you can do this."

A sweet shot of adrenaline ran through Stanley's body. He was ready. He would win, if only for Mary.

She backed away and joined the spectators on the sidelines, her eyes never leaving Stanley.

"Are you actually going to race that piece of junk?" One boy shouted.

"Hey, Stanley, I hope you don't choke on Mark's fumes...Try to keep it on the road," another jeered.

Ignoring them, Stanley walked up to Mark. The two boys faced off while the ground rules were established by one of Mark's football buddies.

"Okay. Let's keep this clean, guys." He grinned at Mark's circle of friends, who laughed and elbowed each other. Turning back to Mark and Stanley, he continued. "The first one to cross the finish line wins. Now shake hands."

Reluctantly, Stanley extended his hand. Mark shook it, applying a bit too much pressure. Then with a laugh, he jumped into his Corvette and revved the engine.

Stanley stepped into his grandfather's truck and looked at Mourda in the passenger seat, his wingman. Oh, if the people out there only knew precisely who is wingman was.

"Just drive, Stanley, the truck will do the rest," Mourda sent his thoughts. "You will win."

Stanley knew he had to win, this race for more than his reputation. But, for the universe.

With his confidence rising, he started the car again. It sputtered, threatening to stall out. He heard the crowd groaning, afraid there would be no race.

"I thought you fixed this!" Stanley yelled at Mourda.

"Believe," Mourda said out loud, not flinching.

He knew that part of the problem was the gas left in the tank. It would have to be used up before the lighter fuel from his ship could kick in.

One of the cheerleaders, a leggy blonde-haired girl with baby blue eyes, extended one arm with a handkerchief dangling from her hand. She looked at Stanley and nodded, then turned her head and gave Mark a wink.

She dropped the handkerchief, Mark's Corvette shot ahead as Stanley's truck stalled. He could hear Mark's laughter floating back through the open window of his car.

Inside the truck, chaos ensued.

Frantic, Stanley kept turning the key, but the truck wouldn't start. "What's wrong? Why won't it start?"

Before Mourda could answer, the truck hiccupped to a start, and the race was on.

Even if Stanley's vehicle had been a faster car, it would still be challenging to catch up. Mark had a substantial lead. As it was, Stanley was losing, losing badly. To make things worse, the truck stalled again.

"That's it. What's the point in going on?" He slammed his hand on the steering wheel.

"You must try, Stanley," Mourda reasoned. Then an idea popped into Mourda's head. "Do it for Mary. She believes in you."

Nodding, Stanley focused and turned the key. This time the truck roared to life and when he stepped on the gas pedal, the vehicle shot out like a speeding bullet, quickly eating up the distance between the truck and the Corvette.

168

"I need more time," Stanley said as he saw Mark approach the finish line. "If it had started like this happened at the beginning of the race, I could have beaten him."

Mourda knew this was true, but he had another trick up his sleeve. Resting his arm on the top of the open window, he leaned out to look at Mark ahead of them. The alien visitor deftly touched a small button on his sleeve, aiming his hand so that Stanley could not see what he was doing. Then touching a button on the cuff of resulting pencil-thin invisible beam at the Corvette. The crowd watched confused, as Mark's car started to slow down, then it suddenly lost power and roll to a stop twenty feet from the finish line. Screaming with fury, he jumped out of his car and tried to push it, looking over their shoulder as the old truck bore down on him.

"Come on, you stupid piece of junk, Mark yelled at his car. "Move it! Move it! Move it!"

Mark was sweating as he watched, from the corner of his eye, Stanley's truck passes him. This is not happening! Mark thought in a panic.

Just then, Stanley's truck sputtered, the engine died, and it began a slow roll toward the finish line.

While this was happening, Stanley caught up to him and eased a couple feet beyond. Just then, the truck sputtered and slowed. Mourda had been able to spare only a small amount of space fuel. He had hoped it would be enough, but he realized that the truck was running on fumes.

Grampa Anderson's old truck crossed the finish line, as Stanley jumped out, hands raised in the air. The crowd at the finish line cheered Stanley, and some of the guys put him on lifted him to their shoulders.

"Eat our dust! Eat our dust!" They all chanted, louder and louder as the crowd grew

Mary ran up, and Roger and Rick lifted her up on their shoulders she was lifted up on shoulders too. Laughing, she reached over and gave Stanley a big hug.

"You did it! I knew you could. All along, I knew you could!"

Sensing the excitement, Mourda jumped out of the truck and joined the kids surrounding Stanley. He had never seen such a display of emotion in earthlings before. He studied his friends, copying their movements, and shouting "Eat our dust." No one would ever expect it was just an act.

Amidst the cheering and loud banter, one voice shouted loud enough to be heard over it all. "I'm not giving you my car!"

Mark's words momentarily silenced the crowd. Although they most had all been behind him at the beginning, they quickly changed sides.

"Cheater!" One kid yelled.

"Spoilsport!" A shout from the cheerleader who had dropped the handkerchief was heard.

The whole crowd started booing Mark.

Stanley held up his hands, quieting the crowd.

"Fine. You can keep the Corvette. Just give me the metal from the shop. Deal?"

" Hey, it's okay. Why would I want that old car," he motioned to the Corvette, "when I have this hot machine?"

The crowd started to cheer. Then Stanley put his hand up again.

"But, you will give me the metal. Deal?"

"Deal," Mark replied.

Once more, they shook hands.

This time it was Stanley who offered his hand.

Mark shook it. "Thanks," he said.

# Chapter Twenty-Two

## Government Officials

Jeet and Drees sailed along an open road in their stolen vehicle, making excellent time. Both were excited because they knew they were almost at their destination.

"Estimated time of arrival?" Jeet asked.

"Ten Earth minutes," Drees replied.

"Finally, we will have the power crystal."

Up ahead, they saw bright lights in the sky.

"Jeet, look! Are those our enemies leaving with the crystal?" Drees asked.

"No, it's probably some of the human's inferior airships," Jeet replied as he turned left down the next road.

"That is good. We must hurry and get the crystal before they can make their escape."

"We're almost there," Jeet assured him.

They passed several farms until five miles down the road, Drees turned right at the next street.

"We will be ready for them," Jeet said as he pulled out his laser pistol.

Both aliens were tense with excitement. Soon, they would be headed home, ready to attack Mourda and Lutsik's home planet. Once they had the crystal core, they would attack, Tau Ceti with no mercy; and then return home as heroes. Their dreams of recognition and further conquests swam in their dark little brains.

"Tau Ceti will be ours. Once we strip it of its resources, we will return back to this barely technological planet and take theirs as well," Jeet said an evil grin on his face.

The road became an S curve, and as they rounded the final corner, they arrived at their destination.

On the left was a large building next to a field of metal towers. The aliens did not know it yet. But, their device had confused the energy reading from the crystal with the power coming from the transformers in the electrical yard.

"This is it!" Jeet said.

They drove up to a large gate and blasted it open. As they sped past the security booth, a guard ran out and started shouting at them. "Stop! Stop!" Pulling out his walkie-talkie, he called for help and then returned to the security booth and pressed the alarm.

The loud noise made Jeet and Drees very nervous. When their device led them straight to the transformers, they jumped from the truck, sure they were close to the crystal. The signal from their locating device was beeping and flashing, but not giving them any direction. Drees switched it on and off and banged it with his hand. Drees tried to locate the Core, but he soon realized the device's mistake.

"The Core is not here," he said, turning to Jeet, and shutting off the device.

Jeet let out a yell, and some nasty words in his language, jumping up and down in frustration.

"Then, turn off that terrible noise!" Jeet said, referring to the piercing security alarm,

Drees couldn't agree more. Pointing his laser at the transformers, he blasted away until the electric station lost power, and the alarm shut off. While he was doing this, different sirens were heard in the distance, and two more security guards ran toward them. They drew their weapons, ready to fire.

Seeing their advanced weapons, the guards turned around. They hightailed it back to the security booth, yelling into their walkie-talkies.

"Call the police," one man shouted, even though he could hear the sirens in the distance. "No, the heck with the police, call the National Guard. They've destroyed the transformers with some sort of blaster."

"We had better leave," Jeet said. "It sounds like they are calling in their military."

The aliens jumped back into the truck and sped right past the two guards, who threw themselves into the security booth, still yelling into their walkie-talkies.

* * *

Fifteen minutes later, General Mitchell arrived at the plant after receiving a phone call from the electric company about the attack.

The general rushed into the plant office. The manager was standing by his desk, talking on his phone. Seeing the stripes on the general's uniform, he hung up. The phone.

"Who are you?" Commanded Mitchell.

"Dan," the man replied, extending his hand. "Dan McDougal. I'm the manager of the power plant that some crazies just shot up."

"Sit down, Mister McDougal," Mitchell invited, ignoring the man's hand. "Tell me what happened here tonight?"

Dan told him the whole story, which he had heard from his security men. "I have to ask you, General, do you know what's going on? Who were those guys? There were only two of them."

"Don't know yet," Mitchell said, "When they left, which direction did they go?"

"Right, toward Habsburg, Kansas."

"I want an all-points bulletin issued."

"What do you want it to say, sir?

"Tell them we're looking for a couple spies who stole some highly classified equipment from the base and warn them not to approach. These men are armed and dangerous," Mitchell said.

The general's aide grabbed the microphone from the radio and switched to the local law enforcement frequency. "This is Lieutenant Stone of the United States Air Force calling the Sheriff of Habsburg, Kansas."

The sheriff had just walked in the door when he heard the call. "I'll take it, Margie." Taking the microphone from her, he said, "This is Sheriff Guthrie. Who am I speaking to?"

"General Mitchell's aide, Lieutenant Stone."

"What can I do for you, Lieutenant?"

Stone repeated the General's orders. "Don't apprehend them. I repeat. Don't make any contact with them. These men are extremely dangerous. If you spot them, call my office immediately, and we will handle it."

# Chapter Twenty-Three

## Scrap Metal

After the race, Stanley siphoned gasoline from one of the student's cars. The young man was more than eager to help the new champ. Stanley followed Mark to his father's place of business.

Unlocking the front door, Mark led Stanley and the other two to a private room, the one where Mr. Whitfield conducted his experiments. Using another key, he opened the door and turned on the overhead lights. Both Stanley and Mourda were amazed at the sight before them. It was a relatively large room and could never be mistaken for anything but a sophisticated laboratory. Fascinated, Mourda walked around, examining everything.

"The stuff is over there on that pile," Mark said, pointing to a large wooden box in the far corner.

Stanley joined the alien, and together, they headed toward the box. Halfway there, Mourda spotted a stack of metal sheets on a workbench. He stopped and picked one up. As he examined it carefully, his eyes lit up with disbelief.

"This is not possible," he said.

"What isn't possible?" Stanley asked.

When Mark joined them, Mourda asked a question. "How long has your father been working on this formula?"

"A couple of years, why?" Mark inquired.

"At your level of technology, this metal should not have been developed for centuries."

"What? What are you talking about?" Mark asked, somewhat defiantly. "My father is the best there is when it comes to metal."

The alien just shook his head. He still could not believe what he held in his hands. He spoke his next words to Stanley telepathically. *Mark's father could not have developed this on his own. This is practically the same metal used in the construction of our spacecraft.*

Stanley looked at Mourda, a puzzled expression on his face.

*To be more accurate, this is the metal from an advanced spaceship. Is it possible that Mr. Carlton somehow got a hold of some metal from a crashed spaceship?*

Stanley turned to Mark. "Where did your dad get this metal?"

Mark thought about Stanley's questions for a while before he answered. "About five years ago, he received a strange, unmarked package. I remember because an armored truck, driven by a guy in a military uniform, delivered it. It wasn't long after when he started working on developing this new metal project."

"Do you remember what the outside of the package looks like?" Mourda asked.

"It was wrapped in brown paper and hand-delivered. The plates on the armored truck were military plates."

"It is as I feared," Mourda said.

"Anyway, that's not the scrap. That's over there in the box like I said. What you have in your hand is the good stuff," Mark said. "I think my father said it was almost perfected."

"Indeed." Mourda examined a few more sheets. "Would it be possible to take some of these sheets? I will gladly pay for them."

Pay him? Stanley thought to the alien. How could you pay for them? You don't have any money, do you? They are probably worth a fortune. Besides, there's no way Mark is going to sell you any of the good stuff.

"No way, man," Mark said. "My dad would kill me if I let any of that stuff leave the building.

"Stanley, please bring me two pieces of the scrap," Mourda said.

Stanley went to the box and retrieved the metal. When he handed them to the alien, Mourda examined them closely and shook his head.

"No, this won't do," he said. There are still too many imperfections in the scrap."

Stanley asked a mental question. Can't you find a way to make it do?

I'm afraid not. It would take far too long to finish the process. Time we do not have.

"You can have as much as you want of the scrap, but you can't have any of the good stuff," Mark emphasized.

I hate to do this, Mourda thought to Stanley. Still, I have no choice. What we don't use for the weld, I can use to finish repairing the damage inside the ship.

You're not going to steal it, are you? Stanley thought back.

No, that is something I would not do.

Then how are you going to pay for it? Better still, how are you going to convince Mark to sell it to you?

Mourda smiled. I have an idea.

"If you allow me to take several sheets, I will give your father the formula to complete the process," Mourda reasoned.

Stanley grew alarmed. No! You can't do that! You said that we shouldn't have developed this metal for a long time yet. Won't that be making things worse?

Yes, it would. But, since your military saw fit to give Mr. Whitfield metal from a crashed alien spaceship. The damage has already been done, Mourda shot back, looking at Stanley.

Mark eyed them both suspiciously. While they didn't speak, he could see they were somehow communicating.

"Wait a minute!"

Mark's eyes grew wide and then focused intently on Mourda. Pointing a finger, his voice changed, "Are you one of those aliens the General is looking for?"

Reaching out, again telepathically, Mourda concentrated hard, sending a message to the young man. When he finished, Mark stared at him, glassy-eyed.

"What did you do?" Stanley asked in a panicky voice.

"I merely placed the information for the formula in Mark's consciousness. Now, it is time to go. We need to get this metal back to your grandfather's farm."

"What about Mark?"

"He will trouble us no further."

Mourda headed for the door with several pieces of the new metal under his arm. Confused, Stanley turned toward Mark, waiting for the jock to try and stop them. To his amazement, the young man walked over to a large black chalkboard, erased some of the formula written on it, and began rewriting it, making the corrections he had been given mentally.

"Man, I hope you know what you're doing," he told Mourda as he hurried after him.

* * *

When they arrived back at the farm, Stanley drove straight to the barn and parked. Mourda handed two sheets to Stanley and took the other four inside the ship to complete repairs. Stanley laid them on the floor next to the damaged part of the ship. "Here it is, Mom. You can reconstruct a new fin and finish welding now."

Caroline went back to work on the repairs.

# Chapter Twenty-Four

## Maintenance

Bored with watching Mrs. Adam's work, the boys decided to look around the barn. When Mary noticed they were touching the equipment, she walked over to them.

"Make sure you don't accidentally damage something. Professor Anderson has worked very hard on these things."

She knew Charles Anderson wouldn't care if his grandson used his things, but since he did not know Stanley's friends, he would not want them touching his stuff. Mary looked at each one and came to a realization. Thanks to the bullies and unkind words they'd heard from the kids at school, all of these boys had low self-esteem. She decided to talk to and, hopefully, distract them from the equipment.

"You guys shouldn't let those bullies at school get you down," Mary said.

"They're always picking on us," Rick said defensively.

"And do you know why?" She asked.

"Because we're nerds," Rick answered.

"Because you're smart. All of you are better students than they are. Sure, they may be good at sports, but not many people can make a career out of playing a game."

"I never thought of it like that," Rick said thoughtfully. "Still, they get all the breaks. The teachers let them get away with stuff just because they're jocks."

"So what? In the end, it will hurt them when they can't get a decent job because they lack the skills they'll need. You're incredibly smart, Rick."

"Still," Roger interjected, "the jocks get better grades than they deserve, just because they're on the football team."

"But they haven't earned them, so the grades are meaningless. Let me ask you something, Roger. When you take your report card home with an A in every subject, how does that make you feel?"

Roger thought about it for a moment before answering. "When I show the card to my Mom, she is so proud of me. It makes me feel proud, too, but it still makes me a nerd."

"So what? When we graduate in a couple years and go on to college, we will succeed because of our brains. Being popular in high school doesn't get someone a great job."

"Now that I think of it, I know some people like that," Roger realized.

"After graduation, Mark will still be working for his dad at the front desk. You, on the other hand, will go on to college and make something of yourself."

"I wouldn't mind becoming a writer, or a newspaper reporter, or maybe even a teacher."

"Or possibly a professor," Mary added. "Whatever you choose, you could make a huge difference."

Roger stared at the floor, allowing her words to sink in.

Like Rick, Roger squared his shoulders and stood straighter, a pleased look on his face.

Mary turned and looked at Stanley.

"I can see you following in your grandfather's footsteps. Your love of the stars could lead to a career in astrophysics or astronomy."

"You really think so?"

"I do. And now that your grandfather is back in your life, who knows? Whatever you choose, I can't see you being very far from a telescope."

*** 

Drees and Jeet drove their stolen truck past Stanley and Caroline's house and headed into town. After the fiasco at the electric company, they were more desperate than ever to get their hands on the crystal. The Greys had escaped before the Sheriff, and his men, the military, and the crowds arrived. As Drees drove through the middle of town, he and Jeet saw more humans than ever.

"This planet is infested," Drees said.

"Yeah, infested with humans," Jeet giggled. "Let's give them a real scare."

Drees's eyes lit up. "What do you have in mind?"

"Why don't you chase them off the sidewalks?"

"Good idea. Maybe we can run over some of them," Drees said as he drove up on to the right-hand sidewalk then across the street and up the left-hand side, peering back and forth.

People screamed and jumped out of the way. Several yelled at them.

"What are you nuts?" One man screamed.

"Where'd you get your driver's license, out of a Crackerjack box?"

The two aliens smiled at the chaos they created. At times, they actually chased some of the people, nearly running them over. Finally, Drees settled down.

"That was fun, but it doesn't help us find the crystal."

"Maybe we should ask someone if they've seen any aliens," Jeet said.

"Good idea."

Stopping the truck in the middle of the street, they jumped out and approached several people asking, "Have you seen any aliens around here?"

Instead of answering, the people just shook their heads and hurried on their way. They didn't know who these two yahoos were, and they didn't want to find out.

"Where are the aliens?" Jeet insisted.

"There are no aliens," an elderly man said. "Just some crazy old farmer who thinks he saw some."

Finally, Jeet spotted a young woman in her early twenties, her arms filled with packages.

Laying his hand on her head, he said, "Drop your accouterments and come with us."

The woman looked at him with a blank expression on her face. "My what?"

Jeet searched his memory for a better word. "Your containers."

"Containers? What containers?"

Disgusted, Drees jerked the packages from her arms and drop them in the middle of the road. They took her to the truck and sat her in the middle of the front seat between them.

"Help us navigate the traffic laws," Jeet said.

Drees nodded his agreement.

"Take us to the crazy farmer," Jeet said.

"Crazy farmer? Oh, you must be talking about Charles Anderson."

"Yes," Jeet said. "Take us to Charles Anderson's farm."

Unable to do anything else, the woman did everything they asked. Unfortunately, they ran a red light as they drove out of town.

"Red light means stop," the woman said after the fact.

They sped through the light just as the sheriff's car pulled up on the cross street. Switching on his lights, he sped around the corner and pulled up behind the truck, giving them two blasts of his siren.

"Now you've done it," the woman said. "Better pull over. The sheriff is going to give you a ticket."

The two aliens exchanged glances.

"Do something," Drees said.

Jeet put his hand on the woman's head once more. "Tell the sheriff that we are your relatives from out of town."

"Do you have a driver's license?" the woman asked.

"No, switch places with me and do what we say," Drees said

Pulling over to the side of the road, Drees shifted into neutral and turned off the motor. Before Sheriff Guthrie got out of his car, Drees changed places with the woman.

"Good evening, ma'am," the sheriff said as he approached the driver's side of the car.

"Good evening, Sheriff Guthrie. Did I do something wrong?"

Leaning down, he looked inside the car and saw the two aliens. "I thought that was you, Emma Waverly. Don't recognize your passengers, though."

"Passengers? Oh, yes, these two guys," she tittered. "They're just cousins of mine visiting from out of town."

"Welcome to the town, gentlemen. Plan on staying long?"

"Just a couple of days, don..." Before Drees could finish his answer, Jeet elbowed him in the side. Drees was about to call the sheriff a donut munching pig.

Returning his attention to Miss Waverly, the sheriff said, "You ran the red light back there. I'm afraid I'll need to see your license and registration."

Emma fished through her purse, which had thankfully been on her shoulder when Drees had taken her packages away from her. Pulling out the license, she handed it to him. "I'm afraid I don't have the registration, sheriff. This is Willie's truck. He's letting me borrow it to pick up a new chair I bought. I'm so sorry about the light, sheriff. I guess I'm just so excited about seeing my cousins that I completely missed it. It's been ten years since I've seen them."

Sheriff Guthrie examined her license and handed it back to her. "Well, I could see how that would be a bit exciting for you. I'll let you off with a warning this time. I wouldn't want to ruin your reunion. Just be careful and try not to break any more traffic laws."

"Thank you so much, Sheriff Guthrie. I promise. I'll be cautious."

The sheriff touched the brim of his hat and nodded. "You folks have a good evening."

***

As Caroline finished the welding, she straightened up, set down her tools, and rubbed her aching back. "That's it. Your ship is as good as new."

Everyone was excited. Mourda and Lutsik came out of the ship.

"We've got everything repaired inside, so I guess it's time to say goodbye," Lutsik said.

As they did, Mourda turned to Stanley. "Would you like to come with us? You would find our planet fascinating."

"No!" Caroline and Mary both shouted at the same time.

"Well, maybe next time," Mourda said. His expression actually showed mild disappointment.

"I'd like that," Stanley said. "Someday, maybe."

Lutsik and Mourda climbed on board the ship and settled in at their stations. Mourda looked through his window and waved. Everyone waved back. Roger even had a tear in his eye. He was going to miss their new friends.

The ship came to life, and the boys opened the barn doors wide.

Across the street, Margaret was looking out her front window. Her husband sat on the couch, watching a football game.

As the saucer eased out of the barn, she shouted, "I knew it!" Nothing could have pulled her away from that window. Leaning forward, she pressed her face against the glass, giving her husband a blow-by-blow account of what was happening across the street.

Jack looked up momentarily from the television set, shook his head, and went back to watching the game.

The ship was barely a quarter of the way out of the barn when it stopped and slowly sank back to the ground.

"What's wrong?" Mourda asked.

Lutsik checked his readings. "I'm afraid I made a miscalculation. We are out of fuel."

Opening the door of the ship, the aliens climbed out of their ship

"What's wrong?" Stanley asked.

"We are out of fuel. When we crashed, we must have punctured the tank," Mourda replied.

"What's it made of? Maybe we can get some more," Stanley offered.

"We don't know in terms of earth resources and percentages."

"My Dad is a chemist," Roger said. "If you can scrape up enough for a sample, maybe he can figure out how to make more."

"I don't know if that's possible, but we must try," Lutsik said.

"We have to hurry," Mourda added. "The Greys could find us at any moment. They have sophisticated technology similar to our own. They are, no doubt, using it to locate us and the crystal."

"You're kidding, right?" Stanley asked.

"Far from it," Lutsik said. "To make things worse, your military is also closing in."

"My dad is the sheriff," Mary said. "Maybe I can talk him into helping us with the general somehow.

"This is bad," Stanley said.

"It gets worse," Lutsik said. "In twenty-three Earth hours, our planet will be out of range for another five years. Without a means of escape, if your government doesn't capture us, our enemies will."

# Chapter Twenty-Five

## The Greys Arrive

Across the street from the farm, the Greys pulled into the Watson's driveway. They parked the stolen truck, totally unaware of what was happening in the barn.

The aliens and Emma climbed out.

"Now what?" Emma asked.

Jeet turned to her and placed a finger on her forehead, but before saying anything, he turned to Drees. "What should we do with her?"

"She's a witness. Maybe we should just eliminate her," Drees replied.

"She is a witness, but with the military and officers close by and looking for the Tau Ceti's spaceship, finding her body could lead to more trouble for us."

Drees looked at the woman like she was nothing more than an insect. "Not if we blast her into nothingness."

"That is true," Jeet agreed. "However, her disappearance could still cause problems. Let's just erase her memory."

"We should only erase her memory of us."

"Good idea." Jeet entered her mind, deleting everything from this moment back to when they had first kidnapped her. When he finished, he removed his finger and said, "Go home, Emma Waverley."

Emma turned around and goose-stepped back to town. After every ten steps, she stopped, wiggled her hips, placed her thumbs against the temples with her fingers widespread, and wiggled them while she stuck out her tongue. "La de la de la." Then she moved forward, goose-stepping ten more steps.

"What did you do to her?" Drees asked with a laugh.

"I just made a little suggestion," Jeet said, grinning evilly.

"How long will she go on like that?"

"Until she gets home."

Both aliens laughed until Drees said, "Enough fun. Back to business."

Jeet retrieved his device from his pocket and scanned the surrounding area.

Do doot, do do doot, do do doot.

Drees his brow furrowed. "Why is it making that strange noise?"

"I don't know. It started after we fixed it with the Earthlings inferior tools." Continuing his scan, Jeet pointed at the farm.

"They are there."

"Are you sure?" Drees asked. He was barely able to contain his excitement.

"Yes, it may sound funny, but the readings are correct." He looked up at Drees, excitement seeming to vibrate throughout his entire body. "We have found them at last!"

"Get the bynoks. I want a closer look," Drees ordered.

Jeet hurried back to the truck, opened the door, and retrieved what appeared to be a small but very powerful pair of binoculars. He ran back to Drees and handed them to him.

When Drees looked through them, six tiny white lights circled the metal around each lens. He watched the property for several minutes, and then his eyes narrowed with evil delight.

"There!"

"Where?" Jeet asked.

"In that large building at the back of the property."

"No one in there can see us or know that we are here," Drees reminded him.

Jeet nodded, and they both scanned the neighborhood, farm, and street. Seeing no one else, they crossed the road and quietly approached the barn. Crouching, they made their way around to a side window and slowly raised their heads to peer inside.

Jeet slowly moved his hand toward the window and pointed the device toward the interior. Immediately, it glowed red. Alarmed, he pulled it back and starred at the small screen.

"This is not good," Jeet said. "It appears that another planet is trying to get their hands on the Core too. The danger factor has increased substantially."

"That alien is dangerous," Drees agreed, looking over Jeet's shoulder at the ominous image on the device.

They exchanged nervous glances and, with a nod, walked back across the street to the truck, glancing over their shoulders with newfound fear.

"We need a safe place to stay where we can keep an eye on everything," Jeet said.

Both aliens turned at the same time and looked at the house in front of them. Nodding, they walked up to the porch and knocked on the front door. When it opened, Margaret peered out at them. It was clear by her expression she did not recognize them.

"Yes, can I help you, gentlemen?" She asked.

The aliens exchanged expressions. Then Drees got an idea.

"We are with the government. There has been some suspicious activity going on across the street. We need a place to keep an eye on things," Drees told her.

She narrowed her eyes and placed her fists on her hips. Margaret Watson was no fool. She'd dealt with this kind of thing before. "Where are your badges?"

Jeet and Drees exchanged looks. There was only one thing left to do. Pressing a button on their cuffs, their holographic human images disappeared. The woman's eyes grew huge. The Greys stood before her in all of their frightening, grey, alien glory. She opened her mouth and screamed.

Terrified and paralyzed, she could only turn her head and look pleadingly at her husband, who was totally consumed by a TV program. She tried to call his name, but she was so frightened, the only sound that came out of her mouth was a squeak. Overcome within the depth of her terror, she fainted.

Drees and Jeet changed back to their human illusions and picked her up. Carrying her over to the couch, they set her down. Her husband, in his recliner, remained blissfully unaware.

"Shhhhhh," Jack told his unconscious wife. "They're just getting to the good part."

For all intent and purposes, the house now belonged to the aliens. Drees pointed to the staircase, and Jeet nodded. They headed up to the second floor for a better view of the property across the street. Walking into the front bedroom, they found themselves in a bedroom belonging to the Watsons' son, who was away at college. Drees glanced out the window. Seeing nothing of interest for the moment, he turned back to the room and found Jeet picking up a stack of comic books from a bookshelf near the bed.

"Look at these!" Jeet exclaimed. "It would appear that the humans know more about the alien races then we had first believed."

The comic books were all about aliens and outer space, and the two Greys were fascinated. Drees grabbed the chair under the desk and carried it over to the window. Then he went back and grabbed the whole stack of comic books.

"Go find another chair. We can look through these while we watch what's happening across the street," Drees said.

Jeet nodded and found a similar chair in the guest room. They spent the night studying every page in the comic books.

"Wow! I never knew they could do that," Drees said, pointing to the Martian, copper-colored, Manta Ray-shaped war machine in The War of the Worlds book he was looking through. "I did not know that they had a base on Mars."

"Who?"

Drees pointed to the picture. "The stupid humans think there are Martians."

Jeet laughed. "That's not surprising. I just don't understand why all this information is here in this room."

"Perhaps this is their command center," Drees said.

Standing up, Jeet went back over to the bookshelf to look for more comics. Instead, he found a stack of drawings. The son, who was an artist. He had done a series of sketches of his mother with different types of aliens. Even though he was in college, he still believed in space aliens, and he believed in Charles Anderson. But because of his mother's suspicious nature, he kept his thoughts to himself.

"We must interrogate the human woman," Drees said.

"Yes."

They went downstairs and woke Margaret up. Although they hid their alien appearance, the woman would never forget their holographic faces. She worked her mouth the way a fish did and fainted again.

Disgusted, Drees and Jeet went back upstairs and reentered the front bedroom.

"I don't understand it," Drees said. "Our leaders have betrayed us. Why were we not informed earlier that there was a command post here."

"Perhaps it isn't an actual command post. We're not sure."

"Jeet, you are inexperienced and naive," Drees shot back. "Look at these historic documents and drawings." He threw some of the comic books at him. "Oh, yes, we are being betrayed and manipulated. Don't be stupid."

Although Drees showed no outward emotion, his words cut through Jeet, making him worry.

Because communication between their planet and Earth was only possible during certain hours of the day when the two worlds were aligned, they waited until midmorning to contact their superiors.

"Are you sure we want to contact them?" Jeet asked.

"We must," Drees replied, staring at Jeet. "They must not know that we know. We now have the advantage."

However, their wrong assumptions made them cautious and slow to believe what their commanders back on the home planet told them.

Anyone eavesdropping on the conversation would have thought they were listening to gibberish. One thing was clear. Whatever they said to each other was more argument than discussion. Their commander finished the communication saying, "for now, don't do anything. There will be a meeting to discuss your situation. Once a decision has been made, I will get back to you."

Closing the communication, Jeet and Drees faced each other.

"What are we going to do?" Jeet asked.

"We are going to do a reconnaissance mission later," Drees replied. "We need to get more information before deciding our next step."

"Then, we are not going to wait and see what the leadership wants us to do?"

"No. We cannot trust them. I will decide what we should do," Drees said.

"If you want my opinion, I think we should destroy the Ceti spaceship," Jeet said. "We'll take the crystal and kill them. Then we can go home. The crystal will be ours, and we will be heroes."

"We'll destroy the Ceti shield, strip their planet of its resources, enslave their people, and then come back for Earth."

# Chapter Twenty-Six

## The Weapon

For the next three hours, the two Greys poured over the comic books, now looking for specific clues, while waiting until dark.

"It's time," Drees said.

Jeet pulled out the bynoks and looked toward the barn. Lights were on. They had to go back, gather information, and find the crystal. Silently they checked their weapons and opened the upstairs door from the command center. The sound of lasers jolted them both, and they dropped to the floor, pulling out their own lasers. Had they been found out?

"Margaret, get me some of that banana cake, will you?" The strange male Earthling called. Lasers and now screams came from downstairs. Jeet pushed the older Grey back, and rolled to the edge of the stairs, his weapon drawn and ready. The woman crossed in front of Jack and handed him a large plate of cake.

"Turn that thing down! I don't know what you get out of those outer space movies! They're so fake. And why in tarnation do you have to have it turned up so loud? Turn it down!"

"Seems more real when it's loud," he mumbled through a mouthful of cake.

Relieved that it was the earthling's entertainment monitor, both Jeet and Drees put their weapons away, crept down the stairs, and out the front door.

"Did ya see that!" Yelled the male Earthling. "Blasted 'em right out of the sky!"

\* \* \*

Earlier, the shield had been lowered to allow Stanley and Mourda to get the metal sheets. After they returned, Mourda forgot to turn it back on.

As the Greys started across the street, a car came out of nowhere, his bright headlights on. Startled, the aliens turned toward the oncoming vehicle. Without their sunglasses, it froze them like a deer caught in the vehicle's headlights.

The driver slammed on his brakes, nearly hitting them before coming to a stop. He stuck his head out the window. "Get out of the middle of the street! What's wrong with you idiots? You want to get run over?" When the aliens still didn't move, he drove around them, muttering under his breath.

Jeet and Drees would have moved out of the way, but the glare from the headlights had temporarily blinded them. As soon as their vision cleared, they continued across the road, heading for the barn. In his hand, Drees carried one of the comic books as their new operational manual on how to fight, using the pictures inside. When they reached the barn, Jeet looked through the window, while Drees checked the comic book, scanning the images by the outside light over the barn door.

Inside, Caroline was still welding.

"I could really use more light, Stanley. Could you bring a spotlight over? I believe there's one on your grandfather's workbench."

Stanley found several. Returning to his mother, he plugged it in a nearby outlet and clipped the light onto an old chair back. But as he adjusted the lamp, he accidentally sent the beam shining through the window and directly into Jeet's eyes. He staggered back from the window and fell to the ground, his hands over his eyes.

"We're being attacked! I think I've been shot," he moaned, mistaking the small round spotlight for a weapon.

"Let me see," Drees said. Removing his scanning device from his pocket, he carefully passed it over his partner's body.

"Am I okay?" Jeet asked fearfully.

"You are fine. They must have missed it. I want to get a look at that weapon." Drees inched slowly up to the window and looked inside. With the spotlight repositioned to shine on the welding, Drees was able to get a good look at it. He turned to Jeet. "I think you're right. It looks like a powerful ET3000 weapon." He flipped to the comic book until he found the page he wanted. "See, it looks exactly like this weapon right here," he said, pointing to a picture.

Jeet leaned up against the side of the barn, careful to keep his head below the window. His fear was profound, making him shake and sweat little purple droplets from his pores. They almost killed me, he thought.

"What did you see before they fired at you?"

Jeet opened his mouth to answer, but no words came out. His fear had clearly gotten the better of him.

"I'm going to take another look," Drees said, sighing over his partner's fear.

Making sure no one was watching, he again inched himself up to the window and looked around the barn. On the workbench, he spotted a least a dozen more lights in a pile. Then he looked up and saw track lights overhead, scattered throughout the ceiling. They had not been turned on.

Using his scanner, he captured images of the lights and everyone inside. Then he dropped down next to Jeet.

"There is a whole arsenal in there," he whispered. "It looks like they have been stockpiling weapons for quite some time."

Having left the barn to sniff around, Professor Anderson's dog started barking without warning, startling both aliens. The purple sweat now popped out on both their bodies.

Fearing they would be spotted before they were ready to attack, Jeet telepathically communicated with the dog. Stop yelling. We mean no harm, he lied.

But Queakly was a smart dog. He didn't buy it. Why are you hiding and spying on my friends in the barn?

The two Greys didn't know that Earthlings could not understand or speak "dog." They were sure he would run in and warn the humans and other aliens. In a panic, they darted back across the street.

Queakly ran inside the barn barking and then darted outside again. Stanley followed him. The dog lifted his nose and sniffed once more. He caught the Greys' scent and ran to a spot halfway between the barn and the house. He didn't find the aliens, but Jeet, in his rush to get away, had dropped what appeared to be a gold coin the size of a silver dollar. The dog got a good sniff, lifted his head, and barked at Stanley, furiously wagging his tail.

"Did you find something, boy?" Stanley asked as he approached the dog. Hunching down, he picked up the gold coin and briefly glanced at it. "This looks like some of the junk Grandpa sells in his alien store." He patted the dog's head. "Okay, boy, time to head back to the barn.

***

"Are they gone?" Jeet asked fearfully.

"Yes," Drees replied. He looked up and down the street. The coast was clear. "Come on. Let's get back to our hideout."

They ran flat out across the street to the porch of the neighbor's house, and then calmly walked inside. Jack remained in front of the television, eating from a bag of potato chips and watching TV.

Margaret had awoken earlier and found no one else in the house, but her husband, went up to the bed, claiming she had a headache. She was in such a deep sleep. She did not hear Drees and Jeet come up the steps and enter her son's old bedroom.

Closing the door, the two aliens went back to their chairs in front of the window. Drees pulled out his communicator and contacted the homeworld. He sent his commander all the information and pictures he had taken across the street. "There are at least fifty books in our headquarters, showing various different war strategies."

"What headquarters?" their commander asked.

"The one you established here but did not tell us about. We were lucky to find it," Drees said.

The commander shook his head. "I told you before. We did not set up a headquarters on Earth for you. It must belong to someone else."

"If that were so, then why isn't the one who established it here?" Jeet asked.

"Maybe it belongs to that dangerous female alien you discovered," the commander suggested.

"I don't think so," Jeet said. "There are no signs of a female in this room, only male. Besides, if that were the case, why are there no weapons here?"

"Maybe it belongs to the Cetis," the commander suggested. "We had nothing to do with it."

Jeet and Drees exchanged mental thoughts. He's lying to us, Drees said.

Jeet nodded. I wonder if they hired that female from Craysus to get the crystal for them. Their females are the best mercenaries in the galaxy.

Let's ask him, Drees said. "Commander, why didn't you tell us that you hired the mercenary from Craysus?"

"What? Absolutely not. If we had, why would we bother to send you?"

"Why, indeed?" Drees asked.

"Listen to me, you are to stay away from her at all costs," the commander insisted. "I recognize her picture, and she is the number one killer in the universe."

"Whatever you say, sir," Drees replied.

"Proceed with caution. We need that crystal."

"Yes, sir," both Jeet and Drees replied.

They cut communication.

"I don't know why the commander is lying to us," Jeet said. "Do you think they hired the female from Craysus?"

"Yes, and the fact that they won't admit it to us and want us to move slowly when it is critical to get that crystal home, is very suspicious," Drees said.

"Maybe they don't want to pay us for its retrieval since they must be paying the mercenary a fortune," Jeet speculated.

"I believe you're right. Let's turn the tables on the commander. Since the Craysus operative is after the same thing we are, we need to become allies. Inside that big red building, we have all the weapons in the world we will ever need. With her at our side, even the human military won't be able to stop us."

# Chapter Twenty-Seven

## The General's Arrival

The next day, a black Suburban rolled into town, followed by a caravan of twenty trucks filled with equipment and soldiers. Through the diligent work of his men using satellite surveillance and other equipment developed to help detect the whereabouts of the aliens, the general's men had finally tracked down the right town.

General Mitchell sat in the back seat with his aide, Lieutenant Stone, rubbing his glove covered hands together.

"Never screw with the red, white, and blue," the general said, reciting one of his favorite sayings.

He was always using some adaptation of those words.

"This will be over quickly, men," he told the officers in his Suburban. I have lived my life for this moment," the general continued. "I want reports right now."

"Yes, sir," the men replied in unison.

"Where's my licorice?"

Lieutenant Stone handed him a partially empty bag of black Twizzlers.

"This time, we're going to kick alien butt," Mitchell said as he handed the Lieutenant a file with the words Top Secret on top. He removed a piece of licorice from the bag and bit into it like a lion tearing off a chunk of meat from a gazelle. "You know, Stone, this all started five years ago when the aliens first arrived here."

He paused to chew up the licorice and swallow. "That crazy farmer Charles Anderson was in the thick of it back then, too. I wanted to lock him up for harboring and aiding the enemy. Still, President Eisenhower wanted me to keep a lid on the whole incident. After Roswell, he didn't want to rile the public up. We were having a hard enough time convincing Americans that the saucer that crashed there was nothing more than a weather balloon. Thanks to that idiot public information officer, Walter Haut, who told the press that the 509th Operations Group had recovered a flying disc on a ranch near Roswell."

"I remember that," Stone said. "It's no wonder so many people don't believe Commanding General Roger Ramey of the Eighth Air Force when he later told the press that it was nothing more than a weather balloon."

"You can bet I wasn't going to let that happen on my watch," Mitchell stated. "When the press wanted information about the aliens, all I had to do was make Charles Anderson out to be a crazy old coot."

"Yes, sir, which makes it easier for you to continue to make him the patsy," the Lieutenant said. Inside, his thoughts were anything but supportive. He knew how the general's campaign had ruined the farmer and his family's life. At the time, Mitchell had had a different aide, a man who hadn't liked what was done to Charles Anderson any more than his new aide liked it now.

"We had to work undercover, which proved to be a handicap. Even so, I almost got them." Mitchell took another bite of licorice and chewed, swallowing before continuing. "This time will be different. This is my moment. This is why I was created. Patton had Italy, MacArthur had the Pacific, Eisenhower had Europe, and I have Wichita. This time, it's war."

As the caravan drove through town, people looked out of store and office windows at the long line of trucks. Kids crowded the sidewalk to watch as the military vehicles passed their school. Everyone knew something was happening. They just didn't know what it was. Several men ran out of the local café to watch.

"What's going on?" One man asked his friends.

"The Russians must have invaded our town," another man replied.

"If that's the case, I'm sure glad the Air Force is here to protect us," a third added.

\*\*\*

Not everyone shared his opinion or his relief. The next morning, Mary and Roger joined Stanley at his grandfather's house to discuss what was happening. They and their friends were the only ones who really knew what was going on.

"Do you think the Air Force will come here?" Mary asked.

"It's a possibility," Stanley replied. "Since the aliens were here five years ago, the general has to suspect that grandpa is hiding them again."

"Maybe not," Roger mused. "General Mitchell must know your grandpa is in the hospital. No doubt the Air Force wants to get their hands on Lutsik and Mourda, but they probably know about the Greys, too. Grandpa didn't mention anything about the Greys coming here the last time."

"You think they may be after the other aliens right now?" Mary asked.

"According to Lutsik, without a doubt," Roger replied.

"You're right," Stanley agreed. "Either way, we need to take this fuel sample to the chemical plant. Hopefully, Roger's dad can figure out how to replicate it. The sooner we get Lutsik and Mourda off the planet, the better."

The three friends piled into his grandfather's truck. Across the street, Jeet and Drees watched through the window in the front bedroom.

"Where are they going?" Jeet asked.

"I don't know, but maybe we should follow them," Drees suggested.

The two aliens hurried downstairs and approached the woman, whom they now had under control."

"Get your keys," Jeet said. "We are going for a ride."

When Margaret didn't move fast enough, Drees hassled her. "Hurry up."

"But I...."

"No, buts," Drees said.

"I'm not a very good drive...."

"Look, lady, do what you're told, or Drees will eat your husband's face off."

The three piled into Jack's blue 1960 Buick Le Sabre. As she backed out of the drive, she hit the mailbox, breaking its wooden post in half.

"Why did you run over that contraption?" Jeet asked.

"I tried to tell you. I'm not a very good driver. My husband does all the driving. He would be upset if he knew I was using his car."

"Too bad," Jeet said. "Just do as you are told."

Pulling forward, she finally managed to get out of the driveway without any further damage. She followed Stanley and his friends at a distance.

As Stanley drove, he began to have doubts.

"Is the world coming to an end?" he asked. He turned his head to look first at Mary and then at Roger, who was seated next to the passenger door.

"Why would you say that?" Mary asked.

"We're just a bunch of high school kids. What can we do to save the universe? We're in way over our heads."

"Listen, Stanley, I have a lot of faith in you," Mary said. "I know we can do this. We can save the day."

"What makes you think that?" Roger asked.

An earnest look crossed Mary's face. "Although adults may not think so, kids can do anything they set their mind to. You and your friends are special, and you don't even know it."

Although the boys all felt better after Mary's pep talk the other night, Stanley's old doubts began to creep back. He wanted Mary to be his girlfriend, which in and of itself was both frightening and exciting. Even though he was on the football team as their goal kicker, the cheerleaders never considered him as a potential boyfriend. He was too shy.

"I'm glad you think so," Stanley said.

Mary looked at him with concern. "I do." Then it dawned on her, this was about more than just saving Mourda and Lutsik. "What's going on, Stanley? Have you forgotten everything we talked about the other night?"

"What makes you want to hang out with me...I mean us anyway?" Stanley asked.

"Why not? I like it. I like your friends too."

"Your dad hates my grandfather, so why would he feel any different about me?"

"My dad doesn't hate your grandfather," Mary argued.

"You'd never know it by the way he treated him five years ago," Stanley insisted.

"I know he may have seemed a bit harsh. After all, being the sheriff, he was put in the middle of everything. I think he was more fed up with the Air Force than your grandfather. That General Mitchell is a real pain in the drain."

"He's nasty, too," Roger added.

The dirt road they traveled over wasn't exactly in the best shape. Ruts and a few deep holes marred its surface. To make things worse, the truck's suspension needed a repair job. When Stanley hit one of those nasty holes, the container with the fuel tipped just enough to spill some of the dangerous contents. It burned a small hole through the truck bed and spilled onto the road.

They continued on without any further damage, but the front tire on the passenger side of the car with the aliens ran over the spilled fuel and blew out. Margaret pulled off the side of the road.

The loud noise of the blowout scared Drees and Jeet, and they pulled out their phasers, thinking that someone was shooting at them.

"What was that?" Jeet asked, looking around for attackers.

"We have a flat tire," Margaret said. "You can put your weapons away."

The three of them piled out of the car.

"What do we do now?" Drees asked.

"There's a spare in the trunk. You'll have to change the tire," Margaret replied.

"No, you need to change it," Drees said.

"I can't. I'm not strong enough," Margaret replied. "I'll tell you how to do it."

Jeet retrieved a spare tire.

"You forgot the jack," Margaret said.

"Forget that," Jeet said. "We have a better way to do it."

Using his remarkable abilities, Drees lifted the whole car into the air. Once it was floating four feet off the ground, Jeet used his equally remarkable power to remove the lug nuts and the tire, which floated in the air while he placed the spare on the axle.

*** 

"How long has Mark been your boyfriend?" Stanley asked.

"He's not my boyfriend!" Mary huffed. "Why does everyone think he is?"

"Because you to do things together and I see you with him all the time," Stanley replied

"We have classes together."

"In the hallway?" Stanley asked.

"Our lockers are side-by-side," Mary easily explained.

"You're also together on the football field," Stanley accused.

"That's where the cheerleaders practice."

"You're a cheerleader, and he's a quarterback."

"So, what? You're the field-goal kicker," Mary countered with a smile on her face.

"Yeah, but field-goal kickers don't go out with the head cheerleader."

"Why not?"

"Would you? If I asked that is?" Stanley felt his heart racing as he spoke.

"Of course, I would!"

"Why? You don't know me," Stanley said, looking into her eyes for the truth of her words.

"Stanley!" Roger said a little too loudly. "Keep your eyes on the road."

"Oh, sorry," Stanley said, facing forward.

"Your grandfather talks about you all the time. His house is filled with your pictures, pictures. He had to go to a lot of trouble to get ahold of. I feel like I have known you for as long as I've known your grandfather."

"Really?"

"Really. If you asked me, Stanley, I would go out with you."

Wishing to strike while he had the nerve, Stanley opened his mouth to ask her out, but as he did, the truck hit a deep rut in the road, and the passenger door flew open. All three screamed, and Stanley quickly put his arm around Mary and grabbed his friend's arm, to keep them from falling out of the truck. Anchored by Stanley's grip, Roger leaned out and tried to grab the door handle. He missed.

Roger kept trying, each time leaning out further. Stanley was so busy trying to keep his friend from falling, that he forgot that all he had to do was to slow down.

"Stanley, slow down," Mary said at last.

"Oh, sorry. I didn't think of that," he replied, blushing.

As soon as the truck slowed to a crawl, the door stopped swinging so violently, and Roger was able to grab the handle and pull it shut.

Even though the danger was past, Stanley did not remove his arm from Mary's shoulders. He grinned briefly, not wanting anyone else to see.

***

When Stanley and the others arrived at the chemical company, they entered the building and walked up to the receptionist's desk in the lobby.

"What can I do for you?" the receptionist asked, smiling.

"We need to speak to my dad," Roger replied.

"Oh my, Roger, I didn't see you at first. Let me call him on the intercom and see if he's available." She did so, and after a brief conversation, hung up. "He'll be right out."

"Roger, Stanley." Mr. Ward greeted them. Then he paused and looked at Mary. "And I don't believe I know your name, young lady."

"It's Mary, Mister Ward, Mary Guthrie, Sheriff Guthrie's daughter."

"Glad to meet you, Mary. What can I do for you young folks?"

"Uh, can we talk in private?" Roger asked his dad.

An amused expression crossed Mr. Ward's face. "Sure, son, let's go in my office."

Roger and his friends followed him down a long hallway that went past labs, storerooms, and offices. Mr. Ward's office was at the end. Numerous windows allowed in what little light leaked through the overcast autumn sky. The furniture was modern metal and black.

"Have a seat," Ward offered, pointing to a small conference table on the left side of the room. Once everyone was seated, he looked at his son. "Now, what is it that you and your friends need to talk to me about?"

"Well, uh, we have this new kind of fuel," Roger said, setting the container on the table. "And we need to duplicate it."

"Problem is, the formula is missing, and we don't know how to make more," Stanley quickly chimed in.

"What is this for, some kind of science experiment?" Mr. Ward asked.

"A little bit," Mary replied hesitantly.

"It's really important that we get more made," Roger added.

"Well, you know how much I appreciate science. Just leave it on the table, and I'll get to it as soon as I get a chance."

"Uh, dad, we really need it now."

"Now? Really?" Mr. Ward asked, surveying the expressions on their faces.

"Yes, sir, we definitely need it now," Stanley replied.

Roger's dad paused a moment before speaking. "I have a feeling that by now, you mean that you need it today."

"Yes, sir, we sure do," Stanley said.

"I'll tell you what. I will do it for you, Mary. I don't know what these two are up to, but being the sheriff's daughter, I trust you."

"Thank you, sir. We really appreciate your help," Mary told him.

"I'm busy right now, but I'll get to it in a couple hours," Mr. Ward said.

He was about to leave the room when Roger stopped him with a warning. "Don't let it drip on anything."

"Why?"

"You don't want to know," Roger assured him.

"Why don't you kids wait in the lobby, so you don't get underfoot?"

The three friends popped up from their chairs.

"Sure thing, dad."

"We don't want to disturb anyone's work," Mary added.

The next two hours dragged by slowly. Stanley was pacing the floor for the third time when Mr. Ward joined them.

"This is going to take a while," he said. "Why don't you have lunch and return later. My treat."

"Gee, thanks, Dad," Roger said as he accepted a five-dollar bill from his father.

Climbing into the truck, they drove to Jim's Diner for lunch.

# Chapter Twenty-Eight

## Negotiations

Having lost sight of them when their vehicle got a flat tire, Jeet and Drees told Margaret to drive them to town, hoping they would find the kids there. They were relieved when they saw the old truck heading down Main Street. The aliens followed, navigating the car slowly until Stanley parked in a spot nearly a block away from the diner. Getting out of the truck, he and his two friends walked down the street towards Jim's Diner.

"They parked the truck," Margaret said. "What do you want me to do now?"

"Find somewhere to put this thing and hurry, before we lose sight of them," Drees ordered.

Since it was lunchtime, very few parking places were available. Margaret had to drive three blocks further before she found an open space.

"Stay here and wait for us," Jeet told her as he and Drees hopped out of the car.

While Margaret was looking for a place to park the car, Stanley and his friends arrived at the diner and found a seat at a booth inside. Jeet and Drees hurried back toward the old truck, but they did not see the kids anywhere. Panicking, they started looking through the windows of the businesses along the street.

Inside the diner, a waitress approached Stanley, Roger, and Mary with a pad and pen in hand. She smiled at them. "What'll you have?"

Having eaten here several times in the past, the three friends knew the menu by heart.

"I'll have a hamburger with mustard and ketchup, an order of fries, and a double chocolate shake," Roger said.

She turned and looked at Mary.

"I'll have a hamburger with tomato, lettuce, pickle, and ketchup," she said with a smile, "and a chocolate soda with vanilla ice cream."

Finally, the waitress turned to Stanley.

"I'll have a hamburger with mustard and ketchup, an order of French fries, and a strawberry shake," Stanley told her.

The waitress walked behind the counter and shouted to the kitchen. "I need a bossy painted red and yellow, an order of frog sticks, and a double black cow. Second-order is a bossy, run it through the garden painted red, and a black and white; third order is a bossy painted red and yellow, an order of frog sticks, and shake one in the hay." She turned, picked up the glass coffee pot, and offered refills to the customers seated at the counter.

"Do you think your dad will be able to replicate the fuel?" Mary asked Roger.

"Piece of cake, my dad's the best. If it's possible, he can do it," Roger assured her.

"I hope so," Mary said in a worried tone. "Lutsik and Mourda need to get the Core home as quickly as possible."

"Don't worry, everything is going to be okay," Roger said.

Changing the subject, Stanley brought up something funny that happened in school the day before. For the first time since all this began, they laughed and were able to relax and talk about normal things.

The waitress delivered their food, and all three dug in.

"I didn't realize how hungry I was," Mary said after swallowing a bite of her sandwich. "I guess I shouldn't have skipped breakfast."

Halfway through their meal, Stanley choked on a French fry when he saw the general walk-in with his aide. Roger pounded him on the back.

"Are you okay?" Mary asked.

Stanley didn't reply. He remembered Mitchell from the video he had watched in class.

Mary began telling the boys a story. She shrugged off his lack of response and continued with her tale.

Stanley continued ignoring her and pulled his hand away from hers as he strained to hear what the general was saying as he approached one of the tables and started questioning the farmers seated there.

Seeing that she was still being ignored, Mary got mad. She didn't see the general and couldn't understand why Stanley wasn't listening to her.

Roger also tried to get his attention, but like Mary, he received no response.

Keeping his eye on the general, Stanley watched and listened to his words. At first, Mitchell made no mention of the aliens.

"Excuse me, folks, but I was wondering if you happen to notice any strange people or happenings here in town."

"No, everything's been pretty much the same as it always is," one farmer replied.

The others shook their heads no. They didn't understand why this military officer was questioning them about their town. As soon as Mitchell moved on to question the couple seated at the next table. The farmers lowered their voices.

"What was that all about?" One of the other farmers asked.

"You got me," the farmer who had spoken to the general replied. "As far as I'm concerned, I think he's crazy."

"Say, wasn't that the same guy who was here five years ago?" Another asked.

"You know, I think you're right," the first farmer agreed. "I wonder what's going on?"

Mary was just getting to the critical part of her story, but Stanley still wasn't listening. In fact, he acted as if he didn't even care. This made her even madder, and she started to get up. Seeing this out of the corner of his eye, Stanley pulled her back down to her chair and motioned with his head toward the general.

Both Mary and Roger looked over and saw him. Now they understood why Stanley wasn't paying attention to Mary's story. All three listened carefully as Mitchell moved from table to table, asking if there were any new people in town.

As if things weren't bad enough, Mark strolled to the door with a bunch of his friends and sat down at the table in front of the windows. One of them elbowed Mark on the side.

"Hey, Mark, look who Mary is sitting with. I thought she was your girl."

Mark looked around until he saw her sitting with Stanley and Roger. His eyes narrowed, but before he could say anything, their server came to the table to take their orders. When she left, he got to his feet and strutted over to their table.

When he got within a foot of them, he pretended to trip, which allowed him to bend forward enough to knock Stanley's arm, spilling his milkshake all over the boy's pants.

"Oops!" Mark had a sarcastic grin on his face.

"Mark! You did that on purpose," Mary scolded angrily.

"Nah, I tripped. Didn't you see me?"

"You only pretended to trip," she accused him.

"What are you doing with these nerds anyway?" Mark sneered.

"They aren't nerds. They're my friends."

Busy wiping the milkshake off his clothing, Stanley tried to ignore the quarterback. Mark's brow darkened. He did not like how close Stanley and Mary were sitting together in the booth.

"You're sitting awfully close for just friends," he said.

Mary glared at him and grabbed one of Stanley's hands.

"It's all right, Mary," Stanley said. He was trying to avoid a commotion so as not to attract the general's attention. "I'm sure it was an accident just like Mark said."

"See? Stanley knows it was just an accident," Mark confirmed. Deciding that he had won, he returned to his table.

Mark and his friends became boisterous until the waitress brought their orders.

"All right, pipe down, you guys, you're disturbing the rest of the clientele."

Just then, Jeet and Drees walked in. Spotting Stanley and his friends, they sat down at the table the farmers had just vacated. From there, they could easily keep an eye on the three kids.

General Mitchell finished questioning two young women. Turning, he realized that the farmers had left, and two men were now sitting in the booth. He walked over to them and sat down, forcing Jeet to scoot over.

"Good afternoon, gentlemen, mind if I ask you some questions?"

The aliens glared at him. When Mitchell sat down, he obscured their view of Stanley and the others.

"We would prefer not to be disturbed," Drees replied, tossing what appeared to be a round gold coin in the air and catching it. He had been doing this ever since he and Jeet sat down in the booth.

"This won't take long," the general insisted.

Sensing the confrontation, the waitress turned around and waited on someone else. It was a good thing, too. Had Jeet and Drees given her their order for one thousand pieces of white bread, it would have made the general suspicious.

"We came here to eat, not talk," Jeet said.

His response angered Mitchell. "Listen up, you yahoos. I represent the always true with the red, white, and blue United States government, and you will answer my questions."

Jeet and Drees exchanged glances. They did not recognize his uniform and wondered if he was another member of the local law enforcement.

While Mitchell asked the questions, he had asked the other diners, Stanley, Mary, and Roger were close enough to hear every word.

Stanley leaned forward and signaled the other two to do the same. "There's something funny about those two," he said, indicating the aliens with a nod of his head. "Have you seen them around here before?"

"No," Mary said.

"They're perfect strangers to me," Roger agreed. "Why do you think that?"

"I can't explain it," Stanley said. "I guess it's just a gut feeling."

Jeet and Drees denied having any knowledge with regard to the general's inquiries. However, Mitchell did not move on to the next table but stayed there, asking even more questions. He had no idea that he was talking to two of the aliens he was looking for. However, like Stanley, he also sensed something odd about the pair.

"We have not seen any strange lights in the sky," Drees said. "What's this about anyway?"

Mitchell lowered his voice, looked around, and leaned closer. "I'm talking about…aliens. You sure you haven't seen any…little grey creatures with a large head and big eyes? They would be about this high," he said, holding his hand up around 4 ½ feet from the floor.

His intelligence far supersedes that of the other local law enforcement that we have encountered, Drees told Jeet telepathically.

You are right, Jeet replied. He must be part of their military, and he's looking for us.

At that moment, Mitchell's aide approached the table and took the general aside to fill him in on a piece of information he had obtained from one of the other diners. With their backs to the aliens, they did not see what Stanley and his friends saw next. Jeet's holographic illusion flickered, and for a few seconds, his alien appearance was visible. Then it returned to his human persona. Drees became alarmed.

Stanley blinked and turned to Mary. "Tell me you just saw the same thing I did."

"It's the Greys," Roger whispered. "It's true. It's really true. They do exist.

"What are they doing here?" Stanley asked.

"Do you think they know that Lutsik and Mourda are staying with you?" Mary asked.

"I don't know," Stanley replied, but we better get outta here."

Pulling the five-dollar bill out of his pocket, Roger tossed it on the table. There was enough to pay for all three meals as well as a generous tip.

When General Mitchell finished listening to his aide, he turned and spotted the empty booth where Stanley, Mary, and Roger had been sitting. He reached out and grabbed the arm of the passing waitress. "Who was sitting at an empty table?"

"Which empty table?" She asked.

"That one," he said, pointing to the booth in question.

"Oh, just some high school kids."

"What are their names?"

She hesitated a moment, wondering why three high school kids would be so important to this man.

"Their names?" Mitchell repeated gruffly.

"Well, there was Mary Guthrie, the sheriff's daughter, Roger Ward, and Stanley Adams, Charles Anderson' grandson."

"Charles Anderson? You mean that crazy old coot who raised such a ruckus five years ago about U.F.O.s?"

"That's the one, but his grandson seems quite levelheaded."

"I'll bet. Is there a back door to this place?" Mitchell asked.

"Sure, it's through the kitchen."

"Lieutenant Stone, did you see those three kids sitting at that table over there?"

"Yes sir, I did," Stone replied.

"Then come with me," Mitchell ordered as he ran through the kitchen, asked the cook if anyone had come through there, and ran out the back door.

When they reached the back alleyway, Mitchell said, "You go left, and I'll go right. Find them."

Fortunately, before either man reached the front of the building, Stanley and the others were in the old truck, headed out of town.

"We missed them, but I know how to find two of them," the general said. "Let's go back inside. There are a couple of guys I want to finish talking to."

They went back into the diner through the front door, but as Mitchell walked toward the table where Jeet and Drees had been sitting, he discovered that they, too, were gone. He looked around confused but determined to find out why five people had left the diner without finishing, or in the case of the aliens, ordering their meal.

# Chapter Twenty-Nine

## Fuel Formula

Stanley, Mary, and Roger headed back to the chemical plant. When they arrived, the receptionist escorted them to Mr. Ward's lab.

"He's over there at that table," the receptionist said, pointing to her boss.

"Thanks," Roger said.

As he and his two friends approached the bench. Mr. Ward looked up and saw them.

"I'm glad you're back, Roger," Mr. Ward said. "I have never seen anything like this. Where did you get it?"

None of the three knew what to say. They did not want to tell him the fuel's original source. For one thing, he wouldn't believe them.

"It blew up the machine I was testing it in." As the silence continued, Mr. Ward turned and looked at each of their faces. "Roger? Stanley?" He turned to Mary. "Mary, come on. I trusted you."

"If you like, believe, and trust Stanley's grandfather, Charles Anderson, then you must trust us," Mary said.

"I can't explain now, dad, but I will," Roger promised. "Just know that it is more important than anything you can ever imagine."

Mr. Ward looked in each of their eyes, his mind whirling with questions. Nodding, he picked up a sheet of paper with writing on it and handed it to his son. "This is a list of the liquid's components, all except one, which I haven't figured out yet. Don't worry. I'll keep working on it. I couldn't stop now if I wanted to."

He was about to say more when the company's hazmat team entered the lab and converged on them. As they prepared to clean up the machine and spill, Mr. Ward explained the corrosiveness of what they were dealing with. He was so distracted by the hazmat team that he didn't see his son pick up the container with the remaining fuel that hadn't been used in the test. Then Roger jerked his head toward the door, and the three of them hurried out of the building and headed for the truck.

"That was close," Stanley said. "I'm glad we were able to get away without answering your father's questions."

"We got away with it for now, but eventually, we will have to tell him what he wants to know," Roger warned.

They climbed into the truck, placing the container with the remaining fuel on the floor between their feet, and headed back to the farm.

"How much time do we have?" Mary asked.

"I'm not sure, but I know we're running out. I hope your dad can figure out the final ingredient quickly. The Greys and the military are closing in," Stanley said.

"More importantly, the time window between Earth and Tau Ceti is closing fast," Roger added.

When they reached the back roads that would take them to Charles's farm, Stanley sped up. In doing so, he had a lot of bumps. When he hit a particularly nasty one, everyone cried out, fearing the worst. The remaining fuel sloshed up and down in the container, but, fortunately, did not spill out.

"You'd better slow down," Mary said. "We don't want to burn another hole in the floor of the truck, and who knows? We may need what's left in that container."

"I'm sorry," Stanley said. "I feel like everything is closing in on us, and I guess that made me drive faster."

They went along in silence until they spotted something up ahead in the road.

"What's that?" Roger asked.

No one answered until they got close enough to see it clearly.

"It's the military," Stanley replied. His voice was filled with dread.

Slowing further, by the time they reached the blockade, the truck was nearly at a crawl. Three cars were ahead of them. However, as soon as they came to a stop, two Air Force officers approached the truck, one on each side.

Stanley rolled down his window. "What's going on? Has something happened?"

"We're conducting a spot check," the officer standing beside the driver's door said. "I need you to turn off the engine and step out of your vehicle."

Stanley, Mary, and Roger climbed out of the truck, careful not to kick the container of fuel, which they left inside. They stood together at the side of the road, trying to prevent the panic they felt from showing on their faces.

"What are we going to do?" Roger whispered. "If they find that fuel and realize what it is, we're sunk."

"Let's not panic yet," Mary said. "We know what they're looking for."

"Yeah," Stanley replied, "the aliens."

"I think you're right," Mary said, allowing a little of her tension to dissipate. "In which case, they can tell, without doing a closer examination, that there is no one else in the truck."

"Maybe they're just going to ask us about the aliens," Stanley said.

"If that's the case, why did we have to get out of the truck?" Roger argued.

Stanley was only partially right. The military was questioning the people in the cars, but they didn't ask them if they had seen anything strange like the general had in the diner. Instead, they were asking questions they hoped would reveal if someone was an alien.

As they waited for their turn, the kids saw another vehicle traveling too fast and coming right at the line of cars. Two of the military officers ran to the back of the truck, shouting and waving their arms.

"Slow down! Stop!"

As the car moved closer, the kids recognized who it was.

"It's the lady from across the street!" Stanley shouted.

Margaret finally realized what was going on, and she slammed on the brakes, but not quickly enough. The soldiers jumped out of the way just before her husband's Buick Le Sabre slammed into the back of the old farm truck.

Stanley ran up to his grandfather's truck and opened the passenger door. A few drops of fuel slowly slid down the side of the container. They needed to get out of there and fast before the fuel hit the floor and burned its way through to the street below. Gently closing the door, he moved to the back of the truck to inspect the damage. As he did so, he saw the two aliens from the restaurant in the car next to Mrs. Weber.

He mostly remembered the neighbor from his younger days when he and his mom still lived with his grandfather. The one thing that stood out in his mind was the fact that she was nosy.

What is she doing with them? She couldn't be a prisoner. Otherwise, she would have jumped out of her car and run screaming to the military. It doesn't make sense.

Whatever happened, because of the fuel, he had to hurry. Nevertheless, this was his chance to take the military's attention off Lutsik and Mourda and place it squarely on the Greys.

He went back to Mary and Roger to tell them what was going on.

"Now is our chance," Stanley said. "The Greys are in Mrs. Weber's car."

"They're asking questions an alien wouldn't know like: What baseball teams are going to be in the World Series? Who are the candidates running for president? Who is the President of the United States?" Roger said.

"Lyndon Johnson, of course." Mary blushed when she realized what she had said. "Sorry, it just came out. I guess I got carried away. Most people would know the answers, but an alien might not."

"Maybe we should tell them to flash a light in their eyes," Roger said.

"That might not work," Stanley said. "Just because the light can hurt the Ceti's, doesn't mean it will do the same thing to the Greys. We don't have a lot of time to wait. I'm going to tell them where the aliens are."

"That might not be such a good idea," Mary said.

Stanley, however, would not listen. He was determined that he would convince the military to inspect Margaret's car. He walked up to an Air Force Sergeant, standing on the sidelines. The line of vehicles was steadily growing more prolonged, and people were becoming impatient.

"You know that car that ran into the back of my truck?" Stanley began.

"Crazy female driver," the sergeant said. "Obviously, she's no judge of distance. We'll get her license and registration for you. Although that truck is so old, I seriously doubt any insurance company would pay to fix it. You may end up having to take her to small claims court."

"She may have done it on purpose," Stanley said thoughtfully.

His answer caused the sergeant to turn and to give him his full attention. "Why would you say that? I believe I overheard you say that she was your neighbor. Does she have some kind of vendetta against you?"

"No, she's a busybody, but otherwise, she's okay."

"Then why would she be under duress?" the officer wanted to know.

"Do you see those two guys in the front seat with her?"

"What about them?"

"I think they kidnapped her. They've been acting kinda strange." Stanley leaned a little closer to the man and lowered his voice. "I think they might be the aliens you are looking for."

Stanley hoped that his words would push the man into action. It did, but not the reaction he was hoping for.

"Who said anything about aliens?" the sergeant asked suspiciously.

"Look, everyone knows why the Air Force is here. That's why General Mitchell was at the diner asking everybody questions."

"I think you been reading too many comic books, sonny."

"I'm serious. If you don't believe me, ask General Mitchell. He can tell you."

"Why don't you go back and stand with your friends? We'll be getting to you soon enough," the sergeant said.

"You have to believe me. Those two guys in that car aren't human. I saw them at the diner. They are wearing some kind of disguise. I know because it flickered for a few seconds on one of them, and I saw what they really look like. They're Greys, just like the ones that crashed at Roswell."

Now he was really pushing it. Not many people knew the truth about Roswell, even in the military. He was so argumentative that it angered the Air Force Officer. Grabbing his arm, the sergeant pulled it up behind Stanley's back and shoved him against the truck.

"How do I know you're not the one with the disguise? It seems to me you're trying awfully hard to place suspicion on someone else."

Mary and Roger ran up to them.

"Stop! What are you doing to him? He hasn't done anything wrong," Mary cried.

"Yeah, leave him alone," Roger said.

By now, the people in the cars in front of the old truck had answered their questions and driven away. Those in the vehicles behind the truck became even more impatient over the delay and began honking their horns.

Knowing they were next, the aliens grew nervous.

Should we go around the truck and break through the barricade, or come out shooting? Jeet telepathically asked Drees.

Wait, I have an idea, Drees replied.

He turned to Margaret. "Start doing what other people are doing."

She turned around in her seat and looked at the cars behind her. "You want me to honk my horn?"

"Is that what is making that annoying racket?" Drees asked.

"Yes."

"Then do it."

Margaret laid on the horn.

By now, people were actually leaning out their windows and shouting.

"What's the holdup?" One man yelled.

"Hurry up. We haven't got all day," a woman in the car behind him strained.

From there, it just got worse.

The officer in charge walked up to the truck. "Is there a problem here?" The lieutenant asked.

"It's this kid," the sergeant replied. "He knows we're looking for the aliens."

"Are you kidding? By now, so does everybody else in this town." He turned toward the other men. "Go on, wave them through. I seriously doubt the aliens are driving around in a car."

By doing this, he was disobeying the general's orders, but he really didn't believe they would find the aliens this way.

He was wrong.

As Margaret slowly past the truck, Stanley locked eyes with Drees.

That human knows who we are, Drees told Jeet.

That's one of the ones in the barn with the Ceti's. If he knows who we are, we will have to take care of him, Jeet replied.

"Excuse me, sir," Mary said. "Can we go?"

"Go ahead. Let the kid go," the lieutenant ordered.

The sergeant obeyed, but as Mary and Roger climbed back into the truck, Stanley couldn't help trying one last time.

"They're getting away."

When he received no response, he climbed into the truck and drove off. They were running out of time.

# Chapter Thirty

## Interference

Caroline, Lutsik, and Mourda continued working on the ship. While Stanley and his friends sat around a table in the barn discussing their strategy.

"The way I see it, we have four problems to solve: The Greys, time, fuel, and last but not least General Mitchell and the military," Stanley said.

"When I went back to get a sample for Lutsik, Dad told me that he hadn't found the final ingredient yet," Roger told them.

"Does he think he will figure it out in time?" Mary asked.

"He is doing his best," Roger replied, almost defensively.

"I hope he can," Mary said. "Otherwise, Tau Ceti is lost."

"Lutsik and Mourda are working on it," Stanley said. "Maybe they can figure it out."

"This wouldn't be so bad if we didn't have to worry about time constrictions," Rick mused.

"What are we going to do about the general?" Roger asked.

Stanley jumped to his feet and started pacing the area near their table. He often thought better on his feet. "General Mitchell is a big problem. I mean, how can we throw off the military?" As he thought, he unconsciously reached into his pocket and pulled out the gold coin he had found outside and begun tossing it in the air and catching it. He was so deep in thought that it startled him when, suddenly, the piece was snatched out of thin air.

Lutsik held the coin and examined it carefully. He turned to Stanley, who had stopped pacing. "Where did you get this?"

"What, that thing?"

Lutsik held the coin so that Stanley could clearly see it.

"Uh, I don't…wait a minute. Queakly found it outside in the yard. It's just some of the junk my grandfather sells in his alien shop."

"I wish that were true," Lutsik said, shaking his head. "However, I can assure you that you will find nothing like this in your grandfather's store."

Mary and the boys left their seats to join them.

"By the sound of your voice, it must be something important," Mary guessed.

"They are here."

"Who?" Rick asked.

"Our enemies, the Greys. This is a medal from their homeworld. It is awarded to those who discover a new planet ripe for plundering."

"Mary, Roger, and I saw them in the diner," Stanley admitted.

"How do you know it was them?" Rick asked. "Did they look like Lutsik and Mourda?"

"If you mean, did they look human? Yes, sort of," Stanley told them.

"Then how did you know it was them?" Rick insisted.

"They use a device that creates a preprogrammed holographic image around their bodies," Lutsik explained.

"For only a moment at the restaurant, that image fizzled out on one of them," Stanley added.

"Apparently, no one but the three of us saw what happened," Roger said.

"They must have followed you back to the farm," Lutsik said. "When did they arrive, and how much do they know?"

"Everything," Stanley said bleakly. "Remember when Queakly ran into the barn barking excitedly?"

"That was right after your ship ran out of fuel and hit the ground," Mary said.

"Your dog barked so much, he must've scared them off," Roger said.

"Mourda and I heard the commotion, but there was so much noise that we couldn't make out what your dog was saying. Since the Greys are also a telepathic race, they knew that he was trying to warn us."

"What are we going to do?" Mary asked.

"The ship has enough fuel to create a force field around the farm," Lutsik said. "However, we can only keep it up for four hours."

"Then put it up for protection," Stanley said.

Mary looked at him, thoughtfully. It was clear by his recent actions that for the first time in his life, Stanley was gaining confidence in himself and his ideas and taking a leadership role.

"I've made a list of items we will need to complete the formula for the fuel that Roger's father is making," Lutsik said, handing the list to Stanley.

"Then, you figured it out?" Roger asked.

"I believe we have," Lutsik said. "We won't know for sure, however, until we have all the ingredients and mix it up."

Everyone crowded around to look at the list.

"Let's divide the list in two and split up," Stanley said. "This way, we should be able to get everything in half the time. Mary and I will take Grandpa's truck and head to the grocery store. Roger, you can go in Rick's car."

"I want to go with you and Mary," Roger said, hoping for a chance to spend more time with her.

"No, you'd better go with us," Rick said.

"But I…."

Rick grabbed his arm, and when Roger turned to look at him, he shook his head and mouthed the words, "Stanley and Mary want to be alone."

Roger sighed in defeat and followed Rick to his car.

Stanley and Mary climbed into the old truck, but as he searched his pockets, he realized he had forgotten the keys. Jumping out of the truck, he ran into the house to fetch them.

Across the street, the nosy neighbor pretended to work in her flower bed in the front yard, but she was actually watching the farm. Having discerned her nature, Jeet decided he could put it to a good advantage. Using mind persuasion, he convinced Margaret to pledge her allegiance to them. He told her to spy on the people across the street. She was happy to oblige.

As soon as Stanley left to get the keys to the truck, she ran into the house, where she met Jeet.

"They're taking off," she told him.

Jeet's expression turned to one of alarm. "You mean they are leaving in their ship?"

"What? No! They're driving someplace," she explained.

"Quickly then, follow them," Jeet ordered

"Which one? Some of them went in a car. The other two are going in Charles Anderson's old truck."

"It does not matter. Pick one, but hurry before you lose sight of them," Jeet said.

"I'll need a disguise," she mumbled to herself as she ran upstairs to her room.

Searching her closet for just the right clothing, she dressed up as a crazy old movie star complete with platinum blond wig and sunglasses. She didn't realize that her disguise would draw attention to herself, instead of helping her blend in with the crowd. Margaret grabbed the car keys and her purse, and as she ran out of the house, she yelled to her husband, "I'm leaving."

Still sitting in front of the television, Jack waved her off. He was so enthralled by the game show he watched that it never dawned on him she would take his vehicle.

Hurrying to her husband's car, she started the engine but waited until Stanley and Mary drove off, before following them. Her disguise was terrible, but she loved it, and she kept glancing in the rearview mirror and grinning. "I am so very clever."

Jeet went upstairs to the front bedroom to find Drees looking out the window.

"Everyone is gone. I sent the crazy female human to follow them," Jeet said.

"Good idea. With the humans out of the way, the Cetis will be alone. Now is our chance. Let's head for the barn. We will eliminate the Cetis and take the Core."

"What about the mercenary?"

"She should be no problem since she is working for our side. If she tries to take the crystal from us, we will simply eliminate her."

"Then we can go home, but are we going to give the crystal to our Commander?" Jeet asked.

Drees' expression turned thoughtful. "If we do, he will claim it, and our leaders will give him credit for its recovery."

"Why should we give it to him?" Jeet asked. "He has been deceitful and untrustworthy."

"Exactly. No, I think we will keep it. It may come in handy at some future time. Besides, all we have to do is wait until the Tau Ceti shield collapses. Our leaders don't really need the crystal for their attack," Drees said.

"Won't the Commander demand that we give it to him?"

"Not if we tell him that his mercenary found it first and took off for her homeworld."

"He will think she reneged on their deal and took both their money and the Core," Jeet said, grinning widely.

"Affirmative, now let's go across the street and get the Core."

Hurrying down the stairs, they ran through the living room and out the front door.

Jack may as well have been on another planet. He had no clue as to what was going on in his own home.

In their eagerness to finish this assignment, the two aliens threw caution away and ran across the street and into the front yard. There they slammed into the force field, which crackled and sizzled and threw them back ten feet. Jeet and Drees landed flat on their backs and spread-eagled. The electrical surge from the force field temporarily scrambled their brains. Had this been a Warner Bros. cartoon, little yellow birdies would be circling their heads and tweeting.

It took several moments before they shook off the effects. When they got to their feet, they had to wait a moment longer to steady themselves.

"The Cetis have put up a force field," Jeet fumed.

"Let's grab a handful of pebbles from the driveway," Drees said. "I want to see how far the shield extends and check for weak spots."

"Good idea."

Each alien scooped up to two hands full of pebbles. Then they slowly walked around the shield, tossing a pebble every two feet.

The shield was kept to a minimum to conserve power and fuel. It started two feet in front of the farmhouse and wrapped around to include the barn and garage and ended back at the farmhouse.

"The shield is solid," Drees said disgustedly. "We'll have to find another way to get through."

"Let's check the manuals in our room," Jeet suggested. "Surely, we will find a way to defeat it in there."

The trip back across the street was once more cautious as they did not want anyone else to see them. Before, when they thought they would get the crystal, they didn't care. Now, they had to go back to being careful. When they reached their room, each grabbed a stack of comic books. Drees returned to his chair in front of the window and set his pile on the other chair. Seeing this, Jeet took the bed.

\*\*\*

The aliens made it back inside Margaret's home just as General Mitchell and his aide pulled in the driveway of the farmhouse, stopping as soon as their car cleared the street. They sat there, staring at the house for several minutes.

"I wish I could talk to them and find out why they are here," the general said wistfully. Little did he realize that he had already spoken to the Greys.

Lieutenant Stone turned and looked at his superior. Is he having a change of heart? He wondered. He shook his head no. When it came to aliens, the general would be relentless until he and his people learned everything they could about their technology.

Mitchell turned his head and scanned the rest of the farm. He was puzzled when he saw all the homemade satellite dishes spread throughout the property. Then it hit him.

"They're here."

"The aliens?" Stone asked. "Which ones?"

"I'm not sure, but I recognize this place. Of course, there weren't as many satellites the last time I saw it. This is where they came five years ago on September 12th." Mitchell was fond of quoting specific historical dates, but this time, he was wrong.

Although he hadn't been serving with the general at the time, Lieutenant Stone knew exactly which aliens were here and the exact date of their arrival. The Greys would not have befriended the farmer or anyone else for that matter. "Excuse me, sir, it was actually September 15th."

"Yes, I believe you're right." Mitchell snapped out of his reverie and became all business again. "Let's go to the sheriff's office. He knows this area better than we do. I want to pump him for information. Let me do the talking. As far as I'm concerned, our conversation with him will be a one-way street. Tell him nothing."

# Chapter Thirty-One

## Warp Speed

General Mitchell and his fleet of jeeps and trucks arrived at the sheriff's office. Lieutenant Stone got out of the vehicle and walked around to the other side to open the door for his superior. Mitchell walked into the sheriff's station like a god, followed by twelve of his men.

One of the deputies hurried back to his boss's office. "You're not gonna believe what just walked in the door, sheriff."

Although Sheriff Stewart Guthrie was not a handsome man, his features were pleasant, and his body tall and muscular. Those who thought he was a stupid backwoods sheriff soon learned to their detriment that they were mistaken. Guthrie had worked initially as a homicide detective in Chicago. When he and his wife were expecting Mary, they made the decision to leave the big city and raise her someplace rural. Where crime was mostly petty things like shoplifting and traffic tickets. Occasionally, something more serious happened, but thankfully not often.

He wasn't happy about General Mitchell and his team of Air Force officers running around his county. He remembered what had happened five years ago, and all the havoc the general had caused, and he wasn't happy about them being there now.

"Let me guess," he replied to his deputy. "Mrs. Wilkins' cat is stuck up the tree again."

"No, Sir, it's not her. It's that highfalutin general and a whole passel of his men."

Guthrie sighed deeply. "I figured he would get around to coming here sooner or later." Standing up, he pushed back his chair and walked to the front of the building, his deputy following closely behind.

When Mitchell saw him, he called out, "Sheriff Guthrie, we need to have a chat."

"Is that so? What about?"

"Why don't we go back to your office where we will have a bit more privacy," Mitchell said.

"I don't have a problem with that," the sheriff said. "There is only room enough for you and your aide."

Turning, he headed back to his office. The general and lieutenant followed.

"Have a seat, gentlemen," the sheriff said, indicating two wooden chairs in front of his desk. "Would you like some coffee?"

"No thanks," Mitchell said. "We're fine."

Guthrie sat in his chair and leaned back slightly, making the chair squeak in protest. He waited for Mitchell to start the conversation.

"I need to know about the people who live on the farms around here," Mitchell began.

"There are a lot of farms around here, general. Which one are you interested in?"

"Well now, I don't rightly know if you could even call it a farm anymore. It seems like the property is full of junk instead of crops."

Guthrie knew which farm the general was asking about, and he didn't like it that the man was coy about it. After the incident of five years ago, he knew darn well that Mitchell knew precisely who lived on that farm. The sheriff liked Charles Anderson. He thought he was a bit eccentric but otherwise, knew he was a harmless old man and a good neighbor. He wasn't happy with the way the Mitchell and his men had treated Charles five years ago.

"Nobody out there but old Charles Anderson," the Sheriff replied. "Why?"

Mitchell had no intention of telling the Sheriff any more than he absolutely had to. "We have our suspicions."

"I live next door. What's up? You're not looking to give old Charles a hard time, again, are you?"

This question threw Mitchell off, but only for a moment. Apparently, the lawman knew and liked the crazy old coot, but that wouldn't stop him from getting at the truth.

"I believe there are some bad guys holding up there. You know…communists? It seems some of them Russian's have snuck into the country during the dead of night. You got anybody that can speak Russian?"

Fortunately, the sheriff had a good poker face. He wasn't sure what was really going on, but he knew it had nothing to do with the Russians. After all, what would they want with a small town in Kansas? Guthrie didn't trust him and knew that Mitchell was lying to him. That made him even more determined to get to the bottom of what was going on.

"Let me assure you, general. Unless they are hiding in the satellite dishes, there are no Russians on Charles Anderson's property. His grandson is there to keep an eye on the place. Aside from a few of the young man's friends, no one else is there that I know of."

"Have you or your deputies noticed anything suspicious going on over there?"

242

"No."

"See any new people you've never seen before?"

"Nope."

"What about any Russians?" Mitchell was getting desperate. Guthrie's one-word negatives were getting under his skin.

"Tell me something, general. How can you tell if someone is Russian just by looking at him? Because if there's a way, I'd sure like to know."

His reply irritated Mitchell even more than the one-word responses.

"Well, I don't suppose you could tell just by looking, but maybe someone in town has overheard someone speaking in a foreign language?"

"If they have, they haven't told me about it," the sheriff replied.

Frustrated, Mitchell came right out and asked the question he hadn't wanted to ask. "What about aliens?"

Guthrie had been gently rocking back and forth in his chair, but when he heard the generals question, he stopped and became pensive. This was just what he feared. He didn't believe that the aliens were here five years ago. Apparently, as far as the general was concerned, they were back.

He opened his mouth to say something, but before he uttered a word, a male high school student, who lived across the way from him, ran into his office, wildly waving a picture.

"Sheriff, sheriff, look at this!"

Guthrie sat up straight as the young man rounded his desk and shoved the picture of the Cetis' flying saucer under his nose.

"See, I told you so. They're here!" He declared, shaking with anticipation.

The sheriff took the picture and studied it while Mitchell stood up and came around to see what all the excitement was about. He knew this picture was the real thing. He had seen the ship before…five years ago.

"That's a very interesting picture," Mitchell told the boy. "Mind if the sheriff keeps it for a while to study?"

"No, sir, I don't. I have more where that came from."

Mitchell looked over at Lieutenant Stone, his expression all-too-familiar. One of the men would be sent to the boy's house to confiscate the remaining pictures and put the fear of God in them if they ever told anyone about what they knew.

"Thank you so much for sharing that with us," Lieutenant Stone said. He got up, put his arm around the young man's shoulders, and escorted him to the door of the sheriff's office. "I wonder if I could ask a favor of you."

"Sure."

"I wonder if you could keep this under your hat for a while?" Stone said.

"You mean, you don't want me to show it to my friends and family?"

Stone suspected the boy may have already done so. Still, the general expected him to convince the young man to keep quiet about the picture. "Could you do that?"

"Well, I guess. If you think it's important."

"I do. We wouldn't want to get everyone upset thinking we were being invaded," Stone said. "Have you shown anyone else the picture yet?"

"No, sir. I came straight from picking them up at the drugstore."

"Excellent, it's very important not to talk about this for now," Stone said.

"Okay, I won't."

"Now, if you don't mind, we need some privacy," the Lieutenant said as he escorted the boy to the outer office. Signaling to one of his men, he whispered in his ear. "Follow the boy home and get all the pictures he has of a flying saucer and anything else he might have. You know what to do."

The man nodded and left.

Stone returned to the sheriff's office, closed the door, and joined Mitchell and Guthrie. The picture was a good one. At the time it was taken, the flying saucer couldn't have been more than 100 feet above the camera lens.

"They're back, Sheriff Guthrie. Those stinking, laser toting universal slime aliens are back. Have you seen anything in town, heard any reports?"

The Lieutenant's expression hardened, and he squeezed his left hand into a fist.

"Nothing, general. Believe me, if any of these folks had seen an alien, they wouldn't have been able to run fast enough to tell me all about it. Are they the Greys?"

One of Mitchell's eyebrows rose higher than the other. "If you didn't know they were here, how did you know they were the Greys?"

"Are you kidding? Everybody remembers Roswell and all the pictures of the so-called aliens that came out as a result. Thing is, I never believed the story was true, but from what you're telling me, that was no weather balloon that crashed back and '47."

Mitchell pinned him with a look. "That, Sheriff Guthrie, is classified information. If it weren't for the fact that they are somewhere in this area, I would never have allowed you to learn that. As a sworn law enforcement officer, you are to keep that to yourself."

This information shook him, but Guthrie's expression remained unchanged. Aliens really were running around his county, plotting who knows what kind of mischief. He needed to be kept in the loop, which meant keeping an eye on the military, and he knew exactly how to do that.

"Say, General, since Charles Anderson is my neighbor, it might be a good idea for you to set up a post somewhere on my property."

"That's very generous of you, Sheriff. We wouldn't need a lot of room, just someplace with a view of the farm, where I could park a command trailer."

Mitchell wasn't stupid either. He knew precisely why Sheriff Guthrie offered the use of this property. I gotta be careful with this one, he thought. He could go off halfcocked and get a lot of innocent people killed.

"I appreciate your cooperation. I need to teach those stinking, laser toting universal slime aliens what you don't mess with the red, white, and blue," the general said.

Once more, Stone's left hand became a fist.

"One more thing," Mitchell said. "I need to go to the farm and talk to Mr. Anderson."

"You won't find him there," Guthrie said. "He's in the hospital. Had a heart attack the night of the alien sighting near his farm. Course, that time, it turned out to be a balloon shaped like a flying saucer and advertising a local car dealership."

Suddenly, like a light bulb going on in his head, the sheriff realized something. He ran out of his office, gathered his deputies, and left the station in a hurry.

"I need to know what hospital the old man is in," Mitchell told Stone.

Nodding, Stone ran after the sheriff, who, like his deputies, was getting into his cruiser. As he closed the door and turned the key in the ignition, the Lieutenant caught up with him and knocked on the glass.

Guthrie rolled down his window.

"General Mitchell wants to know what hospital Mr. Anderson is in. He needs to interview him."

"St. Bartholomew's General Hospital. Warn him not to be too hard on Charles. After all, the man did just have a heart attack."

"I will," the lieutenant replied.

As soon as he stepped away from the vehicle, Guthrie and his men took off. Stone wondered where they were headed, but he had not asked because he did not believe the sheriff would have told him.

As the last of the cruisers pulled away, General Mitchell joined him.

"Come on, let's find that hospital. If Anderson is knowingly harboring fugitives, I'll slap him into federal prison so fast, he won't know what hit him."

# Chapter Thirty-Two

## Galactic Diplomacy

Stanley parked the truck, and he and Mary ran into the grocery store. They both grabbed a cart and were soon out of breath from rushing through the aisles to find the things they needed on their list. Time was a luxury they did not have.

Pulling into the parking lot a moment later, Margaret was right on their heels. Grabbing an empty cart, she followed the first one and then the other, picking up several things she wouldn't normally purchase. She wanted to keep an eye on Stanley and Mary, so she grabbed whatever happened to be at hand, drawing as many strange and curious looks from the customers as the kids did.

"Okay, here's what we need," Stanley said, showing Mary the list. "We need a cart full of fruit, lemons, and corn. Why don't you get those, and I'll look for some of this other stuff."

"Right, as soon as I fill up my cart, I'll leave it by one of the registers, and grab another one."

Stanley nodded and took off, looking for the pet food section. When he found it, he grabbed a fifty-pound bag of dog food and put it on the lower part of the cart.

Checking the signs hanging over the aisles, he ran two aisles over to his right, where he picked up several bottles of Tabasco sauce and cooking oil. He also found the black olives there and loaded several cans into his cart.

In his hurry, he accidentally knocked over a jar of pickles. It was a big jar, and it hit the floor with a loud crash.

"Cleanup on aisle five."

With no space to get by, he ran up to the checkouts, where he spotted Mary's produce filled cart. The clerk gave him a puzzled look, but Stanley figured that Mary had already warned her there would be numerous carts. The clerk wasn't the only one to watch the two of them race about the store. The customers also watched in amazement, wondering if they were witnessing some type of prank.

Stanley found Mary pulling out an empty cart. He grabbed one and showed her the list again. "Why don't you get the Twinkies, marshmallows, rice, sugar, and the bags of beans? he said, handing her the list. "I'll get all the charcoal they have."

"I'm on it," Mary replied as she ran off. Stopping by one of the clerics, she asked, "Where can I find bags of beans and rice?"

"They're on the left-hand side of aisle three," the clerk responded.

Mary hurried off. As she tossed the bags of beans and rice into her card, one of the plastic bags of beans hit the edge of the cart, burst open. Beans scattered across the floor.

"Cleanup on aisle three," came a voice over the intercom.

Mary wondered how they knew about the mess so quickly. She didn't realize that her and Stanley's actions had troubled the store manager. Who sat in the office where the monitors for the security cameras were located, watching the whole thing unfold before his eyes. Like his customers, he thought this might be some kind of teenage prank. Lifting the phone receiver, he called the sheriff.

By now, Stanley was at the register, his cart piled so high with bags of charcoal, he could barely push it. Mary joined him a moment later, and they lined up the carts at the checkout with the shortest line. Neither one could stand still, they kept glancing at their watches. Time seemed to fly abnormally fast, and they gave each other anxious looks.

One customer was in front of them. A little old lady who took forever to place the few items she had in her cart onto the conveyor belt. When it was time for her to pay, she fumbled through her purse, looking for her wallet, and then seemed to take forever to extract the bills and change she needed to pay for the purchase.

Stanley pressed his lips tightly together to keep from yelling at her to hurry up. Behind him, Mary glanced over at a rack, next to the candy and gum behind the conveyor belt, which held three different magazines. Two were legit, Life and Woman's Day. The other was an oversized rag featuring stories and altered photographs that were outright lies, which the publisher claimed were true, but weren't. Normally, she ignored the rag, but as her eyes passed over Life Magazine, she did a double-take. On the cover was a picture of two Greys, along with the sensational title, The Aliens are Back! Story inside.

There was only one copy left. Mary grabbed it and stepped forward to show it to Stanley.

"Get rid of that thing!" He whispered.

Mary quickly stuffed it behind the remaining six copies of Good Housekeeping.

With the elderly woman finally gone, Stanley and Mary loaded the stuff from their carts onto the conveyor belt. They were so busy, they did not see Margaret sneak up and grab the magazine Mary had hidden.

As soon as everything was rung up, bagged, and returned to the carts, Stanley pulled out his wallet and paid for it, using money he had been saving for a down payment on a used car.

The cashier looked at him and asked, "party?"

"An out-of-this-world party," Stanley replied.

He and Mary each pushed one cart and pulled another behind them, with Stanley handling the two heaviest. They had just finished putting everything into the back of the truck when the sheriff's car arrived with its lights flashing. Spotting his daughter, he stopped behind the truck and turned off the lights.

"Mary, don't look now, but your dad's here."

Placing the last bag of lemons in the truck, she turned and smiled at her father as he left his car and walked up to her.

"Mary, Stanley, what's all this stuff for?"

She looked at Stanley with a hint of panic in her eyes. They needed to think fast on their feet. They hadn't expected to run into anyone, let alone Mary's dad, who would require an explanation of their purchases.

Smoothing her features, she turned back to her father and said, "We need it for a science project."

It was a good thing Sheriff Guthrie was as good as his daughter at hiding his emotions. He knew she was wasn't being totally truthful, and it broke his heart that she didn't think she could trust him to tell him what was really going on. His expression changed to one of doubt, and he reached out and placed a hand on her shoulder.

"Is there something you need to tell me, sweetheart?"

Mary swallowed hard. Although this really was a science project, she hated to deceive her father. It was something she had never done before. "Just that, dad, a very important science project."

He nodded. He knew something was up, and he suspected it had something to do with the aliens, but he decided to play dumb for now. He returned to his squad car and parked in a space in front of the store. He was about to go inside to talk with the manager when Margaret flew out of the store. She had gotten stuck in a long line. Pushing the cart with its purchases, she ran over to where she parked her car at an angle, taking up three parking spaces. Throwing her shopping in the trunk of the car, she shoved the cart away, but as she hurried around the car to climb inside, she stumbled and fell.

Seeing this, Sheriff Guthrie hurried over to help her up. As he did, he took a good look at her face, wondering who this person was. Looking past the wig and sunglasses, his brow wrinkled as he wondered what the heck was going on.

"Margaret?"

Her eyes opened wide, and she ran her thumb across her throat. Then turning, she bowed with their hands together and said, "So nice to meet you, Sheriff. I am Lily Flower from Canada."

Mystified, the sheriff removed his hat and scratched his head.

She gave him another big-eyed look and shifted her eyes toward his daughter and Stanley, who were driving off. Before slamming the hood of her trunk, she reached inside and pulled out the rag publication. Thrusting it into his hands, she slammed the trunk, went around to the driver's side, jumped in the car, and took off after them.

"Is the whole town going crazy?" The sheriff asked himself aloud as he stared after her car. Absentmindedly, he glanced at the magazine. "Holy cow!" Running to his cruiser, he jumped in and took off, forgetting all about talking to the manager of the store.

\*\*\*

General Mitchell, Lieutenant Stone, and nine other Air Force officers marched down the hallway toward Charles Anderson's room at County General. They startled both visitors and hospital staff. Before they reached the doorway, the heart surgeon stepped out of the room. The surgeon was about to make some notations on Charles's chart when he realized that all these men were headed for his patient's room.

"Hold it right there, gentlemen. Mr. Anderson is recovering from a heart attack. I can't have all of you crowding into his room and distressing him."

"I have some questions for him," Mitchell said. "Are you refusing to allow me to question him?"

"I'd rather you didn't. I don't want to risk him having another attack."

Mitchell drew himself up, reminding the surgeon of a puffed-up rooster.

"This is a matter of national security," he stated firmly.

Understanding the doctor's position, Lieutenant Stone stepped forward. "Would it be all right if just the general and I went in? We must speak to him. Otherwise, I wouldn't ask."

Stone had used a friendly, compassionate voice. Having heard about Mitchell's reputation, the doctor capitulated, realizing that the man would not take no for an answer.

"Well, if it's just the two of you, but if I see Mr. Anderson becoming agitated, you will have to leave." Pulling the chart from the bracket on the wall, the doctor began to write and make notes. Then he stopped. "And your men can't stand around out here blocking the hallway. Should there be an emergency, the necessary personnel would not be able to get through to care for a patient in dire need." He pointed down the hallway. "They can stay in the waiting room down the hall."

Mitchell did not like anyone ordering him around unless, of course, it was the Commander-in-Chief. He felt like the doctor was trying to bully him, and no one bullied the general.

Knowing that his superior officer was about to blow a gasket, Stone stepped in once more. Turning to the other nine men, he said, "Dismissed. Go to the waiting room down the hall and remain there until I come for you." Then he turned to Mitchell. "I'm sure the doctor is simply looking out for his patient's best interest, sir. Shall we proceed?"

Mitchell's expression was still that of an angry man, but his body relaxed slightly. He turned and entered Charles's room.

Having heard the commotion outside, Stanley's grandfather was not surprised when the general strolled in as if he owned the place. This was the last person in the world he ever wanted to see again, and his own anger rose. Raising the head of his bed slightly, Charles looked the General straight in the eyes and glared.

"What do you want?"

"I have some questions, and I need answers," Mitchell stated simply.

"I'm not telling you anything. You ruined my life."

"There are times when the needs of the many outweigh the needs of the few," Mitchell explained.

Charles turned over and showed him his backside. "Get out!"

"Not until I get some information first."

Charles closed his eyes and tried to ignore him.

Mitchell walked around to the other side of the bed.

Once more, Charles turned over, giving his backside to the general.

"They're here."

Charles's eyes opened.

"I wouldn't know anything about that," he said, pushing the Polaroid photo Stanley had brought him of Lutsik and Mourda under his pillow. He turned over. "Why did you ruin my life?"

"I'm sorry."

The apology was totally unexpected. Still, Charles was not ready to forgive and forget. "Sorry, won't change the last five years. Because of you, my daughter and grandson moved away. You made me look like a fool in front of the whole town."

"Have the aliens tried to make contact with you?" Mitchell asked.

"I have nothing to say to you."

"Why are they here?"

"They missed our television shows," Charles replied sarcastically.

The general slammed his fist on the table over the bed. "I need your help!"

"You gave up any chance of that when you left town without defending me." Charles's voice was filled with anger. "I'm tired." He closed his eyes. "Now, get out."

Lieutenant Stone backed up, accidentally hitting the tray, knocking over a partial glass of water, which splashed onto the general's uniform. "I'm sorry, sir."

While Mitchell disgustingly dabbed the water off his uniform, the Lieutenant removed his gloves to supposedly clean up the water. Grabbing some paper towels from the sink that the doctors and nurses used in the room, he returned to the bed and mopped up the spilled water. As he did, he showed Charles the palm of his hand. Stone and Charles locked eyes, their exchanged glances were filled with meaning.

Wiping the last of the water from his uniform, Mitchell looked at Charles. "I'll be back, Professor."

"I can't wait."

As soon as the general headed for the door, Lieutenant Stone looked at Charles one last time and nodded ever so slightly. The gesture filled the old man with hope.

# Chapter Thirty-Three

## Arrested

"Shoot," Caroline muttered when she realized that she had run out of the anode she used to make the welds. "I need to run home and get more anode sticks," she told her son.

"Are you taking grandpa's truck, or do you want one of us to take you home?" Stanley asked.

"Rick, you take me. Is that okay with you? This way, I can come back in my own car."

"Sure thing, Mrs. Adams," he replied.

"I'll be right back," she called as she followed Rick out of the barn.

\*\*\*

When she arrived home, Caroline ran back to the barn and retrieved the items she needed. Carrying them to her car, she tossed the anodes in her trunk and headed back to her father's farm. She made good time until she was just down the street from her destination, where she had to stop so as not to plow into the side of the black Suburban backing out of the Guthrie's drive.

As the vehicle backed up, the general looked out the window.

"Stop the car!" Mitchell ordered his driver when he realized that Caroline Adams was driving the stopped vehicle. Turning to the Lieutenant, he said, "I want that woman detained."

"Pardon the question, sir, but who is she?" Stone asked.

"She is the daughter of Charles Anderson. I remember her from five years ago. She caused me almost as much trouble as he did. Since her son is in the thick of it, aiding and abetting the aliens, she knows what's going on, and I am going to make her talk."

Going against his better judgment, because he had no choice, the Lieutenant got out of the car with General Mitchell. Both walked over to the driver's side of Caroline's car.

As soon as she rolled down her window, the Lieutenant spoke. "I need you to get out of the vehicle, ma'am."

"Whatever for?" Looking past him, she saw Mitchell. "Haven't you caused enough trouble for my family, making my father look like a fool?"

"Your father did that all by himself," Mitchell said. "I just did what needed to be done. Now get out of that car."

Caroline's eyes narrowed, but before she could say anything more, Stone spoke up.

"I'm sorry, Mrs. Adams," he apologized. "Please do as the general asked."

"I don't have time for this nonsense right now," Caroline said heatedly. "I have work to do."

"What kind of work?" Mitchell wanted to know. "Are you helping those aliens? Because if you are, that makes you a traitor to your country. Which means you will have to answer to the red, white, and blue."

Caroline's face grew red with anger, and her eyes shot sparks at Mitchell. "How dare you? You have no right to accuse me of treason. I'm not going anywhere with you."

"This isn't a request," Lieutenant Stone said. "I'm afraid I'm going to have to place you under arrest."

His words both confused and infuriated her. She got out of the car, but not quietly.

"You have no right...."

"I have every right to have you arrested," Mitchell said. "This is a matter of national security."

As the general spoke, the Lieutenant turned her toward the open door of her car, her back facing him, then grabbing her arms one of the time, he slapped a pair of handcuffs on her wrists. Closing her car door, Stone guided her to the Suburban and into the back seat of the general's vehicle. As if that wasn't bad enough, as soon as she was inside the vehicle, a black cloth bag was drawn over her head.

All this was observed by Sheriff Guthrie, who had been keeping an eye on the general. He wanted to interfere and stop Mitchell from arresting the poor woman, but he realized that there was nothing he could do, at least for now. As soon as the Suburban pulled away, he followed them to see what would happen next.

***

Ever since Mitchell's visit, Charles Anderson had grown increasingly anxious. He knew that Mitchell would be back. He did not want to see him again, and he had no intention of telling the man anything. Above all, he was determined to protect his grandson, Lutsik, and Mourda, from the general's stubborn, misguided determination. He knew that if Mitchell got his hands on his alien friends, he would do anything he could to garner every scrap of technical knowledge and information from them. He also knew that if necessary, the general wouldn't think twice about railroading Stanley and his friends to get what he wanted.

Making up his mind, Charles got out of bed. He was glad that the monitors were removed when the doctor had him transferred from the Critical Care Unit to a regular room. Otherwise, removing them would have brought a nurse, at the very least, running to his room to find out what was wrong.

Searching the drawers of his nightstand and a small chest, used to hold the patient's personal things, he found everything but his clothing. Soap, toothbrush, toothpaste, baby powder, shampoo, a little black comb, and even a small round basin to use for washing up, when a patient was unable to use the shower. Next, he checked the other side of the bathroom door. His clothes weren't there either.

Slipping over to the door of his room, he peeked out and looked both ways. No one was in the hall, and the nurses were either seated at desks in the nurse's station or standing around talking. None of them looked his way. It was time to make a move. Pulling the back of his hospital gown together, he hurried across the hallway and entered a small office that the doctors with patients on this floor occasionally used.

There he found a doctor's white coat, hung on the back of the desk chair. It would help, but he needed more. Looking around, he spotted a change of clothes, hanging on a hook on the back of the door, and a duffel bag on the floor, containing black socks and a pair of dress shoes. Apparently, the physician had plans for when he got off work.

Sorry, Doc, Charles thought. I need these more than you right now.

Charles quickly pulled on the clothing, which fit him fairly decently. The shoes were a size too large, so he stuffed the toes with Kleenex from a box on the desk. Then he put on the doctor's white coat. When he left the room, he looked every bit like a regular doctor. *If I walk with authority and act like I belong here, no one will know the difference.*

Without hesitation, he left the room and started down the hallway in the opposite direction of the nurses' station. Reaching the end of the hall, he turned right and continued toward the elevators. *So far, so good, this was going to work.*

At the nurses' station, one of the nurses, seated at a desk and going over the chart, asked, "Has anyone seen Doctor Turner?"

"I think I saw him heading for the elevator just now," another replied.

Charles was only a few feet from the elevators when running footsteps approached him from behind.

"Doctor, Doctor Turner, I have a question about one of your patients," the nurse called out.

Charles continued to the elevators and pressed the down button.

"I'm sorry to bother you since you are leaving, but I need an answer. This way, I won't have to disturb you at home."

"What do you need?" Charles's question was firm and slightly gruff. He had seen this doctor in the hallway a time or two, and he tried his best to emulate the doctor's voice and personality.

Since Charles never looked at her, she didn't see his face and had no idea that she was talking to an imposter.

"It's about Mrs. Cornell. She's very agitated, and in her condition, I'm afraid it could bring on another heart attack."

"Are there any visitors with her?" Charles asked.

"Yes, her son and daughter-in-law are visiting."

"Does she get along with them?"

"Well, not so much with her daughter-in-law, although I understand it's not the poor girl's fault. Her son told me that for some reason, his mother hates her, although neither of them can figure out why. Whenever the poor girl is around, Mrs. Cornell is nasty to her and often makes her cry," the nurse replied.

"Then it's simple. Tell them to leave, and if she doesn't calm down after that, give her a sedative."

"The same one you gave her before?" The nurse asked.

"Yes." Inwardly, Charles sighed with relief. Naturally, he had no idea what kind of medication to give the woman. Had he needed to come up with the name of something, it would have blown his cover.

"Thank you, Doctor," the nurse said. "Have a nice evening."

She walked away just as one of the elevators dinged, and the doors opened.

It was empty except for him, and once the doors were closed, he pressed the button for the first floor and said aloud, "If you ask me, what that woman needs is a swift kick to the backside." From time to time, Charles had heard Mrs. Cornell's tirades, always complaining that the nurses were too slow, always wanting them to wait on her hand and foot.

When the elevator reached the first floor, Charles strolled out and headed for the exit. It wasn't until he arrived at the parking lot that he remembered his truck was still at home. He had been brought to the hospital by ambulance, and he had no way to get home. He knew that if he called his daughter to come to get him, she would refuse, saying that he needed to stay put until the doctor released him.

"Now what?"

Charles looked around, bewildered. Then he remembered that the front right pocket of his borrowed trousers had something in it. Reaching into the pocket, he pulled out a set of keys that contained a house key, and ignition key, and the trunk key. Now, all he had to do was find the doctors' parking lot. He was pretty sure it was located to the left of the emergency entrance. Turning around, it took him ten minutes to find the right parking lot.

"Now, which one belongs to the good doctor?" He looked at the key and saw that it belonged to an Aston Martin. "Woo wee!" There was only one parked in a lot. It was white, and it was a beauty. Charles was reasonably sure it was the current model. He couldn't help admiring the automobile from every angle before unlocking the door. Since it was a sports convertible, it sat low to the ground. His old bones creaked and complained as he climbed inside. However, once he was comfortable, he looked over the gauges and extra features. He admiringly ran his hand over the smooth black leather seats.

"Sure wouldn't mind having one of these," Charles said.

Turning the key, he started the car and listened to the engine purr. Then he remembered why he was running away from the hospital. Backing out of the parking space, he shifted the four on the floor to first gear and headed for the farm.

## Chapter Thirty-Four

## Sheriff Guthrie

The general's driver turned around in Charles Anderson's driveway and headed back toward the outskirts of town. Lieutenant Stone drove Caroline's car. Mitchell did not want the vehicle abandoned on the street, knowing that someone would notify the sheriff. He didn't want that backwater lawman interfering with his investigation.

Handcuffed and blindfolded, Caroline sat in the back of the Suburban with Mitchell. Her stomach was in knots. Fear made her tremble. She had no idea what would happen next. Logically, she knew that if he learned that she was helping the aliens, she could be in big trouble. It wasn't fair. They only wanted to save their planet.

She had no idea where they were taking her, but she knew she would be questioned and quite possibly bullied. Determined, she decided that she would not tell the general anything. I must put up a brave front, she told herself. Whatever happens, I can't give in to fear. Lutsik and Mourda are no threat to Earth. They must be allowed to return home with their crystal to save their planet.

The car finally came to a stop. She heard the car doors open, and someone gently took her arm and placed one hand on her head so she would not bump it. She was taken across a concrete surface and inside some type of building. As she moved further inside, she heard men talking and the sounds of people working.

"Where am I?"

She may as well have asked the wall. No one answered her question.

Then she heard another door open, and she walked several steps inside what she assumed was another room and guided to a hard, wooden chair. They left her standing there, preying on her nerves until finally, a hand-whipped the bag off her head.

"Sit down," Mitchell ordered.

Caroline complied, but not before looking around first. There wasn't much to see. It was a large room. What she didn't realize was that it was part of a converted warehouse, where the general had set up operations, so that he could be close to the action. It wouldn't have made sense to travel back and forth to the Air Force Base in the middle of an important investigation.

She sat down on the only chair in what was otherwise a barren room. The only other object in sight was a floor lamp with three lights. Only one was turned on, and it was aimed right at her face.

Lieutenant Stone stood near the door with his hands behind his back.

Taking a deep breath, she focused on Mitchell, a determined, wise look on her face.

"Mrs. Adams, you seem to be spending a lot of time on extracurricular activities," Mitchell said.

She remained silent.

"Mrs. Adams?"

"Yes?"

Inside, she was still frightened. How could she not be? She had no idea what Mitchell wanted of her. On the outside, she appeared confident and calm. She wasn't sure if he was an enemy, or just an overzealous Air Force Officer full of himself.

"What are you doing in your father's barn, Mrs. Adams?"

"Why do you want to know?"

"It's of no concern...."

She cut him off. "Oh yes, it is. If you want to know what I'm doing, I want to know why. I have every right to be at my father's place. Am I under arrest?"

"No. Yes." Mitchell was frustrated and tired of people who wouldn't answer his questions. He decided to take a softer approach. "Look, don't be afraid."

His words relieved her fear, but now she was mad.

"You grabbed me, threw me into your car, and put a bag over my head. Yet you stand there and tell me not to be afraid? This is America. I am a citizen. You have no right! When I get...."

"Mrs. Adams, this is about America," Mitchell said passionately. "This is about saving America. The Russians...."

"Don't give me that. I'm not stupid," Caroline said heatedly. "This is not about the Russians!"

"Ah! Then you do know something." He put his face in front of hers, his expression threateningly in hopes of frightening her.

She realized that maybe she had said too much. Dumb, dumb, dumb. I should've played along and pretended that it was the Russians.

"Tell me what you know." Mitchell's voice was back to being nasty. "Tell me...."

"Tell you what? What do you want her to say?" Sheriff Guthrie demanded as he entered the room, his hand resting on his gun.

Surprised, the general jumped back.

266

"Steve, thank God!" Caroline closed her eyes and breathed a sigh of relief.

The sheriff crossed the room and helped her out of the chair, his hand still resting on his gun.

His actions exasperated Mitchell. He felt threatened, confused, and angry.

"You stupid, small-minded idiots, don't you get it? They're here! The aliens are here. Right here in your precious little podunk town. This is war. I'm talking about the end of our country, the end of everything! And your little sweetheart here knows more than she's telling. For all we know, she may be helping those grey, laser totin' alien slime."

Now Caroline was confused. Grey, laser totin' alien slime? Is he talking about the Greys like the ones they say crashed in Roswell? She wondered. Are they here, too? She was full of questions she dared not ask. Apparently, Mitchell had no idea what Lutsik and Mourda looked like. Well, she had no intention of correcting his misconception. If he knew there were other aliens here, he would really become paranoid.

"Are they hiding on your father's farm? Where's their ship? Are they the same ones that came here five years ago? Are they advance scouts for an invasion? When do they plan to attack? Are they hiding their mother ship behind the moon? Is there more than one ship waiting to wipe out humanity or enslave us all?"

By his questions, Caroline realized that if Mitchell ever got his hands on Lutsik and Mourda, he would hurt them. His accusations were stupid. They wouldn't hurt a flea. She had not realized that the Greys were here, too. And although the people of Tau Ceti were peaceful, the Greys were not. Why does he think that with the presence of aliens, there will be a war of the worlds?

Furious, she remained silent, wondering how she would extricate herself from this situation. "I want a lawyer."

"No can do. Not in a time of war," Mitchell said.

His words brought back fear. She had seen movies where people were taken away by the military and were never heard from or seen again. She had also followed the Roswell situation seventeen years ago. The government had retracted their statement and denied the existence of the flying saucer that crashed on a ranch in New Mexico. Afterward, she remembered reading about how civilian witnesses were threatened and bullied by the Air Force, treated even worse than they had treated her father five years ago.

"She is entitled to legal representation," the sheriff disagreed. "Even in a time of war, although no war has been declared, except in your mind. Unless you have cause to arrest her, she's leaving."

His words angered Mitchell.

Caroline looked up at Steve, hope in her eyes. Hope and admiration replaced her fear, and the old feelings from their past began to resurface.

Had Sheriff Guthrie not been there to intervene, Mitchell would have detained her for as long as he wanted, days, weeks, possibly months if he felt it necessary. Then what? Would she have disappeared from the face of the Earth, locked in a prison somewhere, her son agonizing over what could have happened to her?

Angry, Mitchell realized that he could not arrest Caroline with the sheriff coming to her rescue. Although he believed his suspicions were correct, the general couldn't charge her with a crime without due cause. His eyes narrowed. As soon as I have proof to the contrary, I will arrest you, and your sheriff won't be able to do a thing to stop me from getting what I want.

"Get her out of here."

They talked about the situation while Steve walked Caroline to her car. A few years back, they had dated, but for some reason, nothing had come of it. Now at this moment, both felt a renewal of their romance begin to blossom.

"Don't worry, he's got nothing he can charge you with," Sheriff Guthrie assured her.

Caroline was puzzled. "How did you know I was here? Did Stanley call you?"

"I had my suspicions of what he might try and have been following him."

"Thank you for coming to my rescue," Caroline said with a smile. "If you hadn't been there, I shudder to think what he might have done."

"What happened to us?" Steve asked out of the blue.

"I don't know. Maybe we just got too busy with our own lives and drifted apart."

"We should never have allowed that to happen."

"You're right," Caroline agreed. "Let's start over, shall we?"

"I'm willing if you are."

"You know, Mary is quite beautiful. I think Stanley is sweet on her."

"Is he? I didn't realize, but then, it seems I've been too busy to pay much attention to her. I don't like it when that happens. I'll have to make it up to her." He looked into her eyes. "Your son is smart, just like my Mary."

"She's good for him. I'm glad they are friends."

He opened her car door. "I'd best get back to work. Call you later?" Steve asked.

"I'd like that…if we both live," Caroline replied.

They smiled at each other, happy that their relationship was on again.

# Chapter Thirty-Five

## Return of the Professor

An hour passed, and Caroline still hadn't returned. Mourda suspected something was wrong. He turned to Lutsik, who was fine-tuning their flight controls. "Caroline has not yet returned."

"Something may have happened to her," his father reasoned.

"I wonder if General Mitchell has taken her," Mourda replied. "I have been monitoring the human's news and shortwave radio chatter."

"Does it mention that she was arrested?" Lutsik asked.

"No, however, from what I gather, the general has set up a base of operations in town. It is possible that he took her in for questioning."

"He must suspect that we are here," Lutsik agreed. "Nevertheless, how would he know that she is helping us? Maybe something else has detained her."

"I do not know what that would be, but if the general doesn't have her, where is she?"

"I fear the Greys may have taken her," Mourda said.

Lutsik studied his son's face, but he could detect no emotion there. "That would not be good."

***

Stanley and Mary drove back to the farm with their purchases. As they approached the farm, Stanley passed Mitchell's car, which was parked around the corner out of sight from the farm.

"The jig is up," Stanley said. "That's the general's car. If he's there, he must know that Lutsik and Mourda are here, too."

"It gets worse." Mary added, unaware of the fact that Mitchell had received permission from her father, "it looks like they have set up a mobile base on our property."

Stanley turned to look at the sheriff's house. The two of them spotted a large trailer parked in the field next to a small copse of trees. Several men were stationed in various spots around the property – spots that were perfect for keeping an eye on his grandfather's farm.

"Who are those men?" Mary asked.

"Military guys wearing normal clothing and hiding behind sunglasses."

"What makes you say that?"

"They have walkie-talkies. See, one of them is talking into one, probably to the general."

"What are we going to do?" Mary asked worriedly.

"I don't know. Let's tell the others and see if they can come up with any ideas."

Lutsik had kept watch for their return and lowered the shield so that they could drive through. As Stanley parked the truck in front of the barn, Rick's car pulled up next to it. Getting out of the car, Rick and the others joined Stanley and Mary, talking excitedly about getting all the items on their list.

"We found everything," Roger said. "How did you and Mary do?"

"We did, too, but we have something more important to discuss," Stanley said. "Mitchell is nearby. I saw his car parked around the corner."

"That's not all," Mary added. "He has men stationed all over my dad's property."

Stanley ran into his grandfather's little store and grabbed a pair of binoculars. When he returned to the others, he handed them to Roger.

"Watch the sheriff's house. We need to know in advance if the military makes a move."

"They won't be able to get through the shield, will they?" Roger asked.

"I don't think so, but remember, the shield will only last four hours, and time is running out," Stanley warned him.

"Got it. If I see something suspicious, you'll be the first to know," Roger assured him.

"Let's park our cars behind the barn. We can take everything in through the back door," Stanley suggested.

"Good idea," Rick agreed.

Stanley and Rick parked near the door at the back of the barn. Then everyone began unloading the materials they had purchased. As they worked, Caroline finally returned. Carrying the welding sticks, she entered the barn and immediately continued working. She decided to hold off on telling the kids about her encounter with Mitchell.

Meanwhile, Roger looked around for a good place to watch what was happening on Mary's farm. Running to the field of homemade satellite dishes, he found exactly what he wanted next to one of the satellites. Raising the binoculars, he looked through them, closely scanning the property. What he saw gave him a fright. The military looked right back at him through their own binoculars. Startled, he dropped his pair and ran to the barn and through the front entrance, nearly colliding with Stanley, who had his arms loaded with packages.

"We're being watched," Roger warned breathlessly. "Several men are using binoculars to keep an eye on what's going on over here."

"Hurry," Stanley told the others. "Let's get this stuff inside. We'll move the normal farm stuff in the open but sneak the rest of it in whenever they aren't looking. Keep watching them, Roger, and let us know when the coast is clear."

Roger nodded and retrieved his binoculars. Moving to the outside corner of the barn, he kept the others apprised, letting them know when they could move the other stuff. Stanley and Rick carried in used tires, fertilizer, animal feed, and weed killer. As soon as they had the last of their purchases inside, Rick closed the barn door.

Stanley called everyone together in the living room of his grandfather's house. "Here's the situation. The general is nearby. Time is running out, and we have no guarantees that the stuff we bought will successfully make the missing ingredient needed for the fuel. We also don't know where the Greys are, but they have to be close."

"I'm afraid they're closer than we feared," Lutsik said. "They have commandeered the house across the street, and even now, they are watching us."

"We need to hurry," Mourda said.

They quickly began organizing everything. As they worked, Mary noticed something different about their alien friends.

"I don't mean to embarrass you, but are you two...twitching?" She asked.

"Since we have no emotions, we do not get embarrassed," Lutsik said. "You are correct, however, about one thing. Whenever we become extremely nervous, our people tend to twitch."

Across the street, General Mitchell approached one of his captains.

"Report," he said in a gruff manner.

"It looks like those kids are just stocking the barn. You know, with things like animal feed, fertilizer, and stuff like that."

"Let me know if you notice anything unusual." Mitchell walked away and entered the command trailer.

Across the street, everyone worked hard to get the stuff organized. About halfway through, there was a knock on the front barn door.

"Did you forget to put the shield back up after letting us in?" Stanley asked Lutsik.

"I'm sorry. I did forget," Mourda replied. "I will do so now." Being a telepath, he already knew who was at the door.

"I'll get it," Mary said. "What should I do if it's the general or one of his men?"

"Play dumb and tried to stall him," Rick said.

Mary nodded, opened the door, and peeked out. The man standing there with his back to the door, watching what was happening at the Guthrie farm, wore the white coat of a doctor. "Stanley, it's a doctor. It must be about your grandpa."

Fear tightened Stanley's insides. He hurried to the door, glanced over at his mother, who did not look up from her welding. Apparently, she had not heard Mary's words.

At the same time, a captain approached Mitchell. "There's a doctor at the barn door."

The general grabbed his binoculars and focused them on the barn door.

By now, Charles had turned around, his back facing the general.

"Must be about Charles Anderson, the crazy old coot. He's either in trouble or dead. I hope it's not too serious," Mitchell said, allowing a brief moment of sympathy to pass, as he watched the doctor knock on the barn door.

Preparing for the worst, Stanley stopped at the door and took a deep breath. He sent up of silent prayer that his grandfather hadn't taken a turn for the worse. Finally, he opened the door and got a good look at the visitor. "Grandpa!"

Charles pushed past him and shut the door. "Why didn't you tell me about the aliens?"

"We were afraid that if we told you about their reappearance, excitement might cause you to have another heart attack."

"I'm not talking about Mourda and Lutsik, I figured that out for myself. I'm talking about the Greys!"

"You were sick, Grandpa."

"Yeah, I'm sick, all right. Sick of being told I'm crazy for the last five years."

"How did you get out of the hospital?"

Seeing Charles, Lutsik and Mourda hurried over to greet him, speaking their own language, and then switching to English.

"Charles Anderson," Lutsik said. "It is so good to see you. Are you well?"

"Lutsik and Mourda, my old friends, I would have come sooner, but under the circumstances…."

"Then it is better that you did not know," Mourda said. "When we heard of your illness, we knew that you needed to stay at your medical facility and get better. How are you feeling?"

"Couldn't be better, now," Charles replied. "I am so thrilled that you're back. Now I can tell the world that you're back, and you're friendly. I can finally prove that I'm not crazy."

"You can't," Stanley objected. "We have to help them get back to their planet with the Core so that they can save the universe. They need to save their planet and ours, too. If we don't give it back to them, the entire universe will at the Greys' mercy."

"I'm afraid it's a little more complicated than that, Stanley," Charles started his explanation. "You see, our friends need their Core. It's the last one. If we don't give it back to them, the entire universe will at the Greys' mercy. They used up their planet's resources ages ago. Now they raid other planets, strip them of their resources, and enslave the inhabitants."

"Oh, we know all about that," Rick said.

"Plus, we already have the Core," Roger interjected.

Charles Anderson bore a perplexed look.

"You told me the location and the code in the hospital, Grandpa," Stanley explained

He turned to Lutsik, "if you already found the Core, then why are you still here then?"

"Unfortunately, our ship was damaged during an emergency landing. The tank was punctured, and we have run out of fuel. Your daughter has repaired it with her excellent welding skills, and thanks to Roger's father, more fuel has been made. Unfortunately, we are missing a major ingredient," the elder alien explained.

"One more thing, grandpa, they need to leave within the next three hours and twenty minutes, so that they can get to their planet in time. Otherwise, their window of opportunity will be closed, and by the time it opens again, it will be too late."

"We need your help once more, my friend, Charles Anderson," Lutsik said. "We're being observed by the Greys as well as your military and General Mitchell. We are fearful that they will forcibly take the crystal Core from us before the necessary fuel preparations are completed."

Realizing that something was going on, Caroline looked up and saw her father. She walked over hesitantly. When she stood no more than three feet away, Charles looked into her eyes and opened his arms wide. She shyly walked into them. Father and daughter embraced each other for the first time in years.

"I am so sorry, dad," she whispered.

"It's okay. This is all Mitchell's fault. He's the one who made me look crazy to the entire world."

Caroline stepped back and gestured toward the aliens. "Well, obviously, you are not crazy."

"Not even a little bit," Charles said with a smile.

Everyone stood still, allowing them to have a moment.

"Well now," Charles glanced at the clock on the wall, "about three hours and fifteen minutes to get this straightened out and the two of you on your way home. Right?"

"Right!" Everyone said.

"What is the missing ingredient for the fuel?" Professor Anderson asked the group.

Lifting his wrist, Mourda showed him a tiny screen. "Here is the breakdown that the chemical test revealed, and here is the one symbol we are missing. It's an element that we are unfamiliar with."

Charles studied the screen and then walked over to the blackboard and picked up a piece of chalk. He wrote down the formula, breaking down its specific elements until he got to the end. Then he walked over to the workbench where the aliens and the boys were working earlier. Examining the ingredients the kids had purchased, he realized what was missing.

"Hmmm, you got everything except alcohol and jasmine. What do we have that contains those ingredients?"

"Perfume, specifically 'Spring Fling' perfume," Caroline said quietly. "I used to wear it years ago. We need to get to a department store in town and buy some."

"We only need two ounces," Charles said.

Just then, there was another knock on the barn door. Everyone exchanged panicked glances as Charles went to the door.

"I thought you were going to put the shield back up," Stanley whispered to Mourda.

Amazingly, a look of surprise crossed the alien's face. "In all the excitement, I forgot…again."

Thinking that General Mitchell was on the other side, Charles opened the door, but instead of the general, Mr. Ward stood there.

"Charles, I thought you were in the hospital. How are you feeling?"

"Fine, fine, is there something I can help you with?"

"Unfortunately, I couldn't figure out the missing ingredient for the stuff Roger and Stanley asked me to make. So, I brought what I have here. I need a couple of the boys to help me carry it inside."

Roger rushed up to his father. "It's okay, dad. Drive around to the back of the barn, and we will bring it in. I'm glad you brought it here. It will save us valuable time. Besides, Stanley's grandfather knows what the missing ingredient is."

His words shocked his father. "How would…."

"It's a long story," Stanley said, stepping forward, "but we need to hurry. Time is running out. I only hope we can finish synthesizing the final ingredient in time."

# Chapter Thirty-Six

## Parental Discretion

The boys turned to look at Mary.

"Do you have any perfume?" Stanley asked.

Mary hesitated. "Um…yes, I do…sometimes."

"You do. I sit behind you in English class, and I smell it all through class," Roger said.

Everyone looked at Roger.

"What? It smells nice," he said, blushing just a little.

"Well," Mary admitted. "I wear perfume at school."

The boys smiled and shook their heads.

"Okay, I have it. I have a bottle of 'Spring Fling' in my bedroom."

Stanley looked at Mary. "I can't believe you're helping me with this."

She smiled and returned his look, then slowly placed her hand in his. "Let's go get it."

"I don't know. You guys are walking right into the lion's den," Roger said, feeling a bit panicky.

"We'll be fine," Mary told Roger. She turned back to Stanley. "I can't think of a better way to save the world than with you."

Surprised, Stanley looked away, then shyly turned back to Mary and caught her smile. He gently squeezed her hand.

"Mary and I will get it," Stanley said.

"I'll go with you." Roger chimed in. He was so focused on the crush he had on her, that he didn't stop to realize that he had no chance. Mary was taken.

"No!" Everyone in the barn shouted. They wanted Stanley and Mary to have this time together.

Leaving the barn, Stanley and Mary crossed the street and walked through the fields toward her house.

"I've never known anyone like you," Stanley admitted.

"Me, too," Mary said. "I mean, I've never known…."

He squeezed her hand again. "I know what you meant. Do you think it means that we were meant to be…together that is?"

"Definitely."

Her words made Stanley's heart soar.

Back in the barn, the others mobilized into an efficient team. They pulled out all the stops, and each used their individual strengths toward completing the fuel and making it work.

"We're gonna need a huge pot and a stove to cook this on," Roger announced.

"I think I saw one back in the corner," Rick said. "Someone will have to help me haul it over here, though. It looks heavy."

Rick and Mourda found the pot and dragged over to the workbench.

"I have a half-dozen hibachis' in the basement," Charles said. "Maybe we can cobble those together somehow."

"It will have to be big enough to heat the pot evenly," Roger said.

His chemistry class and all the science books he had read over the years would prove to be a big help. Roger had taken a lot of guff over the years from the football players, who never passed up a chance to make fun of his intelligence. Little did they or anyone else know that he would save them all.

Roger and Charles headed for the basement.

"It's a good thing you bought all that charcoal," Charles said. "Will we be able to make the fire hot enough?"

"Do you have any lighter fluid?" Roger asked.

"There's a can in the basement next to the hibachis," Charles replied.

"That should do it then. We'll need some matches, as well."

"There's a box in the kitchen cupboard next to the sink."

They gathered everything up and hauled it out to the barn.

Across the street, the Lieutenant followed them with his binoculars. Must be having a really big barbecue over there, he thought to himself. I wonder if they're going to make ribs. He licked his lips. Those sure would taste good right about now.

Back in the barn, since the pot was so large, Roger decided to set up his makeshift stove on the floor. Grabbing a broom, he cleared the straw away from a large area. He didn't want to risk accidentally setting the barn on fire.

"My dad and I did something like this on a smaller scale once," Roger said. "I should be able to put this together in no time." He liked to build things. The shelves in his room were filled with model airplanes and cars that he had put together over the years. Each one was a work of art, painted to perfection.

Charles helped him rig everything up and fill the hibachis with charcoal. Then Roger poured the charcoal lighter over the briquettes. After placing the pot on top of it, he struck a match and lit the charcoal. The fire blazed up nicely.

Roger was good at math and physics. He and Charles worked out the formula they would need. Their figures would have to be precise, and Roger made sure that his measurements were exactly what they needed to be. As they made the fuel, the others brought them the ingredients they needed.

***

Mary and Stanley headed for her house, still holding hands. Unfortunately, Mitchell spotted them and turned to the sheriff, who had joined him moments earlier.

"We need to find out what's going on in that barn."

Guthrie remained silent, and the two men stood on the front porch, watching the kids approach. The moment they arrived, Mitchell pulled them inside the house. Sheriff Guthrie followed them. The living room was filled with men and equipment, which angered Mary. She felt like her father had betrayed her, even though she didn't think he knew what was going on.

She turned to her father. "What's he doing here?"

"Aliens," he replied.

"You're kidding, right?"

"I'm not kidding."

"What are you kids doing in the barn across the street?" Mitchell asked, interrupting their conversation.

"We are working on a science project," Mary replied.

As she spoke, Stanley took a step toward the door, but the general blocked his way so that he couldn't leave.

"Young man, you aren't going anywhere," Mitchell said. "You are under arrest."

Here we go again, the Sheriff thought. The man has no finesse. He's like the proverbial bull in a china shop.

"For what?" Stanley asked.

Mitchell thought for a moment.

"What are you doing here?" Mary asked, taking the offensive.

"Never mind that," her father interrupted. "What's going on in Anderson's barn? I want to talk to you."

"Sure, dad, I just need to use the bathroom first. I'll be right back."

Knowing she had to find the perfume and somehow get it back to the barn, she ran upstairs to her bedroom to retrieve the perfume.

Guthrie wasn't happy with his daughter at that moment, but he allowed her to brush past him with a frown. Mitchell would have stopped her the way he had stopped Stanley, but one look at the sheriff's expression made him step aside.

While she was upstairs, Mitchell turned to Stanley and pushed him down on the couch. Then he reached over and removed the lampshade from the lamp, creating a bright glare of light that hurt Stanley's eyes.

Mary grabbed her perfume and stuffed it into the front pocket of her slacks. Then she picked up her constellation book and stuffed it in her back waistband, pulling her shirt over the top of it. Heading down the steps, she returned to the living room and sat down next to Stanley, looking expectantly up at the general with a look of total innocence.

"You're both going to tell me everything I want to know," Mitchell sternly declared.

Guthrie looked uncomfortable. "You can question Stanley, but I'm going to speak to my daughter alone."

He looked at Mary and indicated the kitchen. Knowing she had no choice, she stood up and went there, her father following closely behind her. When they entered the room, he took her by the arm and led her to the far corner, out of the way of listening ears.

"Mary, I've always trusted you. You know, if you tell me the truth, you will never get in trouble for it. That's what I need now, the truth." He proceeded to tell her about Mitchell's idea that the aliens were here.

"I thought you believed that the aliens only existed in Charles Anderson's vivid imagination?" She questioned her father.

Her father frowned, and he changed the subject. "What made you start hanging around with Stanley and his friends?"

"Don't you like him? He really is sweet. His friends are nice too."

"Of course, I like him. Stanley seems like a nice boy, but…."

"I met him the night Mark took me out to look at the stars. I should've known that Mark was only interested in one thing."

Guthrie's frown deepened.

"Anyway, when I discovered that Stanley was staying at his grandfather's house, I brought him some supper. Later we had a date, and I really enjoyed myself. Stanley's not like the others. He respects me, and he loves the stars, too."

"Then tell me. What are you doing over there now?" Her father asked.

"Now?" She wanted to reply that she was talking to him, but that would be smarting off to her father, which she never did. She respected him too much to talk to him that way.

"Oh, we're just working on a science experiment, and you know about the telescope Mr. Anderson built, right? You can see a lot of..."

"Enough, Mary, I need the truth. I have a sickening feeling that a lot depends on your telling me the truth."

# Chapter Thirty-Seven

## Negations

Jeet sat in a chair in front of the bedroom window, watching everything that was going on outside. What he saw alarmed him, and he turned to Drees. "Mreep mreep saka tooie."

"Speak English. We should keep practicing," Drees admonished him.

"Two humans left the barn and have crossed the street to the other house."

Drees jumped up and hurried over to the window to see what was going on for himself. "What could they be doing?" He stuffed his mouth with marshmallows, making his words almost unintelligible.

"Collaborating, they are. Seeking reinforcements. The Earth's military and the local law enforcement are working together. This is very bad...critical! We must find out what they are doing."

The Greys turned and faced each other, then looked at the books strewn about the floor.

"We must present ourselves as a friendly Earth neighbor," Drees said.

"Good idea. I will morph into Margaret, as I speak the best English," Jeet decided.

They walked into the women's room and looked through her closet. A box of Halloween costumes lay strewn about the floor.

"No, no, not this one, none of these are any good," Jeet said.

Drees examined the costumes on the floor in the box. He held one up. Jeet turned himself into Margaret and tried on the ridiculous outfit.

Drees shook his head. "No, no good."

Next, Jeet tried on a clown costume.

Drees giggled.

"What's so humorous?"

"Go. Look in the mirror."

Jeet did, and as soon as he saw his reflection, he, too, giggled.

"No, it can't be that one either," Drees said.

"Too bad, this one suits her so well."

When they both stopped giggling, Jeet tried on the third outfit. It looked just like the one worn by Barbara Eden in the I Dream of Jeanie television show.

"Yes, yes, that is the one," Drees said excitedly.

Downstairs in the kitchen, Margaret finished decorating a cake she had baked earlier. Clearly, cakes were not her forte. Two-layered and lopsided, she had overly decorated it in garish colors and designs, none of which made any sense.

The two aliens came downstairs and entered the kitchen. Drees walked up and touched the top of Margaret's head. "Who occupies next-door residence to the farm?"

"Sheriff Guthrie lives there with his daughter, Mary."

He asked no further questions, and without saying another word, Margaret went to the living room and sat down next to her husband, who was watching football.

The two Greys followed her.

"Yeah! All right!" He turned to his wife. "Did you see that?"

"Did you see that?" She responded, sounding more like a robot than a human being.

Jack gave her a strange look. He would be the first to admit that he did not understand his wife. Believing this was her way of trying to support his interest, he placed an arm around her shoulders and went back to watching TV.

"Did you see that?" She yelled again as she stared at the screen.

Exchanging glances, Jeet went back to the kitchen, picked up the outlandish cake, and walked out the door.

***

"Where are those two?" Charles asked Roger. "They should have been back a long time ago.

Roger looked through the binoculars again but saw no sign of Stanley or Mary.

Caroline walked across the barn to stand next to her father. Taking his hand in hers, she squeezed it.

"We've lost out on a lot of years," she said softly. "I've missed you."

Charles smiled at her through his worried expression.

"He's a smart kid, dad," she said, trying to reassure him. "Not like me. I should have believed you back then. If I hadn't made such a fuss about it, Stanley would have believed you, even if he didn't admit it to anyone else. I'm sorry."

"It's okay, kiddo. You believe me now, and so does Stanley. I have my family back." He gave her a quick hug and kissed her on the top of the head.

A tear slid down her cheek. It would be a long time before she forgave herself for the five years they had missed out on.

"Being a family, a brilliant family, we will get this straightened out. You can beg for my forgiveness on your hands and knees," he teased, "after we save the world."

Caroline laughed. Giving him a quick hug back.

By now, all the ingredients, except the perfume, were mixed together. Suddenly, Lutsik burped. Then Mourda burped. Charles Anderson was next, and within seconds, everyone else was burping, too. Wide-eyed, the kids turned and looked at Lutsik and Mourda.

For the first time in his life, Lutsik smiled. This amazed everyone more than the burping. He was experiencing emotions for the very first time.

"This is perfect," Lutsik said. "It means that the formula is working and almost ready."

Everyone continued burping nonstop, unable to talk. They raised their eyebrows.

"It will last exactly three minutes, and then it will stop," Lutsik informed them. "Brrruuuurrrrrrp!"

* * *

General Mitchell stood over Stanley, who was still seated on the couch in the Guthrie household. He opened his mouth to badger the boy further, but the doorbell rang, interrupting his chain of thought. Lieutenant Stone answered the door and was met with a bizarre sight. Disguised as the nosy neighbor, Jeet stood in front of the door with the ugly cake in his hands.

"I saw everyone over here and thought I would make you a cake," the fake Margaret said.

"What's going on here?" Mitchell asked as he joined the Lieutenant. "Who are you?"

"Live next-door," the false Margaret replied, straining to see around him and into the room. "May I come in?"

Confused by her bizarre outfit, Mitchell continued to block the door. "What do you want?"

"Why, hi there. General Mitchell, isn't it?"

"Yes, ma'am. What can I do for you?"

"Why, I just heard that the Sheriff Guthrie is entertaining some of you fine military men. I just thought you might enjoy one of my unusual and exceptional cakes."

"Ma'am, we don't have the time to…."

"Well then, is the noble sheriff in?"

Mitchell tried to close the door.

"I believe this is his favorite cake," the fake Margaret insisted as she continued trying to see around him.

"We have a situation here, ma'am."

"Oh, a situation? Dear me." Her expression changed to appear that she was concerned.

"Yes, we're swamped." Mitchell tried to close the door. She was driving him crazy. Every time he tried to shut the door, she would ask him another question.

"Is it those aliens we've heard about?"

The general opened the door a bit further. "What you know about aliens? There are no aliens."

"Oh. Well, I am certainly happy to hear that."

"Russians."

"Russians?"

"Yes, the Russians are invading this sacred soil. Russians! Do you hear me?" The general yelled.

"I'm not deaf," the alien Margaret said indignantly.

Mitchell squeezed his eyes closed and looked at her outfit again. He was puzzled as to why she would be dressed that way.

During that moment, he missed seeing Jeet's hands momentarily morph back to their real, long-fingered appearance. The same thing had happened at the diner when his head briefly changed from human to alien.

Shaking his head, Mitchell started closing the door.

"Just one little bite?"

The alien Margaret held up the cake, but Mitchell slammed the door, shoving the cake right in her face. She looks startled and then licked her lips. "Yum." Turning, the fake Margaret walked back to the house, licking her lips. "Yummmm!"

Mitchell returned to the couch and towered over Stanley. "If you don't tell me what's going on in the barn, I'm going to ruin you."

Anger infused Stanley's face, and he asked, "Like you ruined my grandfather five years ago?"

"I did it for the sake of the red, white, and blue," Mitchell replied.

"You cost me five years with a terrific grandfather, and you caused me a lot of grief. Thanks to you, everyone said I was living with a crazy family. That wasn't fair."

The phone rang. Sheriff Guthrie answered it in the kitchen.

"Hello."

He paused, listening to the person at the other end, and then walked into the living room and picked up the extension. As soon as he did, Mary hung up the kitchen phone.

"It's for you, General."

"Is it the President?"

"No, it's Caroline Adams."

The general shook his head and took the receiver. "Are you ready to tell me what's going on?

"I have a message for you, sir," Caroline said, her voice shaky. "If my son and his friend Mary do not return within the next five minutes, there will be nothing left of the sheriff's farm, my father's farm, or anything else on the planet Earth. Five minutes. Just the two of them…alone." She hung up the phone.

The sheriff returned to the kitchen. He and Mary sat down at the small round breakfast table to talk.

"I'm sorry, dad. I have never tried to deceive you before, but I wasn't sure you would believe me."

"With everything that's been going on, I think I will believe whatever you have to say," her father assured her.

She lowered her voice and told him everything she knew about the good aliens, the bad aliens, and the universe coming to an end.

"So, you see, what we're really doing is trying to formulate more fuel so that Lutsik and Mourda can return to their planet. We are running out of time. The window between their planet and ours will close before long. If they don't take off soon, they'll never arrive home in time to reinforce the shield around their planet. Mourda said if that happens, once the Greys strip their planet of all its resources and enslave their people, they will come here next and do the same to us. After that, they will prey on yet another planet, and another, and another. Destroying countless sentient beings and their homeworlds."

"If they can't get through the shield to attack the Tau Ceti's planet, what's to keep them from just coming back here and attacking us?" her father asked.

"If they don't have to defend their own planet, Mourda promised that they would attack the Greys. Since we're helping them save their planet, he said that their ruling council would band together with their allies on other worlds and stop the Greys from attacking anyone else," Mary explained.

***

Jeet hurried into the house and up the stairs, transforming back to his alien form, which made the costume droop comically on his thin body. He stepped into the bedroom. When Drees saw him, he burst into uncontrollable giggles. Jeet set the cake down on the dresser. As he did, he saw himself in the mirror, and he, too, giggled hysterically.

"Wait," Jeet said when he finally regained control himself. "There is another enemy. They are called the Russians. The Earth people are preparing for their invasion."

"What planet are they from?" Drees wondered. "I have never heard of them."

"I don't know, but they are not looking for the Tau Cetis or us. They are going to war with these Russians. We must get the crystal and return to our planet quickly. Perhaps they will blow themselves up and save us the trouble."

"I hope not," Drees said. "If that happens, we won't be able to drain their resources. We must let our commander know and get away before the war begins."

"Oh, one more thing. You must try this…." Jeet shoved a handful of cake into Drees' mouth.

Their already large eyes grew even bigger.

"Yummmmmm!"

Jeet changed back to his human disguise, and both started stuffing themselves with cake.

***

Sheriff Guthrie came out of the kitchen, looking stern and pulling his daughter along behind them. He placed her on the couch next to Stanley. "You stay here and don't you move. I'll deal with you when I get back." He turned to Mitchell. "General, I want to show you something." He headed toward the door.

"But dad…."

"Mary, I don't want to hear it. I've heard enough."

She sat quietly next to Stanley.

"General Mitchell, I need you to come with me, and bring a couple soldiers with you."

"We have reinforcements coming," Mitchell said.

Lieutenant Stone joined them, and as soon as they left the house, Mary grabbed Stanley's hand and took him to the door that led down to the basement. They went downstairs. Mary then grabbed a stool and set it down in front of the washing machine.

"Hurry," she told Stanley. "My dad is creating a diversion so we can slip away." She pointed to the window above the washer. "We can climb out here."

***

Mary and Stanley rushed into the barn. They saw Charles deep in discussion with Mourda. As soon as they were spotted, everyone ran over to them.

"Do you have perfume?" Roger asked, his voice filled with hope and excitement.

"Yes," Mary reassured him.

They gathered around the pot, and Mary pulled it out of her pocket.

"You should have the honor of adding it to the mixture," Stanley said.

"How much should I pour in?" Mary asked.

Roger handed her a measuring cup. "Just two ounces, no more, no less."

Removing the lid on the bottle, she carefully measured out two ounces and poured it into the mixture. A moment later, the mixture began to boil. Sparkling bubbles appeared and popped. The kids reacted with alarm.

"No, it's okay," Mourda said. "That's supposed to happen."

At the other side of the barn, Rick and Stanley started talking about the nosy neighbor.

"I think the neighbor across the street is on to us," Rick said.

Stanley grimaced. "Yeah, that's why I took the phone off the hook. I don't want her to call here and bother us. Even though she creeps me out, I have to be nice to her. But once the aliens are gone, I don't have to put up with her shenanigans any longer."

Mary came toward them, hearing only the last two sentences of what Stanley said. Turning away, tears ran down her cheeks. Slipping out of the barn, she went home feeling hurt and sad.

***

Mitchell stood around the sheriff's dining room table with five of his officers. "We are going to sneak in, quietly."

"But General Mitchell, sir," Lieutenant Stone said. "They're just kids."

# Chapter Thirty-Eight

## The Raid

In the darkness, the Air Force contingent, dressed in navy blue uniforms, circled the property and quietly made their way toward Anderson's barn from all sides. Team leaders carried walkie-talkies, conferring with each other in whispers whenever necessary. As they slowly crawled through the grass and approached the barn, the men were on high alert, sweating and nervous that any minute, the aliens might fire on them with their lasers.

For the most part, the leaders of each team used hand signals to communicate with their men. Although the stars were bright, the moon was little more than a crescent, much to their relief. Although anyone familiar with nature would have realized that something was up. The night was still. Even the crickets that usually filled the night air with their song had quieted, disturbed by the presence of so many humans.

These men were brave. Many of them had seen action in the Korean War, but that was a war fought with weapons they understood. Facing technically advanced aliens from another world made the men uneasy and fearful. Some of them were old enough to remember the 1938 radio broadcast of War the Worlds. Although the story was a work of fiction, these men couldn't help wondering if the alien weapons were as powerful as those depicted in the broadcast. The thought of being evaporated by an alien laser gave pause to even the bravest.

At the Guthrie house, the general and his men had left to take part in the raid, all except for Lieutenant Stone. He was left behind to keep an eye on Mary and the sheriff. Mitchell wanted to be sure they could not warn Stanley and the others of their approach.

Mary sat on the couch next to her father, her emotions a jumbled mix of anger, fear, and anxiety. She had spoken to her dad prior to the raid, bringing him up to date on what was happening across the street.

The sheriff was also conflicted. If there were indeed dangerous aliens involved, he understood the need for the Air Force to secure them. At the same time, he did not want Charles and his family to get hurt in the process. Thanks to his daughter, he now understood that there were two sets of aliens involved. One pair, if Mary was to be believed, was benevolent, wanting simply to return home with their crystal to save their planet and the universe from the other set of aliens, the Greys from Xylanthia. The Greys were more like universal pirates, bent on taking what they needed from other worlds and enslaving the inhabitants.

Unfortunately, the general and his men were descending on the good aliens.

"If they are captured, the general will imprison them," Mary told him. "And if that happens, Tau Ceti will be captured, and the rest of the universe, including Earth, will be destroyed."

The sheriff eventually made up his mind to warn Charles about the upcoming attack, but his expression must have given him away. Mitchell took Steve and his daughter prisoner, leaving Lieutenant Stone behind to keep a watch on them.

Mary glanced up at her dad. His worried expression did nothing to ease her anxiety. Stanley deserves this. He's a jerk. She glanced at the lieutenant, who stood in front of the window, gun drawn, dividing his attention between what was happening across the street, and keeping an eye on her and her father.

Even so, I should help him. Lutsik and Mourda only have three more hours before their planet is out of range. They don't deserve this. Her thoughts returned to Stanley. What if he's lying? Can he really be trusted? Or is he just manipulating everyone for some reason? No, this is real. Even if I can't believe Stanley, I know I can trust Lutsik and Mourda.

"This is no way to make friends."

Stone turned and looked at her. "What's that?"

"The aliens," Mary said. "Don't you think it would be better to befriend people who are smarter and more technologically advanced than we are?"

"General Mitchell doesn't see it that way."

"That doesn't make it right."

"I never said it did, but he's the boss."

"Don't you ever disagree with him?" Mary asked.

"Frequently," Stone admitted. "That doesn't mean I want to be court-martialed."

Mary thought about what he said. Then she got an idea. "My boyfriend and I had an argument."

"I'm sorry to hear that. I have a daughter your age. I know how stressful that can be for a young person like you. Maybe you can work things out."

"Maybe," Mary replied thoughtfully. "For that to happen, we need to talk. Can I call him?"

Stone thought about his own daughter and her on-again-off-again relationship with her current boyfriend. Her mood would swing between happiness and depression, depending on whether the relationship was on or off.

"There's nothing else to do but wait," Mary continued. "If I could just talk to him, maybe I could get things straightened out. It would sure make me feel better."

Seeing the sadness in her eyes, Stone gave in. "Go ahead."

Mary stood up and headed for the kitchen.

Stone followed her to the doorway. "Promise you won't leave the house," he said.

Picking up the receiver, she gave him a sincere look. "I promise. I'll stay here in the kitchen and returned to the living room when I'm done."

Stone believed her. Turning around, he went back to his post in front of the window. Where he could also keep an eye on her father.

Mary quickly dialed the number of the phone in the barn, but all she got was a busy signal. She tried over and over, each time feeling more desperate than the last. Who's on the phone? Come on. Hang up. I have to warn you before it's too late! She tried for a full ten minutes before giving up and returning to the living room.

"That was quick," Stone said.

"His phone was busy," Mary replied. "I'll try again in a few minutes."

***

In the barn, everyone was busy finishing the fuel. When it was ready, they used buckets and a large metal funnel to pour it into the fuel tank of the spaceship. The binoculars had been left on the ground, so no one was watching the general, and the occupants in the barn had no idea they were about to be attacked.

302

Lutsik approached Stanley. "We are so proud of you and your friends and what you have managed to accomplish. Without your help, we would never make it back to our planet in time. Once our mission is accomplished, and the Greys have been removed as a threat, I will inform my people of your heroic deeds. You will be honored among us."

"That's nice, Lutsik, but the only thing important is that we get you home in time."

Lutsik nodded and stretched. It had been a long day, and like everyone else, he was tired, so tired that neither alien had their minds open to danger. He walked across the barn to the front door, intending to step outside for a breath of fresh air, hoping it would revive him. Then it hit him, and he knew they were about to be attacked. He hurried back to the others to warn them.

"Mourda, the shield has failed, and the general and his men are about to invade us. We must move quickly."

"What are we going to do?" Stanley asked.

"You and your friends get busy doing something innocent. Mourda and I will engage a holographic deception."

Moments later, the ship became a piece of artwork, like the kind that Caroline frequently made using her welding skills.

Caroline smiled. Looking around, she spotted an old car muffler, picked it up, prepared to look busy when the soldiers arrived.

Head for those two empty stalls, Lutsik told Mourda. We will disguise ourselves as female bovines.

Stanley was about to tell them to hide but could not find them.

Moo!

Startled, everyone looked around and spotted the cows standing in the last two empty stalls.

"Great idea!" Stanley said. "They'll never find you now."

"Wow, I wish I could do that," Roger said.

"Shhh," Stanley hushed him. "Quick, everybody look busy."

Stanley and his friends got busy cleaning the barn. Even Charles pitched in. Grabbing a pitchfork, he tossed fresh hay into each of the stalls, occupied by the hidden aliens.

A moment later, the front and rear doors of the barn slammed open, and the general's men stormed into the barn, followed by Mitchell himself.

"Hands up! Don't anyone move!" One man shouted.

Everyone stopped what they were doing and gazed in mock surprise at the intruders. No one, however, was more surprised than the general and his men. Scanning the interior of the barn, they could find no sign of the aliens or their ship. With nothing more than an old man, a middle-aged woman, and a group of teenagers, the soldiers lowered their guns but did not put them away. It was evident by the expressions on their faces that they felt embarrassed by the unnecessary show of force.

Still, Mitchell strutted to the center of the barn like a king coming to take back his throne. His arrogant expression faltered when he looked around. He seemed uncertain as to what to do next until he spotted Caroline standing next to the disguised ship.

Determined to interrogate her, he walked over and was about to reach out and touch the art piece, but she stopped him.

"Don't touch," she warned. "It is still fragile. I just finished welding it."

Neither knew that had he actually touched her so-called art piece, he would have realized that it was nothing more than an illusion hiding the spaceship.

Charles marched over to the general. "What is the meaning of this?" he shouted indignantly. "This is private property, and you have no right to storm in here with your men like this was a military invasion or something. In case you haven't realized it, Mitchell, the war is over. It's been over!"

For once in his life, the general was at a loss for words, but not for long. "I have every right to be here," he blustered. "You've been hiding the aliens. You are aiding and abetting the enemy. Now hand them over, or I will arrest every one of you and take you back to the base for interrogation."

"There ain't no aliens here," Charles shouted. "Are you blind, you insufferable dirtbag? I'm not about to let you run roughshod over my family and me like you did five years ago. I'll sue! Do you hear me? I'll sue…."

Suddenly, Charles grabbed his chest and collapsed. Surprisingly, Mitchell caught him and gently lowered him to the floor. Caroline and Stanley rushed over.

"Get out of my way. Stand back," she shouted at the soldiers. "Can't you see what you're doing? All this commotion has caused my father to have another heart attack, only this one is a lot more severe." Trying not to panic, she looked up at Stanley. "Dial the operator and tell her to send an ambulance."

The soldiers cleared a path for Stanley as he ran to the phone. That's when he discovered that the phone was off the hook. Hanging it up, he waited several precious seconds for the dial tone to return. When it did, he dialed zero.

"Operator."

"Operator, quick, send an ambulance. My grandfather is having a heart attack!"

"What's the address?" She asked.

Stanley told her and then hung up the phone and returned to his grandfather's side.

Rick pushed through the soldiers and joined him. Roger was about to do the same until he stumbled over the binoculars. Picking them up, he wandered over to the barn's front window and looked through them at the house across the street. His eyes quickly fastened on the Greys, who stared right back at him. It was the first time he saw them without their human disguise. Roger yelped and rushed over to Stanley and the others.

"Stanley, the aliens…"

"Not now, Roger, can't you see that my grandfather is having a heart attack?" Stanley replied. Fear filled his voice.

"But…." He turned to Rick. "The aliens. They're across…."

"Not now, Roger." Rick jerked his head sideways at the general. "There are no aliens," he half-whispered.

With all the confusion going on, Roger could not get anyone to listen to him. He looked around for Mourda, and when his eyes fastened onto the cows, he remembered they were aliens in disguise. He rushed over to the stalls. Stepping inside one of them, he whispered in one cow's ear, telling him what was going on.

One of the soldiers look over, and when he saw what Roger was doing, he shook his head and looked away. Poor kid, he thought. The stress has made him looney.

***

Watching the military attack across the street, Drees and Jeet panicked.

"We must leave here and quickly," Drees said. "There is a human army across the street. They will take the Cetis. They will take the female warrior."

"And don't forget the Russians," Jeet added.

"Yes, they will take them, too. Then they will come for us next," Drees warned. "We must leave...now!"

"No, we must retrieve the Core, first," Jeet whined.

"We can't overpower all those soldiers to retrieve it. We will return to our space ship. The only way we can win is if we use the weapons on our ship against them," Drees concluded.

"How are we going to leave without being spotted?" Jeet asked. "There are more soldiers in the street. Surely they will see us and take us, prisoner."

"We'll change into dogs," Drees said after a moment's thought. "No one pays any attention to other people's dogs. It's our only way out."

Running into the kitchen, Jeet placed his hand on top of Margaret's head. "You will drive us to our spaceship."

"I will drive you to your spaceship," Margaret repeated is a voice devoid of emotion. She walked into the living room to her husband. Jack still had no idea what was happening in his own home. He was still watching TV.

"I must take them to their spaceship," Margaret repeated.

Engrossed in his program, Jack paid no attention to what she said. With his eyes still fastened on the TV set, he waved at her. "Hurry back."

Grabbing the keys to the Grand Marquis, Margaret, Drees, and Jeet headed into the garage. She slid into the driver's seat. Jeet and Drees climbed in beside her, shut the passenger door, and changed themselves into a holographic pair of bulldogs.

*Boy, are you ugly*, Jeet giggled telegraphically.

*Not as ugly as you.* Drees also giggled until he looked into the rearview mirror. *Ugh, we're both ugly.*

The two aliens giggled almost hysterically.

Margaret glanced at them when she heard the dogs snorting and panting, their tongues hanging out of their mouths, which were open, revealing a doggie grin. "Boy, are you two ugly!"

The bulldogs dissolved in outright doggie laughter, rolling on the seat until Jeet fell off the seat and onto the floor, bringing even more laughter.

"Straighten up," Margaret warned. "Here comes the Air Force."

Backing out of the driveway, she pulled onto the street, passing several Air Force personnel.

"Evening, ma'am," one officer said as he indicated he wanted her to stop.

"My, such a handsome man in uniform. Is something wrong…" She tilted her head, looking for his rank, "…sergeant?"

"Nice evening for a ride," the sergeant said.

"Yes, indeed. I'm taking my two little pooches out for a run in the park. They don't get nearly enough exercise. They're getting fat and lazy." She patted Jeet's head, pulling her hand back just in time to avoid getting bit. "Is something going on?"

The sergeant looked at the dogs and hid a grimace. Boy, are they ugly, even for bulldogs. "No, ma'am. Have a nice drive."

"Thank you, sergeant," she said and drove off.

*Stupid humans do not realize they have allowed us to escape.* Drees told Jeet telepathically.

Jeet laughed in his mind. *Yes, but when we return, they will know we are here as we eradicate everyone and take the Core for our own.*

# Chapter Thirty-Nine

## Captured!

"They found it, Sir," Lieutenant Stone said.

A thrill rushed through General Mitchell's blood. "Finally! Is there a debris field?"

"No, sir, the saucer appears to be undamaged."

"Excellent, get the truck onsite, and have them load it on as soon as possible. I want it taken to the warehouse outside of town, where we set up our field office," Mitchell ordered.

"You don't want to send it back to the base?" the Lieutenant asked.

"Not yet," the general said thoughtfully. "We're going to use it as bait. I want you to head over there right now and get everything ready to receive the saucer. Now that we have a working model in our possession, the scientists should be able to accomplish the reverse engineering a lot easier."

"What about the sheriff and his daughter?" Stone asked.

"Forget them. We have everything secured here. It no longer matters where they go. It's too late for them to warn their friends."

The two men finished speaking just as the ambulance pulled up. The ambulance attendants backed it up to the barn door and brought the gurney inside. After taking his vitals, they loaded Charles on it and wheeled him outside.

"Wait," Caroline called to the attendants. "I'm coming with you."

"No, you're not," the general said.

Just then, Sheriff Guthrie and Mary ran across the street and approached the ambulance.

"Let her go," the sheriff said. "You have no right to keep her from her father's side."

"I can do whatever I please," Mitchell snapped back.

Caroline turned on him. "I don't care what you think. I'm going with my father, whether you like it or not."

"You may as well let her go," Guthrie said. "I guarantee you won't get any useful information out of her if you keep her from his side."

It was clear by the look on his face that Mitchell did not want to allow her to leave, but reason finally convinced him that the sheriff was right. "All right, go ahead. I'll talk to you later."

Caroline turned to Guthrie and mouthed the words, 'Thank you.'

"I'll join you as soon as I can," the sheriff told her. Once the gurney was inside the vehicle, he took her hand and helped her inside.

After the ambulance pulled away, Mitchell lined everyone up on the left side of the barn, except Mary and the Sheriff, who stood protectively next to his daughter. The general was about to speak when one of his men exited the barn, one hand firmly grasping Mourda's arm.

"Who's that?" Mitchell asked. "Where did he come from?"

"I found him in one of the stalls," the sergeant replied. "I don't know where he came from. One minute, the stall was empty, the next time I looked, I spotted him."

"Cuff him and the Adams boy and put them in the backseat of my car," Mitchell ordered.

"Wait!" Mary looked up at her father. "Do something, Dad."

"I'm sorry, honey. My hands are tied for the moment."

As the general climbed into the front seat, he overheard Mourda talking to Stanley.

"You don't have to stay involved in this for me," Mourda said.

"No way," Stanley assured him. "I'm with you until the end."

The general turned around in his seat. "End? What end? What do you know?"

Stanley and Mourda ignored him, neither saying another word.

They were about to drive off when Roger ran up to the car and banged on the window.

Mitchell lowered it. "What do you want? Are you ready to confess?"

"What? No…I mean, you have to listen to me," Roger stammered. "The Greys…the evil aliens are across the street in the Weber's house!"

"Finally! The truth comes out." Mitchell stepped out of his car and addressed his men. "You there," he called to the sergeant. "Stay with the prisoners. The rest of you come with me. The Greys are hiding in the house across the street. Let's go get 'em!"

With far less stealth and finesse, the soldiers surrounded the Weber home, and when the general signaled, they attacked. Men slammed open the doors and crawled in through the windows. Checking every room as well as the basement. When they found no one but the husband sitting in front of the television in the living room, Mitchell ordered his men to ransack the house.

"Check everything. They may have left some evidence here that will tell us where they went."

Two men entered the kitchen and found every available surface covered with cakes, all frosted with outlandish colors and designs.

One man looked at the other. "Bizarre!"

"I'll say," the other replied.

The Lieutenant headed upstairs and called down a moment later. "General Mitchell! I found something up here," Stone shouted.

Anyone else might have run up the steps, but not the general. He had his dignity to maintain. When he reached the upstairs landing, Stone pointed to the front bedroom.

"In there, sir."

The room was littered with equipment, cake, and numerous comic books.

"As you can see by the chairs and binoculars in front of the window, they must have used this room to keep an eye on what was going on across the street," Stone said.

The general looked around and picked up one of the comic books. "What's this?"

"Comic books, sir, specifically space comic books."

"I know they're comic books," Mitchell replied. "What were they doing with them?"

The Lieutenant shrugged. "Reading them? I guess they don't have anything like that back on their planet."

Mitchell shook his head as one of his men came into the room and saluted.

"What have you got?" Mitchell asked.

"We've finished searching the premises, sir. The aliens are gone. The only one here is Jack Weber, the homeowner."

The general scowled. "It's time to question him," he told Stone.

The two men headed downstairs to confront Jack.

"Where is your wife?" Mitchell demanded.

Jack continued watching the screen. "She left, took the dogs with her."

"Follow me," Mitchell told his men, but before he walked out the door, Jack spoke again.

"Wait a minute." He paused and looked up, a confused expression on his face. "We don't own any dogs." He finally shrugged and went back to watching the television screen.

Mitchell turned to Lieutenant Stone. "I want an APB put out on that car. Now!"

"Yes, sir." Stone rushed out to the car and used the radio to set it up.

"Send some of the men around to the houses in the neighborhood. Give each household one of my cards and tell them to be on the lookout for anything suspicious. If they see something to call the number on it.

As soon as Mitchell joined him, they drove Stanley and Mourda to a portable jail cell. With sturdy bars and thick walls, it had been set up inside the warehouse where their temporary headquarters were located.

***

Miles away on the road headed toward the place where Jeet and Drees had left their spaceship, Margaret slowed down, careful not to exceed the speed limit.

314

We don't want to be stopped by any other forms of law enforcement, Jeet had warned her telepathically.

The two aliens, disguised as dogs, were now in the back seat, their heads stuck out the open side windows with the wind blowing against their smiling faces.

***

Mary and her father entered the barn, where they found Roger and Rick. Having dropped his holographic cow disguised, Lutsik stood nearby.

"What's the general going to do to Stanley and Mourda?" Mary asked.

"I don't know," Rick replied.

"We have to get them back," Lutsik said. "Look at the time…."

"Guys, guys!" Roger interrupted. "I've been trying to tell you. Mrs. Weber took off in her husband's car doing something like sixty, and I think the aliens were with her."

Rick turned on him. "Jerk, why didn't you say something earlier, and how come you told the general they were across the street."

"I tried to, but everyone was screaming, I said the wrong thing, and then the general started yelling and ran across the street before I could correct myself. No one would listen," Roger explained.

"Man, she is coo-coo, just like Stanley said." Rick shook his head.

Mary rushed over to them. "What? That was Mrs. Weber? Stanley was talking about Mrs. Weber?"

"Yeah, who else would he say that about?" Ricke asked.

Mary looked contrite and hurried out of the barn to catch a glimpse of the general's car, disappearing down the road.

"How could I be so stupid?" Sighing heavily, she returned to the barn. "What do we do now?"

"We finish fueling the ship," Lutsik replied. He glanced at the clock on the wall. "Time is running out. I don't want to do it, but if we can get him back in time, it looks like I will have to leave Mourda behind and come back for him the next time the planets realign."

The thought of leaving his son behind for the next five years made his heart heavy, but what choice did he have? He knew that the needs of the many outweighed the needs of the one, regardless of who he was.

# Chapter Forty

## The Cell

A line of black Suburbans drove through town, heading for the field office Mitchell had established. Strangely, the streets were filled with people standing silently watching the procession. More people came out of businesses, shops, homes, and apartments and joined the others. No one said a word as they solemnly watched the procession.

Stanley and Mourda looked out the back-seat windows at the people staring at them. People who eventually would be dead or enslaved if the crystal did not reach Tau Ceti in time to defeat the evil emperor attempting to control the universe. What the boys saw only deepened the dread that filled them. All was lost.

"Would your father leave without you?" Stanley asked.

"I don't know," Mourda admitted. "I can only hope that he will. I dislike the thought of being separated from him for the next ten years. But better that than the destruction of our people – both yours and ours."

"I don't think my mom could do it," Stanley said.

"I fear the same is true for Lutsik. He will want to even convince himself that he must, but the bond between father and son, mother and daughter, is powerful. It lessens only when the offspring takes a mate. It is this bond that will prevent him from leaving without me."

As he finished speaking, the line of cars stopped outside the field office. A team of ten Military Police waited outside for them. When the general's vehicle stopped, the

MPs moved forward, five on the left side of the car, and five on the right. Opening the back doors, a set of five agents surrounded each boy. They were led into the field office and placed in a room that contained a 10' by 10' portable jail cell with heavy-duty, reinforced steel bars and thick cement walls. Security cameras followed them every step of the way.

Extra soldiers were called in to create a high-security perimeter, stationing men around the four exposed sides of the cell as well as in the corridors leading to the room that contained it. Armed guards were also placed at every exit, making escape nearly impossible.

The cell contained two cots and nothing more. Stanley and Mourda were shoved inside. The loud clang of the door sliding in place and locking sounded like a death knell to them. Feeling lost and hopeless, they sat on the cots and hung their heads.

Stanley looked up and scanned the faces of their guards. They might as well have been statues. Standing ramrod straight, the only expression on the men's faces was solid determination. Sighing, he turned his head back to look at Mourda. He, too, was examining their guards. Finally, they looked at each other.

"We were so close," Stanley said. He kept his voice low, but in the surrounding silence, he may as well have shouted.

"You are a true friend," Mourda replied.

The alien's words offered little comfort as Stanley realized how bad a friend he had been to Roger, and Rick.

***

"I have to clear something up with Stanley," Mary told her father.

"I need to clear something up with Caroline," he replied.

"Okay, let's go to the hospital first," Mary remembered that her father had been friends with Stanley's mother. Still, she was very young at the time, so most of her memories were vague.

When they arrived at the hospital, they headed straight for the Coronary Care Unit. Caroline was just leaving her father's room, her face a mixture of worry, concern, and fear. As soon as she noticed Steve and Mary, she stood up and rushed into his arms. Tears rolled down her cheeks as he hugged and comforted her.

"I'm sorry. I'm so, so sorry," Steve whispered, stroking her hair.

"Thank you for coming." Stepping back, she turned to Mary and took her hand. "You, too, Mary, Dad told me about all the time you have spent with him, bringing him meals and desserts. It meant a lot to him. It means a lot to me."

"I enjoyed his company. He's been like a grandfather to me," Mary said. "He is an extraordinary person."

"How is he?" Steve asked.

"Dad's in bad shape," Caroline said as she fought back the tears. "There was some major damage this time. They think he has a blocked artery."

Dr. Fisher, Charles's heart surgeon, stood next to the door, writing something on Charles's chart. When he finished, he closed the metal binder and slid it into a plastic holder on the wall next to the door.

Turning to Caroline, he said, "Could I speak to you in private, Ms. Adams?"

Steve placed a hand on her back. "Go ahead. I'm going in to see Charles. There is something important I need to discuss with him."

He and Mary went into the room, and the sight that greeted them frightened Mary. Charles was hooked up to numerous monitors and IV bags. Tubes seemed to be coming out of him everywhere. A blood pressure cuff was wrapped around his right upper arm, and wires attached to an electrocardiogram stuck out in various places from his pajamas. On the meters, lighted numbers beeped and occasionally changed, indicating heart rate, blood pressure, heartbeat, and the settings for the IV drips.

Charles was awake and a little drowsy from the medication being fed into his system.

"How are you doing, Charles?" Guthrie asked.

"Not so good. At least, that's what my doctor tells me." He looked at Mary. "Thanks for bringing Mary to see me. She's like a granddaughter to me."

"I know, but that's not the only reason I'm here. I came to apologize. I should have believed you. I should have ignored what people thought and said."

"I forgive you, but it's harder to forgive you for breaking my little girl's heart," Charles said. "Caroline still has feelings for you. I could see it back at the farm. It's not too late, you know. Maybe for my heart, but not for Caroline's."

Caroline's divorce had been nasty, and the process had seemed to drag on forever. The sheriff had been called out to her home, whenever her husband showed up on her doorstep looking for trouble. Over the months, she and Steve became close friends, and before long, he was the rock upon which she leaned upon.

After the divorce, their relationship had grown into something more than friendship, until five years ago when Lutsik and Mourda first visited Earth.

Finishing her talk with the doctor, Caroline entered her father's room.

Guthrie turned to look at her. "I'm sorry I let you down, Caroline. I allowed everyone's opinion to dictate our relationship. I should have stayed by your side. Breaking up with you was cowardly. It's a decision I have regretted for the past five years."

"No, you did the right thing, Steve. I see that now. All the negative publicity heaped upon my father, thanks to Mitchell and the press, proved to be our undoing. Because of it, your reputation began to suffer. You were painted with the same brush of skepticism as my father."

"That's no excuse. I should have stuck to my convictions."

Shaking her head, she crossed the room and placed a hand on his arm. "Sticking up for my dad would have been political suicide. Your job was on the line. As a widower and single father, you had to put your daughter's welfare above everything else. I should have understood that when you tried to explain it to me, but I was so angry and distraught that it blinded me."

A nurse came into the room to check Charles's vital signs and attach a new bag of saline solution to his IV. When she finished, she turned to Guthrie. "I'm sorry, sheriff, but visitors are restricted to family only."

"I understand," Steve replied. When the nurse left, he turned to Charles. "I need to go anyway. There's something important I need to take care of."

As soon as he and Mary were out of the room, Mary turned to him. "Dad, you want to explain that to me?"

He smiled and lifted an eyebrow. "Really, Mary, I think you understand."

Mary grabbed her dad's hand and squeezed it. "You know, Stanley's grandfather is right. It's not too late. Where are we going now?"

"To see General Mitchell. I have an idea that might just work."

"Good, then maybe I can talk to Stanley and get something straightened out as well," Mary said.

***

As they headed to the field office, Mary told her father about the crystal, their time restraints, and the importance of getting Lutsik and Mourda back to their planet in time.

"Please, dad, you have to help them. The clock is ticking, and they are nearly out of time."

"Would Lutsik leave his son behind?"

"No, even though he says he will, if necessary," Mary said.

"I agree. He's not going to leave with his son a prisoner. I'm sure he realizes that Mitchell would never release Mourda. Knowing the government, they would perform all kinds of experiments on him, putting his life at risk."

Mary was shocked. "They would do that, even if it ended up killing him?"

"Even if it ended up killing him," her father replied. "The boy would be treated no better than a lab rat."

"That's terrible! Please, dad, we have to figure out a way to help him escape."

"I'm working on it."

Sheriff Guthrie parked his vehicle near the door of the field office, and he and Mary went inside. He was astounded by the number of men Mitchell had guarding the boys. Realizing that the general was going to win the battle but lose the war, he approached him.

"General, I just learned that the other alien was in hiding during your raid. One of the boys has taken him away from the farm and is on his way out of town," Guthrie said.

"Why are you telling me this? Up to now, you have withheld the information you possessed."

"That was when I didn't believe there were any aliens. I see that I was wrong," the sheriff said.

"Are they en route?"

"Yes, heading east, according to one of my deputies."

Guthrie wasn't certain the general would fall for his story. However, Mitchell telephoned his men stationed at the sheriff's house and gave orders to go after them. Little did he realize that they were being sent on a fool's errand to allow Lutsik time to escape.

While he was on the phone, Mary found the room containing the cell that held Stanley and Mourda, prisoner. It wasn't hard. All she had to do was follow the trail of guards. She walked into the room and up to the cell bars.

Stanley stood up and came to her.

"I want to apologize for walking out on you today."

"That's okay. It was all just a misunderstanding," Stanley replied.

"What do we do now?"

Before he could answer, Mitchell walked in. "I want you out of here."

She gave Stanley a worried smile and joined her dad.

"It sure seems like a lot of men to guard two boys," Guthrie drawled, setting the bait.

"That's none of your business," Mitchell replied.

"Yeah, you're right. However, if it were me, I would send most of these men after the alien on the run, and the two Greys. From what I've heard, the Greys are armed and dangerous. They are the ones who want to take over the planet and destroy our very lives."

"Who told you that?" Mitchell demanded.

"I have had several incidents of people disappearing and being forced to do things they wouldn't normally do. The kids vouch for Mourda and Lutsik. They claim they have been with them the whole time they have been on this planet," the sheriff said.

"Are you sure you have your facts straight?"

"Positive."

Mitchell briefly thought over Guthrie's words, and then called his men to him. "Lock the door of the room the cell and put a guard on the entrance and exits. I want the rest of you to find those Greys before they bring the whole armada down on us."

"Yes, sir," everyone replied. They rushed out to their vehicles.

Except for three guards, the placed emptied out. The hunt was on. The general remained until Sheriff Guthrie and Mary left for the farm. Then Mitchell, Stone, and the general's driver piled into his vehicle and drove off.

\*\*\*

"Where did everybody go?" Stanley asked Mourda.

The alien's eyes took on a distant look for several seconds. Blinking, he looked at Stanley. "The general sent them after the Greys, which is good. Sheriff Guthrie shamed him into doing it. Those stationed across from the farm have been sent after Lutsik. Mitchell believes that one of your friends drove away with him seeking refuge in another town."

"That was brilliant. Now's our chance. I just wish we could find a way to get out of here."

Mourda cocked his head. "What would you want to do? There are still three guards left on the premises."

"Look, I know you have all kinds of powers. I saw some of them when we were looking for the crystal. Is there some way you can destroy the lock on this cell and make a hole in the warehouse wall behind it?" Stanley asked.

A look of concern crossed Mourda's face. "Yes, but to do so, I would be destroying someone's property."

Stanley became excited. "I believe that in this case, it would be justified. We have to get you back to the farm so you and Lutsik can leave. Time is almost up," he reasoned.

"Using that much power will drain me. I will be weak and maybe even sick," Mourda warned him.

"I don't think we have a choice," Stanley said. "Go ahead. Do it."

Mourda stood up and faced the lock in the cell door. Closing his eyes, he concentrated on unlocking it. After only a moment, they heard a click. Stanley moved to the door and gently pushed it open. He grinned at the alien, and both moved to stand in front of the back wall.

Mourda's concentration deepened, and sweat beaded his forehead. A crack ripped through the air, and when Stanley looked at him, the alien's face was a vivid bluish purple.

"Mourda? Are you okay?" Stanley asked worriedly. He had never seen a person's face turn that color unless they had a nasty bruise.

"Mourda?"

Crack! Boom!

The wall shattered, creating a hole large enough for them to step through. The effort, however, was too much. Mourda staggered.

Stanley reached out and supported him. "Let's get out of here before the guards come."

They hurried through the hole at the back of the building.

"There," Mourda said weakly, pointing to one of the Suburbans. "Take that vehicle."

"I don't have a key," Stanley protested.

"Don't need it."

After helping him into the car, Stanley ran around to the driver's side. He climbed in, but as he closed the door, one guard came through the hole, and the other two from the sides of the buildings.

"Halt! Stop, or I'll shoot!" one of the men yelled.

With a panicked look, Stanley turned to Mourda, but before he could say anything, the alien used the last of his power to start the car. Stanley shifted into drive and slammed his foot against the gas pedal.

"Wooo weee!" He shouted jubilantly, glancing in the rearview mirror.

The guards ran after them but soon stopped, knowing they could never outrun the car.

"Looks like we took their last vehicle," Stanley crowed. "This is way cool."

When he glanced at Mourda, however, his excitement dried up. The alien was slumped unconscious in the seat. Thinking quickly, he flipped the switch that turned on the vehicle's siren and sped back to the farm as quickly as possible. When they were a block away from the farm, he pulled over to the side of the road and stopped.

"Mourda, Mourda, can you hear me?"

The alien moaned. "I am so weak."

"I know, and I'm sorry. Look, I can't drive up to the house. The car will attract too much attention. Can you walk?"

"I don't think so."

Stanley jumped out of the car, ran around to the other side, and opened the door.

"I'm sorry, Stanley. I don't think I can make it." Mourda's words were barely above a whisper.

"It's okay. I've got you."

Using a fireman's carry, Stanley lifted his friend onto his back and carried him to the farm. He felt bad that he'd had to ask Mourda to do something so dangerous to his health. Determined to make it up to him, he used his feelings to give him added strength. When they arrived at the barn, Lutsik, and Rick ran over and carried Mourda to a chair. Stanley dropped to the ground next to him, exhausted.

"It is good that you are back," Lutsik said. "I did not want to leave you behind to be imprisoned.

Rick pulled a handkerchief out of his pocket and handed it to Lutsik, who used it to wipe the sweat from his son's brow. "You are very weak. You must have used up a lot of power."

"I had to," Mourda replied. As he rested, his face returned to its normal coloring. "I knew you would not leave without me."

"Good call." Lutsik turned to Stanley. "How is your grandfather?"

"I don't know. I'll call my mom." Standing up, he went to the phone and dialed the hospital. It seemed like it took forever, but he was finally put through to the nurses' station outside the CCU. Moments later, he spoke to his mother.

"Mom."

"Stanley, is that you? Are you okay?"

He could hear the tears in her voice. "It's all right, Mom. Mourda and I have escaped. We're back at grandpa's house."

"Thank heavens, you're safe, but Stanley, you need to get here as soon as possible."

Her words made him realize that his whereabouts weren't the reason she was crying. "Mom, what's wrong? Is grandpa okay?"

She sniffed. "He's…Stanley, he's had another heart attack. It doesn't look…." Her words trailed off. She was unable to speak as her tears threatened to overwhelm her.

"He's what? Mom?"

"He's dying, Stanley. Just get here quick," she sobbed.

Stricken, what he had learned was all too obvious by his expression.

"You must take me to him," Lutsik said.

"Look at the time," Mourda argued.

"I must see him," Lutsik insisted. "Are you strong enough to finish fueling the ship and get it ready?"

Mourda took a deep breath. "Yes, we'll be ready when you return."

# Chapter Forty-One

## The Deadly Return

Later that evening, Margaret returned home alone with explicit instructions that Jeet had given her. She pulled her husband's car into the garage and closed the door, but before going inside, she hurried crossed the street and snuck up to peek in the barn window. If what the Greys suspected was true, she would find the other aliens and their ship still inside. And if that were true, she was to do whatever it took to stop them.

***

Stanley and Lutsik got out of Charles's truck and ran into the front entrance of the hospital. They approached the front desk.

"Where is the coronary care unit located?" Stanley asked.

"Take the hallway on my right and follow the signs," the receptionist said. "You can't miss it."

They followed her instructions, making numerous turns until they reached the nurses' station in the coronary care unit. From there, they followed the room numbers on the door frames until they found the one they wanted. Entering the room, they found Caroline seated in a chair beside the bed, holding her father's hand. Charles's complexion was white and pasty, and although he was unconscious, his face was turned toward his daughter. His breathing was slow and heavy, and as Stanley checked the monitor, he saw that his grandfather's pulse was frighteningly slow.

Stanley went up to her, took her other hand, and squeezed it.

"Any change?" he asked.

330

"He's the same," she replied with a negative shake of her head.

Lutsik walked around to the other side of the bed.

"I cannot leave without helping you, my friend." Placing one hand over Charles's heart, Lutsik placed the other hand over his own heart. Then closing his eyes, he concentrated.

Stanley and his mother were amazed when the hand Lutsik placed on Charles's heart began to glow. They exchanged glances. Suddenly, Caroline felt an odd tingling sensation in her hand. She quickly jerked it away, fearing that whatever Lutsik was doing to her father might also affect her, but in an adverse way.

"Is he…?" Stanley was unable to finish his question.

Hope-filled Caroline's eyes and she shook her head slightly, indicating that she didn't know the answer.

Just then, the lights in the hospital started flickering. A moment later, things returned to normal. Lutsik dropped his hands and smiled, but Charles remained unconscious, with no apparent change in his condition.

"Goodbye, my friend." He turned to Stanley. "Come, we're almost out of time."

Stanley looked from his mother to Lutsik and back. Whatever his friend had done, it's apparently wasn't what he and his mother had hoped it would do. Knowing he had to get Lutsik back to his ship so that he and Mourda could depart, he turned to his mother.

"I'll be back, Mom, just as soon as Lutsik and Mourda have taken off."

They left, leaving Caroline wondering and disheartened. She was grateful that Lutsik had tried to help, but apparently, whatever he had done did not work. She reached for his hand again and bowed her head. Suddenly, she jerked her head back up when the television popped on, and the machines inside the room went nuts, blinking, beeping, and acting strangely. Terrified, she was about to call for the nurse. When the woman, along with a doctor, ran into the room.

"Get the crash cart. Now!" The doctor yelled.

***

Margaret peeked through the barn window. She saw the flying saucer along with Mourda and the boys scurrying about, finishing up last-minute preparations for the aliens' return home.

General Mitchell has been tricked, she thought. Jeet and Drees warned me that this might be the case. I must tell the general, but how? Then she remembered the card she had been given with Mitchell's phone number on it, and the words the airman had spoken. 'If you see anything suspicious, anything at all, call my office immediately.' She ran back to the house, headed into the kitchen, and grabbed the receiver off the wall phone. Picking up his business card, she dialed the number on it.

When a male voice answered, she said, "I need to speak to General Mitchell right away."

"I'm sorry. The general is in the field. May I take a message?"

"Yes. You need to get a hold of him as soon as possible."

"Who's calling, please?"

"Margaret Weber," she replied. "Tell him he's been fooled. The spaceship and its occupants are still here. He needs to return to the barn."

"It's going to take some time to reach him, but I'll do my best to get a hold of him right away," the man assured her.

Hanging up, he flipped the switch on the intercom. "Code red! Code red! This is not a drill. We need to get a hold of General Mitchell right away. Tell him that the alien's and their ship are still here. He needs to return to the barn."

***

Stanley drove up to the barn. He and Lutsik got out and ran inside.

Seeing them, Mourda shouted. "Almost ready, there is just one more thing we need to do."

"We must hurry," Lutsik said. "Our window of opportunity is rapidly closing, and if we stay here much longer, we might have to fight our way clear.

***

Mitchell and his men had been driving for several minutes. After finally tracking down which boy would be driving the escape vehicle with alien inside, and getting a description of Rick's car, the general called for a helicopter. When it reached his location, he ordered it to fly ahead to try and spot the vehicle. The chopper traveled the route for some time without locating it. He returned to Mitchell's location.

"I'm sorry, sir," the pilot radioed. "I've flown beyond the furthest distance the car could have reached within the time it left ahead of you. There's no sign of it."

Mitchell fumed. "Return to base and await further instructions."

"Yes, sir."

The pilot's report made the general suspect that Sheriff Guthrie had sent him on a wild goose chase. "I'll have his badge for this. Aiding and abetting a hostile alien is a criminal offense. He'll pay for this. I'll see that he spends the rest of his life in federal prison with no parole. Take me to the area where they found that spaceship," he ordered his driver.

"Yes, sir."

When they arrived at the location of the Greys' spaceship, it still had not been loaded on the truck. The general got out of his vehicle. A strange noise emitted from the ship, but Mitchell paid no attention to it. He was too incensed that his men had not done their job in the time he expected it to be done.

"Surround this thing," he ordered his men as he hurried over to the sergeant in charge of the operation. "What's going on here? Why hasn't this been loaded on the truck and taken away?"

The man did not answer. He just stood there staring out into nothingness.

"Answer me! What's wrong with you, Sergeant?"

Still, the man did not answer. Suspicious, Mitchell looked around at the other men under the sergeant's command. Every one of them stood as still as a statue, staring at something he could not see.

"Lieutenant Stone, find out what's wrong with these men."

"Yes, sir, I wonder if the noise coming from that spaceship has anything to do with it."

The general looked startled. Although he had heard the sound as soon as it exited his car, he was so angry when he saw that the ship had not been removed yet, he had ignored it. A look of panic crossed his face.

"Get these men out of here!" He shouted.

It was a good thing, too. They no sooner removed the men standing in close proximity to the ship, when the sound increased, and the saucer shot up into the air and took off so fast that it seemed to just disappear.

"The men still appear to be locked into some kind of trance, sir," Stone said. "What should we do with them?"

"Put them in the back of the truck. Assign other men to drive their vehicles."

He was about to say more when the phone in his car rang. His driver answered it.

"What's that? Are you sure? Okay, I'll let him know."

The driver jumped out of the car and ran over to the general. "Sir, I just received a phone call from the base. Apparently, the neighbor, who lives across the street from Charles Anderson, telephoned your office. She claims that the other aliens and their flying saucer are still in his barn. She said that you have been deceived."

Mitchell's face turned red with anger. "Why should I believe her? She's the one that helped the Greys escape. This could just be another ruse to throw me off their trail."

Lieutenant Stone said nothing.

"Then again, since she works for the Greys, maybe she wants the other captured. Everyone back to your vehicles," he shouted. "We're heading back."

"What about the truck and the other men?" Stone asked.

"Send them back to basecamp and have a couple of doctors look them over. Maybe he can figure out what the enemy did to them."

Mitchell and his team looped around and headed back toward town, driving as fast as they dared. Ten cars sped down a two-lane road, headed for Charles's farm.

Frustrated and feeling like the enemy was getting the best of him, the general went crazy and began screaming orders. "Drive faster! Hurry up. They're going to get away!"

"Yes, sir. Right away, sir," the driver said as he floored the gas pedal.

***

The military wasn't the only one headed for Charles's farm. The Greys would arrive before them, bent on grabbing the crystal and destroying the Tau Cetis.

"I still can't get the shields working so that the ship is cloaked," Jeet said as he angrily kicked the instrument panel on their ship. "The humans will see us now."

"It doesn't matter. We have forty-seven minutes to obtain the crystal and get off this planet if we are going to make it home in time to begin the invasion," Drees replied.

"What will we do if Earth's military is there waiting for us?" Jeet asked as he continued working on the malfunctioning shield.

"We'll destroy them with our weapons," Drees answered. "That's why we returned for our ship. One way or the other, we are going to get that crystal, even if we have to destroy everything in our way to get."

***

With blue emergency lights flashing, the government cars sped down the two-lane highway and eventually entered the town. If everything went right, they would arrive at Charles's farm in time to stop Lutsik and Mourda from leaving. If they were successful, all would be lost.

# Chapter Forty-Two

## The Battle Begins

The last of the fuel was finally loaded into the spaceship. As Lutsik sealed the tank, Mourda went inside the ship to run some preflight tests. He was about to sit down when he glanced over at the slot with the crystal had been placed. It was gone. He checked everywhere, and when he did not find it, he ran out of the ship, stopping at the top of the ramp.

"The Core is gone."

This announcement grabbed everyone's attention.

"Isn't it in the slot on the instrument panel?" Lutsik asked.

"No."

"Did you look in the ship?" Rick asked.

"Of course," Mourda replied.

"Everywhere?" Roger asked.

"Naturally," Lutsik reassured him. "It's only this big," he said, pointing to his vessel.

"It must have been dislodged when we crashed," Mourda replied.

"Then it's probably on the floor somewhere," Lutsik reasoned.

"No," Mourda repeated. "I told you. I looked."

"Where can it be?" Stanley asked.

As the words left his mouth, Mary and Sheriff Guthrie walked into the barn. They knew something was wrong when they saw the expressions on everyone's face.

"What's the matter?" Mary asked. A look of concern crossed her face.

"The Core is gone," Stanley replied.

"Did someone take it?" Mary asked.

"Has someone stolen it?" Her father asked.

"I don't think so," Stanley replied. His brain whirled as he thought about where it might have rolled. Then his expression lit up. "It must be in the grass somewhere between here and the place where you crashed. Everyone! Flashlights! Grab those lanterns. We only have forty minutes to find it!"

Everyone ran outside, spreading out in a line from the barn to where the spaceship had crashed. Stanley's guts clenched, and he was pretty certain that the others were also experiencing the same stress. They had to find that crystal and fast!

Stanley looked at his watch. Ten minutes had passed. Please, Lord, help us find it before it's too late.

"I found it! I found it!" Roger yelled as he straightened up with the crystal-shaped Core in his hand.

Everyone ran back inside.

"Thirty minutes!" Stanley shouted. "We have only thirty minutes left."

The words no sooner left his mouth when General Mitchell drove in the driveway and up to the barn, followed by his men. Stanley quickly took the Core from Roger and hid it behind his back so that Mitchell would not see it. If he did and realized its importance, he would confiscate it, and all would be lost.

It was time for a final confrontation. Stanley stood in front of his friends and family. Mitchell entered the barn and stood facing him, backed by his military might.

"Sir, I know this looks bad. And you probably have no reason to trust or listen to me, but please, just give me two minutes to uh…explain the…uh situation. Two minutes, please, sir," Stanley pleaded. He glanced at the clock on the wall. "After that, we will surrender. All of us, if that's what you want."

"You have two minutes, Mr. Adams. Make them count," Mitchell said.

"These aliens are not the enemy. They aren't the ones you're seeking. The Greys are our enemies, but Mourda and Lutsik, from Tau Ceti, are our friends and comrades. They actually saved us…saved the Earth from an attack by the Greys. If we stop them from leaving our atmosphere within the next eighteen minutes and prevent them from them returning to their planet, the Greys will destroy it. After that, Earth will be their next target."

Stanley took a deep breath. "The people of Tau Ceti are our protectors, our unknown allies. If it weren't for them and their crystal, we may have already been obliterated. General, this is the time to join forces with a powerful, influential ally. You, sir, will be hailed as a hero for recognizing the difference and making the call. You, sir, will have saved our people from enslavement and our planet's resources from being stripped and hauled away to another world. This is your hour. We place our very survival as a species in your hands."

Just then, Charles and Caroline walked into the barn through the backdoor and stood next to Stanley.

"He is absolutely right, general. This is where we choose, and it's your call," Charles said.

Stanley's mouth dropped open, and he turned to look at his grandfather. "Grandpa! What are you doing here? The doctors…Mom said, you…."

"Our friend and ally, Lutsik, saved me. He fixed my heart. I'm 100% healthy. See?" He jumped into the air and clicked his heels. "And General," he turned and fixed his gaze on Mitchell, "why would he bother to save me, one old scientist farmer if he was planning to destroy our world?"

Mitchell looked conflicted. His eyes darted from Charles to the aliens and back again.

"We have only fifteen minutes remaining. They must leave with the crystal by then, or all will be lost," Mary said.

The general snarled. "This is poppycock. You're all a bunch of nut jobs. Don't you think my intelligence information would know if an alien fleet was getting into position for an attack? They would have informed me. Why should I listen to a bunch of kids and a…a crazy old U.F.O. nut?" He pointed to the two aliens. "You two get over here."

Mourda and Lutsik started ambling toward the general until Mary stepped between them.

"First of all, we're not a bunch of kids. We're United States citizens, and Stanley has as much right as you, or anyone else, to save our world. As for you, with all due respect, you work for us, the citizens of this country and this planet." She took Stanley's hand.

"With all due respect, sir, sometimes I think you hide behind your rank and your medals," Mary continued. "I think you believe you are only worthwhile as a person

340

because you are a general. That's not true. You're a good man who wants to do what is right. You want to protect us, the country, and the planet. It's just that you sometimes get caught up in what you think everyone else expects of a general. The reality is…the real you, Allen Ryan Mitchell, is a much better man, and a much better leader."

Roger's eyes got big as he looked at Stanley and whispered in his ear. "Sometimes you do that too, you know? That whole football jock thing. When really, you are a much cooler guy. You know, just being yourself."

Stanley looked at Roger and smiled. "I know." He looked back at Mitchell. "Together, we can protect our planet, all of us, working as friends, sharing all our information. That's what real friends do. They never hide the truth from each other, because truth creates trust, and a real friend is someone you can trust."

Mitchell stared at him, saying nothing.

"You have to know who your true self is, and who your true friends are and stand with them. Sometimes you can't tell who those friends are by outside appearances, but friendship demands truthfulness and honesty."

When the general still did not speak, Stanley continued. "The Greys are probably on their way here right now in their ship. They want the Core, too. They want it so that they can attack Tau Ceti and Earth. Afterward, every planet with the resources they need because they can't be bothered with searching for an alternative energy source. They would rather just steal everyone else's."

Mitchell thought over what Stanley said.

"We're wasting time, General. The Greys will be here any minute," Stanley concluded.

Mitchell motioned Lieutenant Stone forward. "All eyes on the sky. Have the men get into position with tanks, anti-aircraft, and everything else we have to throw at them. It's time to roll out the big guns."

* * *

The Greys flew their saucer only a few hundred feet above the ground. As they passed, televisions, radios, and cars stopped working. That and the bright lights of the ship brought people outside to stare up at the sky and point at the alien vessel. It was so close that no one could mistake it for anything but a real flying saucer. Terrified, some people hurried into their bomb shelters. Then the lights inside and out flickered off, as did the street lights.

On a back road, a couple making out in the front seat of a car stopped kissing to look up at the ship. Their hair stood on end, and looking at each other, they laughed, unaware of the threat the aliens posed.

Dogs, cats, birds, and all kinds of farm animals set off a cacophony of sounds, terrified by something they did not understand. Residents looking through the windows of cafes and gas stations followed it with their eyes.

For a moment, the world seemed to hold its collective breath. Then the dam broke. People flooded into the streets and ran helter-skelter, incapable of figuring out where they should go…where they could hide, and their screams joined the cries of the animals.

The end of the world was at hand.

# Chapter Forty-Three

## War Between Worlds

Although Mitchell sent his men to prepare for battle, he still hadn't said what he would do with Lutsik, Mourda, Stanley, and his friends.

No one moved as they waited for his answer. Lieutenant Stone returned after giving orders to the men outside.

"General Mitchell, sir, I agree with the intelligence you have just received."

The general nodded, convincing himself that what he heard was the truth.

"Except for one thing," Stone said.

"Yes, Martin, what would that be?"

"You have been infiltrated, sir."

"What?"

"Yes, sir, at the highest level."

The general grew alarmed. "What? Not the president?"

"No, sir. You, sir."

"What? What are you talking about?"

"Do you believe in me, sir?" Stone asked.

"Of course, I do. You have been by my side these past five years," Mitchell reassured him. "As far as I know, you have never lied to me.

"Me. I'm one of them." The Lieutenant showed him his hand, exposing the mouth within his palm.

Mitchell gasped.

"We have been here for a long time. Many of us. These two," he said, pointing to Lutsik and Mourda, "are some of our very best agents. In fact, as far as I'm concerned, they are the best in the universe. We have not only been monitoring but protecting Earth for centuries. We are at a critical time for both Earth and the entire solar system. These two agents must leave with this crystal in eleven minutes, or we'll all be doomed. And general, there will be no memory of you or anything you've done…ever! Your decision, sir?"

As he finished speaking, the Grey's spaceship came into view. Everyone panicked as lasers from the ship's weapon system hit the ground and other objects, causing them to explode. The civilians in the barn started screaming, and the animals also cried out, which added to the sound of the explosions made a nearly deafening noise.

Mitchell ran to the barn door, shouting orders to his men. "Fire! Hit that ship with everything you have!"

His men opened fire, pummeling his saucer with tank fire, rockets, anti-aircraft guns, and in the case of those not operating larger equipment, even rifle fire. They may as well have been using pea shooters. As soon as the ammunition hit the saucer's shields, they exploded, doing absolutely no damage to the ship or shield.

Knowing there was no place safe for Charles, Stanley, and the others, Lutsik and Mourda gathered them together. "Hurry, we need to get as many of you as possible inside our ship," Lutsik said. "It's the only safe place."

"Not all of you will fit, though. I'm afraid the most we can fit inside is five of you," Mourda added. "You must choose who will go."

344

"That's easy," Charles said. "The kids should climb into the saucer. The rest of us will fight."

"No!" Stanley shouted. "We can help."

Charles shook his head. "I'm sorry, son, but you and your friends are the future of our people. It's important to keep you safe."

Stanley opened his mouth to protest, but Lutsik cut him off.

"No arguments. The rest of us must leave the barn. It's a big target, and the Greys will be tempted to fire on it. As long as you are inside the ship, we will not have to worry about your safety. Now go."

Mary laid her hand on Stanley's arm. "Come on, Stanley, let's do what he said. We'll only get in the way."

"All right," Stanley finally agreed. "Come on, people. Get a move on."

As soon as they were inside, Lutsik sealed the hatch.

Sheriff Guthrie walked over to Caroline and took her arm. "Come with me. I may only have my service revolver, but if those aliens get out of their ship, it can hurt them if necessary, unless they happen to have personal shields to protect them."

She looked at him with adoring eyes. "I know you will protect me as much as you can."

Joining hands, they ran from the barn, ducking behind trees and any available cover until they were free of the immediate battle zone. Charles, Lutsik, and Mourda also left the barn. The scene before them was like something out of a nightmare. The saucer flew overhead, surrounded by explosions that hit their shields, but caused no damage.

The Greys fired at the tanks and other weapons, picking them off one by one.

Having retrieved their hand lasers from the ship, Lutsik and Mourda also fired at the ship.

"If we concentrate our weapon fire so that both hit the same spot on the saucer, we might be able to create a weakness in their shields that would allow the humans' ammunition to get through and damage their vessel," Lutsik said.

Charles was torn between fear and elation over participating in a real alien battle. He ran for the house, dodging around the general's men and their equipment. He was amazed at how fast he could run. I haven't been this limber since I was a young whippersnapper, he thought. Heading inside, he went to his bedroom closet and pulled out a shotgun, and as many rounds of bullets, he could stuff in his pockets. Then he loaded the gun, and headed back outside, joining Lutsik and Mourda.

"I'll shoot at the same spot you're aiming for," he told them. "Maybe with the three of us concentrating our fire, we can put a chink in their armor."

Taking aim, he fired, but their teaming up did not go unnoticed by Jeet and Drees, who fired their laser at them. All three men dove to the side as the ship's beam cut an eight-foot-long ditch right along the very spot they once occupied.

"Where are my X-15s," Mitchell yelled into the radio of his Suburban. "I need them here now. We're in the middle of a battle with space aliens, and they're kicking our butts!"

"They're on their way, general," the man at the other end said. "There are only four available, but they should reach your position in ten minutes."

"We'll need more than four," Mitchell shouted. "Those Greys are melting down our equipment like a marshmallow in a campfire. Nothing we hit them with is doing any damage!"

The laser hit one of the tanks, shearing off the muzzle of its weapon. The driver tried to steer the tank away from the line of fire, but a second shot along its metal treads lifted the tank into the air and flipped it over. Two more tanks came to its rescue, firing at the saucer and giving the two men inside the damaged tank a chance to crawl out to safety with only minor injuries.

As the general left his vehicle, Lutsik ran up to him.

"Your weapons are doing little to no damage to the shields. Have your men concentrate their fire on a single location. That, added to Mourda's and my laser fire might create a small crack in their shields. It may not work, but it's worth a try."

"Good idea."

Mitchell passed the order along to his subordinates, but several of their weapons were already damaged beyond repair. Men were forced to abandon their equipment and dive for cover as the saucer approached and fired.

***

Inside the town and surrounding areas, everything was dark as pitch. Some people stopped running, their eyes pulled to Charles's farm outside of town. Many covered their ears as the piercing sounds of weapon fire, lasers, and explosions sounded like the end of the world was near. Others ran and hid while still more were frozen in place, their fear so overwhelming that they were incapable of moving.

Then another sound sped through the sky. Flying so fast and so low that those who hadn't already covered their ears, did so now.

"What is it?" One woman shouted.

"I don't know," her husband replied.

"Maybe it's the mother ship," another man shouted.

As the sound came closer and closer, people turned from the battle scene to see what new terror was approaching. Then suddenly, cheers erupted from the mouths of many. The Air Force's X-15s were coming!

"Look!" One man shouted, pointing at the fast-approaching jets. "It's the Air Force!"

"Go get 'em!" Another woman shouted.

"Show them they can't mess with the good ole U.S. of A!" Mark Whitfield yelled.

"Wait!" His father hollered. "There are only four! We need more than that. Where are the rest of them?"

His words dampened the hopes of several, and people began to cry and bemoan their situation.

"Maybe that's all they need," Mark offered.

"There must be more on the way," a man said. "Maybe these are just the forerunners."

*** 

Back on the farm, the battle was going badly. The F-15s were their last hope, and the jets joined the battle, their comrades on the ground also cheered. Flying in formation, the jets closed the gap with the saucer.

Inside the alien craft, Drees flew the ship, while Jeet fired their lasers.

"Evasive action!" Jeet yelled.

Drees complied. "I don't think their weapons will be any more effective than the ones on the ground," he said, "but a spot in the shields is weakening."

The saucer zoomed in and out. Flying so close and accomplishing impossible maneuvers that the jets, which were firing rockets at it, had to break formation. When the rockets hit their target, the shield sizzled and popped, but held steady.

Jeet fired several shots at the jets as their saucer flew past. Most missed, but one hit a newly fired rocket that was too close to one of the F-15s. The resulting explosion rocked the jet.

"Mayday! Mayday! I'm hit and losing altitude," the pilot radioed.

"Find somewhere safe to land," the team leader radioed back.

"I can't land on the road. They're backed up with cars full of panicked civilians," the pilot asked.

"Then put her down in one of those open fields but stay with her. We can't have civilians crawling all over our equipment.

"Aye, sir."

Dense smoke poured off the jet, but the pilot was able to set it down on a nearby farm and douse any flames with a fire extinguisher.

The battle continued. Drees flew in and out between the jets, playing chicken until the last minute and then pulling away, barely avoiding numerous crashes.

With their payload used up, the disheartened pilots had no choice but to fly back to base and call for more help. Unfortunately, the bulk of the pilots were off on maneuvers, too far away to be of any help.

***

With most of their resistance nullified, Drees and Jeet celebrated by shooting at barns, houses, and other structures along the way before finally returning to Charles's farm and landing their spacecraft.

Lutsik returned to the barn and let the kids out of the ship.

"What's happening," Stanley asked.

"It's over. We have lost," Lutsik replied, shaking his head sadly.

Mary burst into tears. Stanley took her into his arms and stroked her hair, trying to comfort her.

As the two Greys approached, the general marched out to confront them.

The aliens no longer used their holographic technology to disguise themselves. Mitchell opened his mouth to say something, but Drees stepped forward and placed his hand on the general's head.

"Kneel!"

Mitchell tried to fight it, but he sank to his knees against his will.

"Now point your weapon at your chest," Drees ordered.

Again, the general tried with all his concentration to fight it, but it was no use.

Drees looked around at the men surrounding them. "Drop your weapons, or your leader will be forced to shoot himself."

What choice did they have? The men did as they were told. This completed Mitchell's humiliation, and he hung his head.

Lutsik stepped up beside the general. "Do not harm him or any of the others."

"I won't if you give me the Core," Drees replied, training his laser on Lutsik's head.

"He doesn't have it."

Drees looked around to see who had spoken. He saw Stanley and the others emerge from the barn. "Stay with him," he ordered Jeet. Taking in the situation, the alien noticed that Mary held tightly to Stanley's arm. I can use the female as leverage, he told himself.

Stepping forward, he quickly grabbed Mary and jerked her away from Stanley. Then he pointed his laser at her. "Give me the crystal or she dies, Earthling."

"Don't do it!" Mary begged. She tried to get away, but Drees had a firm grasp of her wrist and would not let go.

"If you will follow me, I'll get it for you," Stanley answered.

Turning around, he and the boys walked into the barn to retrieve the crystal. Which he had placed on a workbench by the phone. Grabbing it, he walked towards Drees, who was now standing in the doorway.

"No, Stanley, you can't," Mary pleaded.

Drees released her wrist and extended his hand. "Give it to me."

# Chapter Forty-Four

## Capturing the Greys

As soon as Drees entered the barn, Rick quickly and quietly headed for the light switch. It was a move the boys had discussed earlier. When the alien grabbed the crystal from Stanley's hand, Lutsik and Mourda each put on a pair of sunglasses. Then Dave threw open the barn doors, and Rick turned on the powerful overhead lights, blinding both Drees and Jeet, who screamed.

"Aaaaaaaaaaaaaaaaaaaaah!

Drees released Mary and dropped the Core. Unable to see, the Greys covered their eyes with their hands, but it still wasn't enough to filter the light completely. They stood absolutely still, frozen in place.

Mourda leaned over and picked up the crystal-shaped Core, which emitted a pulsing green glow as soon as he touched it.

Stanley and Roger rushed forward and disarmed Drees and Jeet.

"Don't move," Lutsik said as fifty soldiers surrounded the two Greys.

"Keep the light on them," Stanley told the soldiers.

The soldiers pinned the aliens with their flashlight beams as Mitchell walked into the barn.

"Handcuff them and put them in one of the vehicles under full guard," he said. "As soon as we wrap things up here, we'll head back to base. Whatever you do, keep that light on them."

"Yes, sir."

The men ushered Drees in Jeet outside and placed them into the back of one of the Suburbans. Two men climbed into the front seat. One turned on the car's overhead lights and then added the beam from his flashlight to the other man's.

"Get that truck back here and load that spaceship on the back," the general shouted.

"Which one, sir?" Lieutenant Stone asked.

Mitchell turned and glanced at the ship inside of the barn. He wanted to take it to see if the new aliens' technology was similar to the Greys, but he realized that he did not have that luxury. "Take the one outside." Then he turned to Stanley. "I have to hand it to you, kid. You seem to know what you're doing."

Mourda, Lutsik, and the others released the breath they'd been holding and gathered around the general, who turned and faced the Tau Cetis.

"I never thought I'd say this, but you are free to go. Save your planet. Save Earth. Save the universe. Who am I to stand in the way? It is obvious that you are far more advanced than we are. On behalf of the President of the United States and the rest of the world, I wish to extend our heartfelt thanks. You could have been like the others," he said, nodding toward the car that held the Greys. "I'm grateful that you're not. Is there anything I can do to help?"

"There is one thing," Stone said. "Can I go home?"

"Yes, you can, as long as you promise to come back and visit." Mitchell reached out and shook his hand. "It has been a pleasure working with you these past five years. I'm only sorry that you have to leave, but I imagine you're anxious to return home. Five years is a long time to be away from your family."

"It certainly is,"

***

Mitchell's men finished loading the Grey's flying saucer onto the truck and fasten down a huge tarp to cover it while the boys pushed the spaceship out of the barn and into the clearing in front. Stone, whose real name was Sonwe, climbed aboard the ship. With only two minutes left before their planet was out of reach, Lutsik and Mourda said a hasty goodbye and hurried after him.

Everyone, including the general and his men, backed away from the saucer, but when Lutsik tried to start it up, it made a groaning noise.

"Oh, no!" Mary cried.

"What's wrong now?" Roger cried out in frustration.

"Now don't go getting yourselves in a tizzy," Charles said. He walked over to the ship and kicked it in just the right spot. The saucer came to life, and he moved away. "Must be the new fuel."

Everyone held their breath and crossed their fingers as the ship briefly hovered and then shot up into the air and disappeared from sight. Cheering erupted, including the military men. Stanley hugged Mary. Caroline hugged her father. Soon, all were whooping, laughing, and crying while hugging everyone else.

They had made it. Stanley, his family, and friends had accomplished their goal, and in doing so, become better individuals.

"I'm proud of you," Charles told Stanley. "I'm proud of all of you. You faced a difficult, nearly impossible situation, but you worked it out."

Mitchell walked up to the group of civilians. "On behalf of the red, white, and blue, I want to extend my thanks to all of you. You helped save the universe and taught me a lesson. I won't soon forget."

He saluted them and climbed into the back of his Suburban. A moment later, all of the military vehicles drove off, headed for McConnell Air Force Base.

# Chapter Forty-Five

## A New World

Three months later, several changes had taken place. A large wooden sign was on display in Charles Anderson's front yard stating: The Aliens Stayed Here! The farmyard had been cleaned up, part of which was now a large parking lot for the hundreds of visitors who came to sightsee. In the spring, Charles and his grandson would repair the damaged satellite dishes.

A long line stretched from the barn doors to the street. Mary showed the visitors the giant telescope and explained how it was built and the constellations visible through it. She especially loved showing everyone where to find Tau Ceti and talking about Lutsik and Mourda's homeworld, its people, and all the amazing things to be found there. Things she had learned during numerous conversations with the aliens.

Stanley showed the tourists a large-scale model mockup of the alien ship he and his grandfather had finally finished. He regaled them with stories of how they met the aliens, and how they got Mourda and Lutsik back to their homeworld in time to save the universe.

Charles was in his glory as he told his story about both visits to anyone who would listen. When the tourists left the barn, they stood in another long line leading to the garage and the U.F.O. And Alien Invasion Preparation Store.

Inside, Rick and Roger sold pictures of Mourda and Lutsik and alien memorabilia, worked the cash register, and restocked shelves. The merchandise flew off the shelves as quickly as they could restock them. After the story hit the news about the alien visitors, all five kids became the most popular kids in school. The boys, in particular, enjoyed their new status, but none of them forgot who their real friends were, each other.

In his spare time, Roger created his own version of a comic book featuring all the aliens and everyone involved in the adventure to save the crystal Core. He was so good at it that he now had a large following of students who couldn't wait to buy and read the next story. He and a cute, shy girl from art class became close friends. She helped him make up new stories and even assisted with the artwork.

***

All the kids now called Charles, Grandpa, which thrilled him to no end. Stanley was still the best and closest to his heart, but he loved the attention. It was like a soothing balm to a man who had been so lonely for the past five years.

Taking a short break before the next group of tourists was brought in, Mary approached Charles.

"How are you doing today, Grandpa?" She asked him.

"Now that I have this new heart, I feel thirty years younger," he replied. "I wake up every morning feeling like a new man."

"I wonder if it's the new heart or the fact that you have been reunited with your family," Mary suggested wisely.

"A little of both, I think," Charles admitted.

"I think it's so sweet that the kids all call you Grandpa now."

"Me, too. When Stanley and his mother moved away, I was so lonely. You were the only one who cared about me, and I'll always be grateful for that. Next to Stanley, you are my favorite grandchild."

Mary hugged him. "And you are my favorite grandpa. I really missed my real grandparents after they died. Truth is, I still do, but you are the best replacement I could ever ask for."

***

Rick was now a member of the Debate Team. He was so good at it that before long, he became their captain. Life all around seemed better. Although things at home hadn't changed much, he had learned to channel his frustration and unhappy home life into his debates, and his mother was very proud of him. Recently he started dating one of the girls in the club.

As he stocked the shelves in another part of the store, they practiced the current topic for their next debate. Each took turns debating the opposite point of view.

"Believing in aliens is childish," she started, taking the counterpoint of someone who did not know better. "I suppose you're going to state the Roswell Incident as a case in point?"

"Absolutely," Rick replied. "If the military hadn't been dealing with a real flying saucer, they would never have released the story to the press."

"Yes, but it was retracted the following day as being just a weather balloon filled with crash test dummies."

"And that statement also tells you that the government is lying. Crash test dummies weren't created and used until the 1950s. The Roswell incident happened in 1947."

"How can I argue against that?" His friend laughed.

They continued to debate as they worked.

A month after Lutsik and Mourda returned home, Caroline put her house up for sale. She and Stanley moved back in with Charles, and the three of them were happier than they could ever remember. A week after they moved in, Sheriff Steve Guthrie came to call.

"Afternoon, Caroline," Steve greeted her at the diner where she worked.

She smiled. "Afternoon, Steve, can I get you a cup of coffee and a piece of pumpkin pie?"

"You bet, but I wonder if you could take a small break and come outside to talk a minute first."

She turned to the other waitress, Sandy, who was busy wiping off the counter.

"Go ahead, you two. I'll cover for you," Sandy replied.

After grabbing her jacket off the hook in the back, Guthrie escorted her outside.

"Walk with me," he said.

"Brrr." Caroline pulled her jacket closer around her.

"It's getting chilly," Steve allowed, but as soon as he placed his arm around her shoulders, she no longer felt the cold.

"Looks like snow," she said, looking up at the dark clouds overhead.

"Seems that way."

She looked into his eyes. "What did you need to talk to me about?"

"I'm glad fate brought us back together," he replied.

"Mmm, me, too," she agreed. "It's funny. I never realized how much I missed the company of a good man."

"Now that you do, I want to start over. Would you like to go to dinner and a movie Friday night?"

She stopped walking and faced him. "Are you asking me out on a date?" she asked, smiling.

"And if I am?"

"Then I accept. I think that would be lovely."

Steve's expression had been serious, but now he broke into a grin. "You just made my day…no, make that my whole week!"

They both laughed and continued walking until it was time for Caroline to return to the diner. Steve was so happy, he forgot all about the coffee and pumpkin pie.

***

That night after the tourists and helpers had all gone home, Caroline sat at the kitchen table with Stanley and her father.

"We had another good day today," Caroline said as she finished tallying up the day's receipts.

"At this rate, we'll have enough money set aside for your college education in no time, son," Charles told Stanley.

"I can hardly believe how everything turned out," Stanley replied.

"Yes, siree," Charles agreed. "Our debts are paid off, and we've even put some money aside for a rainy day."

"Oh, I almost forgot," Caroline interrupted. "We sold the house today!"

"Wow, that's great, mom."

"Can you believe it? The family that bought it did so because of you, Stanley."

"Me?" Stanley was perplexed. "How so?"

"The family loved the house, but they also have a nine-year-old boy who just had to have your room. He couldn't wait to tell all his friends."

Everyone laughed.

Yes, life was good now. Charles had his daughter and grandson back in his life, and everyone respected him. Stanley was no longer teased at school or Caroline at work, and all three were pleased.

"You know this won't last forever," Caroline warned her father. After a while, the tourists will dwindle down to just a few."

"I know," Charles said, "and that's okay. Come next summer, I'm thinking of building a full-sized space ship, maybe even a ride of some sort that people can explore and have fun with. And who knows? In five years, Lutsik and Mourda and maybe even soon, we will be back for a visit, and things will pick up all over again."

"That's a great idea, Grandpa," Stanley said. "I can't wait to get started on it."